SINCE THE WORLD IS ENDING

SINCE THE WORLD IS ENDING

INDYANA SCHNEIDER

SCRIBNER

London · New York · Amsterdam/Antwerp · Sydney/Melbourne · Toronto · New Delhi

First published in Great Britain by Scribner, an imprint of
Simon & Schuster UK Ltd, 2025

1 3 5 7 9 10 8 6 4 2

Simon & Schuster UK Ltd, 1st Floor
222 Gray's Inn Road, London WC1X 8HB

Simon & Schuster Australia, Sydney
Simon & Schuster India, New Delhi

www.simonandschuster.co.uk
www.simonandschuster.com.au
www.simonandschuster.co.in

The authorised representative in the EEA Is Simon & Schuster Netherlands BV,
Herculesplein 96, 3584 AA Utrecht, Netherlands. info@simonandschuster.nl

Simon & Schuster strongly believes in freedom of expression and stands against
censorship in all its forms. For more information, visit BooksBelong.com.

A CIP catalogue record for this book is available from the British Library

Hardback ISBN: 978-1-3985-0113-3
Trade Paperback ISBN: 978-1-3985-0114-0
eBook ISBN: 978-1-3985-0115-7
eAudio ISBN: 978-1-3985-4131-3

Typeset in Palatino by M Rules Ltd.
Printed and Bound in the UK using 100% Renewable Electricity at CPI Group (UK) Ltd

SINCE
THE
WORLD
IS
ENDING

For Lell and Pap

To study music we must learn the rules. To create music, we must break them.

—Nadia Boulanger

I wish the world were ending tomorrow. Then I could take the next train, arrive at your doorstep in Vienna, and say: 'Come with me, Milena. We are going to love each other without scruples or fear or restraint. Because the world is ending tomorrow.'

—Franz Kafka, *Letters to Milena*

FRIDAY

My phone buzzed just as she kissed my neck. And I loved it.
The little shock, the erotic synchronicity:
My humming back pocket,
her hot lips on my throat,
hands on my thighs.
It buzzed again as she traced her mouth along my jaw, again
as I tasted the red wine we'd shared on her lips. Silky, aromatic.
The buzzing had stopped by the time she clawed at my clothes,
scratched down my chest, sighed into my mouth. Now I'm
lying next to her, her dark sleeping body twisted in the sheets,
and my phone is somewhere with my clothes on the floor.

For a moment, I watch Vienna's vicious morning wind lash-
ing a tree outside Lucia's window. Then I creep out of the bed
and rescue my phone from the floor. Dead. Who would have
called so late anyway? The floorboards croak as I tiptoe over
to her bedside table.
'*Buongiorno*, Maya,' she whispers, her eyes still closed.
'Morning,' I say, 'do you mind if I plug my phone in
here?'
'*Certo.*'
Her dark eyes are open now – sleepy, velvety brown. She
looks my naked body up and down. Lust hushes my mind, fo-
cuses my thoughts, melts any lingering drowsiness. I usually
try to avoid sleeping with other musicians, though they're
sordidly good in bed. Something about the rhythm, maybe,
or the coordination, or the dexterity. Oh well. This is casual.
I lean into her. Soothing lust, playful lust, slows everything
down so I can feel things

one

at

a

time.

Her warm lips,

the flick of her tongue,

the gentle bite of her teeth.

—

Sitting on the edge of her bed, wrapped in sheets. Lucia is smiling at me, a misty, playful, *desire-ful* smile, as she strokes the side of her middle finger with her thumb. *Desire-ful.* Something has happened to my English in the few months since I moved here. Language feels free, *potential-ful*. I no longer take for granted just how many English words I have at my disposal. These days, my mind swirls with adjectives, unbound grammar, and almost-tautologies. *Hot, heated, sexual, sensual.*

She pulls the sheets from her body and I wonder what movements chiselled her stomach that way, two vertical lines carved into each side, equidistant from her belly button. Exquisite brown symmetry. Then I notice it's a scar she's stroking, a long, pale line along the inside of her middle finger.

'What happened there?' I ask.

Her eyes crinkle, 'It is nothing so serious. My cello string snapped when I was a child. Don't you have any scars from tired violin strings?'

I shake my head, raising my scarless hands for inspection.

Lucia sits up. Vienna's spring sun decorates her body in patches of soft mandarin light. Last night was all too *frenzied, frantic, desperate, passionate* to think to close the blinds.

'I like scars,' Lucia continues, examining my hands, brushing her warm fingers along my palm.

I shiver despite the heat.

'They turn our bodies into archives, *archivi.*'

'Mm,' I hum, closing my eyes.

'Show me one of *yours.*' I can hear the smile in her voice. 'I am sure you have a few.'

I open my eyes, lift my feet onto the bed, and point to a dark circle where my calf meets my ankle.

'Only this one from a motorbike exhaust pipe.'

'A motorbike? You are more adventurous than I thought!'

She's laughing, soft, silky, *tease-y.* Our scars meet as she traces the dark circle with her finger.

'No, no. Well, not anymore,' I lean closer, 'I was more adventurous in my early twenties, I think.'

'Yes, you're a very serious musician now. No more time for adventure.'

She curls cool fingers around the back of my neck and pulls me towards her.

'Uh huh. Very serious,' I repeat into her mouth, 'no time for anything else, really.'

———

I button up yesterday's white shirt and forgo shorts. Lucia wraps herself in a silk robe and I follow her into the living room.

This is my fifth, maybe sixth, time in Lucia's apartment and I'm still enthralled by her elegant décor – her white marble kitchen island, elaborate speaker system, thick rose curtains and matching velvet sofa, the eclectic mixture of art on the walls.

'I can't get over how beautiful this apartment is,' I say.

'Yes, well, I am very lucky. Tea?'

'Please.'

She flicks the kettle on. It's blue, retro-looking. And I like her style.

'I like your style.'

'*Grazie, cara.*'

And I like the way she calls me *cara*.

While the kettle boils, I stare at a painting in a thick silver frame beside the fridge – bright colours, wobbly circles arranged concentrically. It looks like an out-of-focus peacock feather. Hypnotic. It's the kind of art you can fall into. I have the vague sense of having forgotten something, but it's probably a symptom of the painting. Lucia hands me a steaming mug and we stand beside each other, shoulders pressed together, looking at the small print. All of Lucia's mugs are decorated with the silhouette of a composer and a word or phrase in German. Today she's drinking from *Brahms, frei aber einsam* (free but lonely) and I have *Schubert, unvollendete* (unfinished).

'It's by Hundertwasser. Do you know him?' Lucia asks, gesturing to the silver frame with her mug. The name sounds familiar, but I can't place it. I shake my head.

'He is an Austrian architect and artist, kind of like the

Gaudí of Vienna. This one is called *A Raindrop Which Falls into the City.'*

Oh, I see it now, the blurry bird's eye view.

'Hundertwasser hated straight lines.' She draws in the air with her tea-free hand. 'He thought it was unemotional to work with a ruler. If you're interested, there is an exhibition of his work at the Leopold at the moment.'

The Leopold Museum has come up in conversation with a few orchestra colleagues in the context of the artist Egon Schiele and a particularly scandalous exhibition in 2005, which, in the midst of a heatwave, promised free entry if you attended naked. The exhibition was called *The Naked Truth* and featured early twentieth-century erotic art. I heard one of the guest conductors joke that he went for the 'live flesh' on display, rather than the paintings.

Lads.

Lads.

Lads.

I am yet to go to the Leopold.

'The exhibition is called *Imagine Tomorrow*, with Hundertwasser and Schiele,' Lucia continues. 'I love Schiele.'

I nod and sip my tea. I don't know Schiele well enough to have my own opinion. I've found the posters of his art I've seen around town quite disturbing – a window into a hidden, ugly Vienna I'm not acquainted with.

We sit across from one another on either side of the marble island. In the centre is a jar of olive oil and balsamic vinegar, swirling together slowly like a delicious lava lamp, and a purple candle shaped like a woman's torso. Part of me can't believe that I'm sleeping with Lucia Rizzo, that I'm right now watching the gentle rise and fall of her shoulders, her arched neck, the light tap of her fingers on the ceramic. Lucia Rizzo, cellist extraordinaire, who was described by *Gramophone* magazine as *'elegant, vibrant, irresistible'*. She removes the teabag from my mug with a spoon and puts it in her own. It feels like an intimate gesture, though maybe she just prefers stronger tea.

Directly opposite us on the wall above the speaker system hangs another colourful print in another thick silver frame. Klimt – I recognise the aged, burnished gold and the decadent patterns from the dozens of Klimt gift shops around town. I've seen *The Kiss* on a hundred different surfaces since moving to Vienna – vases, pencils, decorative plates, candles, totes, pillows, espresso cups, tea towels, even leggings, even condoms. When I first visited the Belvedere Museum, I was surprised by how moved I felt by Klimt's art. Not by his skill, not at all, but by the women he painted. No, 'moved' is the wrong word. I felt *seduced*. The way his *Judith* looked at me with her half-closed eyes and her bared teeth and her sex hair. I almost didn't notice the severed head she carried.

'You know, this apartment could be a gallery,' I say.

'I make sure my homes are always filled with art, no matter which city I'm living in.' She pauses. 'So, what would you call my exhibition?'

'Oh! Okay!' I stare at the print – at the women's elongated

bodies, at the colourful dots and arabesques, at the simulated gold leaf. Yes, you could say there was something *mystical, mythical, ethereal* about the setup, but

But

But

It also looks like an underwater lesbian orgy.

'I think the title of your exhibit would be—' I start the sentence before I know the end.

'*Sì*?'

'—Hypnotised.'

'Really? Why?' she asks, like I have given this more than four seconds' thought.

'Yes! What about a room where the art changes based on who's inside? Depending on what would hypnotise them. Like, everyone sees Hundertwasser's wobbly circles, but then the rest depends on their personal brand of hypnosis.'

Lucia is laughing and I feel quite pleased with this answer.

'So for you and me, the magical exhibition turns into sexy, naked women?' she asks, leaning towards me. Under the table, she strokes my bare leg with her foot. I fucking love how much she touches me.

I laugh, too. 'And all-female orchestras!' I point to another painting near her sofa – an orchestra of Black women with a cellist in red at the centre. I'm briefly saddened by how shocking the sight of so many women playing together is. I would never double-take a painting of an all-male orchestra. In fact, I'd probably just call it an orchestra.

'My father painted that one.'

I stand and walk towards the painting. The cellist in the

centre wears a red suit, similar to one I've seen Lucia wear
in concert. Her hair is familiar, too – dazzling, bouncy coils.

'It's beautiful.'

'Actually, this painting is the reason I wanted to become
a cellist. My father painted it when I was three and I kept
pointing at the cellist in the centre saying, "*sono io, sono io,*
that's me!" And eventually my parents understood and
rented a little cello from the local *conservatorio*. This painting was their – how do you say – parting gift to me when I
moved to Vienna.'

I don't tell Lucia that my mum's parting gift to me was a
long hug and a thumbs-up in our kitchen. She was already
in her scrubs and had an agitated I'm-going-to-be-late energy,
though her shift started a full ninety minutes after I was due
to leave. My sister Lisa drove me to Gatwick and, in her car at
the entrance to the terminal, handed me a shoebox of things
I might need in Vienna – a new key chain (copper, shiny and
bare), a UK-EU adaptor, the iron tablets that don't make me
constipated, Marmite, printed copies of my passport, apartment contract and employment contract (I don't know how
she got these), and a white plastic framed photo of her, me,
and mum from my 'graduation' at the Royal Academy. It's just
the three of us in a bleak, empty room because the rest of my
class had graduated six months prior.

'Obviously put the shoebox in your checked luggage,' Lisa
said as she hugged me awkwardly, one arm still on the steer-
ing wheel. I stared at her because her voice sounded strained,
and I could just make out a half moon of water at the base of

each eye. 'Because of the Marmite. It counts as a liquid.' She returned both hands to the wheel.

'Because of the Marmite, got it,' I repeated and climbed out of the car.

'What do you like about the painting?' Lucia asks, pressing her palms against the cool marble countertop, then to her cheeks.

'I love that it's the conductor's view of the orchestra,' I say, 'I feel kind of powerful looking at the musicians from this angle.'

Her tone is suddenly very serious.

'In rehearsal last night, when you were playing the Mendelssohn, I was thinking about the boss of the room. Normally, we would say the conductor is the boss of the room, yes? Especially in the Phil, when we are all "emerging artists" or whatever they call us. But I think that yesterday, it was you, Maya. You were the boss. You were *enchanting.*'

My stomach twists as she says my name. I silently chastise my body for being so predictable. She grins.

'Who taught you to lead the room like that?'

My throat catches. 'Hey what about you? I've never heard musical authority like when I hear you play solo.'

I worry that this is too *intense*, too obvious a deflection, though I mean it. Lucia just shrugs, 'I feel most powerful when I'm playing music I've written.'

'Wait, you compose?' I picture Lucia in her red suit alone in the centre of an audience circle. *Lucia Rizzo, star cellist, composer* . . . I can't tell if I feel jealousy or awe. Though they're not mutually exclusive.

'*Certo!* I studied cello and composition at the *conservatorio*.'

'What kind of music do you write?'

'Whatever is in my head.'

I laugh, but she is being serious. 'Can I hear one of your pieces?'

'*Sì!*'

She clasps her hands together and disappears back into her bedroom. I carry our mugs to the sofa. I lie down, à la Freud, and cross my bare legs. I realise we're likely not far from Freud's actual sofa – strange – and gaze at Lucia's far-away ceiling.

Freud would probably have enjoyed hearing about my childhood. According to my Reception teacher, after my dad died I was 'in my own world', 'newly socially awkward', and 'difficult to communicate with'. Contrastingly Lisa, who had just begun Year 3, started coming top in her classes. Mum asked my teacher how to 'fix me' and my teacher told my mum 'she's not broken'. But my mum pushed, and eventually the teacher recommended I take up some sort of art to 'get back in touch with my feelings' – something visual, dance, music, singing. Mum bought me a violin that same week. I don't know why she chose the violin. I expect she considered it the most erudite option. But God, I remember that first lesson so clearly. The weight of the violin in my tiny hands, the sudden, devastating sense of purpose. My first teacher, Mrs P, sat me down on her little green futon, played me vinyl after vinyl of Brahms, Vivaldi, Bach, Shostakovich, and watched as my four-year-old world came back into focus.

—

Lucia returns with a cello, a darker instrument than the one she plays at the opera, almost reddish. She sits opposite me and I roll on my side to look at her, at the soft lines of her shoulders, her dark, flawless décolletage. The curve of her breasts. Fuck me, her breasts. Lucia transforms when she holds her cello. Her easy bedroom smile shifts. Glamour, success, ready for the concert hall. She tunes quickly, ending with a perfect, Mozartian cadence.

'You ready?' she asks me and I nod, a little dizzy, cloudy, *lust-ful*.

The first time I heard Lucia play, I imagined her cello was filled with bodily organs. An instrument with lungs, that breathed when she breathed, whose beating heart kept time with hers. I stood outside a practice room, my ear pressed to the door, and listened to the blood in her music. It haunted me, how the sound she made felt more human than weeping or laughter. If the melody was a kiss, the *stringendo* bit at my lip, then pulled. And, God, there was a sweetness in her lower register that tasted of hot caramel. I can taste it again now as she plays. She crosses upwards through the strings, notes light and slow, but lush, creamy, toffee-flavoured. Then falling, again. The drops grow heavy, almost mighty, almost dangerous. There's something *modern, electronic, hypnotic* about the bowing. I feel my own pulse quickening. I love watching her play like this – no conductor, no accompaniment. I can hear her sharp intake of breath between phrases. Her eyes catch the light, gleaming like dark jewels.

—

'That was stunning.' My voice sounds soft after her musical storm.

'*Grazie.*'

She leans her cello against the speakers and collapses on the sofa beside me.

'When did you start composing?'

'When I realised my playing would never be like the sounds in my head. I wanted to find something closer,' she says. 'I struggle with words sometimes, but I can say whatever I want to say with music.'

'I get you,' I smile and she nods.

'The piece is called *Tuono della Vita*, Life Thunder. I knew you would understand it because I hear this thunder when you play the violin. *You* play like the sounds in my head, Maya.'

I swallow. I roll my head to the side so that our mouths are centimetres apart, 'Thank you for my morning concert.'

'*Prego.*'

Her lips are warm, soft, tender at first, then more demanding. There's an elegance to the way she wants me this morning. A kind of sensual tenderness. It's playful, how she pulls at the hair at the base of my neck, teasing. The music in my head is Widor's *Piano Quartet*. The second movement. Each deep kiss is rich with harmony, each moment of almost-ecstasy stopped short just before release. Breathless sex, yes, but languid. We're gasping not because of urgency, but because we're indulging in each breath. I don't know if the music makes the sex or the sex makes the music.

—

Lying together on the sofa, panting, satiated. Lucia's phone buzzes, and I'm reminded of last night's ignored calls.

'Oh! I'm just going to go check my phone in case they've written to us about rehearsal today.'

She sips her extra-strong tea, holding my gaze above the rim, 'Take your time. I have nowhere to be until work.'

God, I love it here.

My phone is alive! Once unlocked, it vibrates against my palm with news updates, social media notifications, professional emails, spam, new releases on Spotify.

And then—

Missed calls (x4) – JOSH

No.

JOSH:
Hey Maya
I know this is out of the blue . . .
But would you give me a call?

Josh, whose contact I accidentally saved in CAPS outside a wine bar in London four years ago. Josh, who eats two mints at once because he likes the feeling of a mint in each cheek. Josh, who would occasionally drink his coffee in the shower because of a scene in a Ben Lerner novel. Josh, whose bedside table was covered with colourful thank you notes from his Year 13 class. Josh, whose late-night page turning was the soundtrack to which I fell asleep. Josh. JOSH, who I haven't spoken to in a year.

'Is everything okay?' Lucia calls from her peaceful living room.

'Yes,' I say, blood flooding into my hot cheeks. 'Yes,' I say again. 'Just a missed call from London. Do you mind if I— I think I should— I'm just going to— call someone!'

'*Certo!*'

—

Her bathroom tiles are cool on my feet, grounding. I'm staring at her bamboo toothbrush as I wait for him to pick up, at the faint line of lipstick near the bristles. I can almost smell the spearmint. Then his liquid baritone floods my speakers and, well, fuck.

'Maya! Hey! You nearly missed me!'

'What's going on, Josh? Is everything okay? Are you alright?'

'Yes. I'm fine. Well, kind of. I'm—'

There's a faint, tinny echo of an official voice in his background, like he's on the tube or –

'—I'm at the airport.'

'Okay?' I pick up Lucia's eucalyptus hand soap. I need something to fiddle with.

'I promise I'll explain more later. But I'm about to go through security.'

'Okay. Where are you off to?'

Silence.

'Josh, where are you going?' I ask again.

'Well,' he sounds nervous, 'I know. I know what this sounds like, but it's not like that. I mean, I promise I'll explain when I get there and I wouldn't come if . . .' he trails off. I don't know what to say.

'Maya?'

I don't know what to say.

'I promise I wouldn't be coming if it wasn't important.'

He sounds different – something about the way he said 'important', like the word was heavy or dangerous. 'Maya? Is that okay?'

'I'm not sure what I'm supposed to say.'

'Right. Okay. Of course. Well, obviously you don't have to—'

'Jesus, Josh. When do you get in?'

I tell him which bus to take from the airport. I am dizzy. I am thinking about tongue twisters in the rain in Kew Gardens, singing with a stranger on a rooftop spa in Budapest, our first kiss before the tube doors closed, Sunday morning massages to the clang of our local church bells. It took me a year to realise he was the reason we never ran out of toilet paper or toothpaste or olive oil.

But then – panic attacks, bow shake, insomnia, mornings alone in my mum's apartment, soggy popcorn in the bath, my sister's London visits, the water she left beside my bed. Months later, my phone was still autocorrecting words like 'breakfast' and 'Brexit' to 'break-up', so texts read:

'We could meet for break-up before rehearsal?' or
'Fuck David Cameron. Fuck break-up.'

I can hear my therapist's soothing voice in my ears: *Take your-self away from the panic. What can you smell? Hear? Feel? See?*
    The sound of my nails tapping the sink.
    My wild-eyed reflection.
    The lingering vanilla of Lucia's perfume.
Good.
Back in the kitchen:
Lucia's fridge humming on a low A-flat.
Colourful fruit and vegetables, like an elaborate still life.

I've come to associate fridge fullness with maturity – re-liable people tend always to have full fridges. See? Coherent thoughts. I'm fine. I can handle this. I am back in the kitchen, handling this.

'Maya, I am craving fruit. I think I am dehydrated from all of our exercise,' Lucia smirks, 'Do you want to share a mango?'

My stomach clenches at the mention of food.

'Mangos are my favourite,' Lucia's accent bounces over the syllables of 'favourite', bubbles over the vowels. 'There is pleasure in waiting for the mango to be ready to eat, no?'

'Yes, absolutely.' I say, eyes on the mango as she slices it open and removes the stone. She smiles at me with messy, sticky fingers. Only minutes ago, I might have reached for her hand, drawn her fingers into my mouth, and sucked at the sweetness. She might have moaned, or closed her eyes, or stepped towards me and kissed me slowly, mango juice on both our tongues. Instead, I watch in silence as she carves small cubes into each half.

'Is there an English word for ready to eat?' Lucia flips the mango inside out so that it resembles some exotic flower, rich yellow flesh jutting out towards her. *Focus, Maya.*

'Yes, kind of. For fruit, we say "ripen". So this mango is "ripe".'

'Ripe,' she repeats with three times as many vowels. She hands me my half of the mango, bringing her half to her lips and sucking on each piece until it glides into her mouth. I mirror her. It dissolves on my tongue, ice cold, juicy.

'I'm sorry we have to speak English together, you know,' I say.

'Why are you sorry? I love English! And it is even more fun when you know Latin and Germanic languages because it is a mixture of both!' She lists a few examples:

Fiore, Blume – flowers, bloom

Dio, Gott – deity, God

Why the fuck is Josh coming to Vienna? Should I say something to Lucia? No, I'm just going to meet him, hear him out, and tell him he can't stay with me. *Focus.*

The crash of tap water hitting the sink, like a roll on a snare drum.

Eucalyptus soap on my hands.

The outline of Lucia's body beneath her thin robe.

'Although, to be honest, English is not a good language for sex.' She picks up the torso-shaped candle, studies it, returns it to the table.

'How do you mean?'

'I don't like your words for the body.' She massages the side of her neck. 'Like "bum"! "Bum" is for children. "Arse" is too rude. "Butt"? "But" is a complaint!'

She grabs her chest. 'You say "boobs" so silly! "Breasts" is for doctors. "Tits"? *Oh Dio, no.* Give me something sexy, *per favore!'*

She touches my arm with wet fingers. '*Braccio,*' she says, 'for example'.

'Arm,' I say with mock shame.

'Arm,' she repeats, smiling, rolling the r so that it sounds like a purr. *Arrrrrrrrrm.* Her hand is still on my forearm, but her eyes are wandering, searching my face for–

'Okay, what is wrong Maya?' She passes me a chequered hand towel. 'You have changed since you went to check your phone.'

'Have I? Oh. I'm sorry. I just heard from this friend of mine in London, which I wasn't expecting. But everything's fine,' I sound ridiculous. 'But hey, I've been wanting to ask for ages how you found an apartment like this in Vienna? I love my little studio, but this . . .'

Tactless. Boring. Obvious. I'm speaking without thinking.

'I am lucky.' A lift of her shoulders. 'When I first arrived in Vienna, I met a conductor who liked the way I played. He and his wife support young musicians in the city. They own this apartment and I rent it from them for not so much money.'

'Oh, wow!' *Did I just say 'wow'?* 'That's a great setup!'

We're hovering by the kitchen sink. *Should I lead us back to the couch? No, I need to get out of here.*

'Hey, I think I'm going to head to the opera early to

practise before the big rehearsal,' I stumble, throwing the hand towel onto the counter. I feel our perfect, sexy morning slipping away.

'Certo, cara. But don't stress about today, you're going to be wonderful.'

—

The Donaukanal could be the love child of Paris and Berlin – graffiti-tattooed walls, waterside bars, groups of all ages drinking, legs dangling over the green river. The first time I came here was with Lucia. I close my eyes and sink deeper into the past like it's quicksand. *Mmm. Pull me under!* Lucia, whose warm thigh pressed against mine in the pub as she smiled, looked straight ahead, so sexy, so nonchalant, sipping from her beer.

It was my first public performance with the Habsburg Philharmonic – Elgar's *Cello Concerto*. My palms were damp as I approached the *Karlskirche*. I remember Svetlomir, our resident conductor, pointed out the Roman columns, Greek portico, and baroque copper dome. He called it an 'architec-tural collage' and 'celebrity of the Vienna skyline'. I wiped my hands on my dress – simple, black, modest – as we, a formless cluster of passionate, underpaid instrumentalists, walked together down Karlsgasse.

Backstage, the acoustics captured each nervous shuffle and cough. Lucia swept past me, her red suit a ruby beacon in our sea of charcoal. Our shoulders brushed and she placed

her hand on my forearm, wishing me *in bocca al lupo*. Even
then, there was something about the way she looked at me
that made me ache. Lucia, who was the evening's soloist.
Lucia who ruled the stage, whose dark eyes glimmered as
she played. She was magnificent.

After the concert, we crowded the tables of Golser, a pub in
the First District famous among musicians for its cheap booze
and anything-but-grand interior, and sipped from ice-cold,
shimmering golden beers. Lucia's glamorous red was even
starker beside the plain white walls. Sure, all she did was sit
beside me, but she might as well have danced on the table. I
was transfixed. *Lust*. I almost didn't recognise the lost sensation – easy blush, hard swallows, such close attention to the
way she sipped her drink, or stretched her neck, or the grace-
ful shape of her hands in her lap. Ten months before, I'd been
weeping alone on an Acton Town kitchen floor, vowing never
to love again. *Desire is strange*, I thought, as I leaned into her.

I told her I'd never seen the Second District. She told me I
should walk her home. I'd imagined men with ironed shirts,
women in staccato heels ... But the Second District was all
ripped jeans, colourful eyeliner, beer bottles, orthodox Jewish
men in small huddles. The sweaty people sandwiches of the
Friday evening London tube felt so far away.

I studied Lucia's stylish, balletic stride, the swing of her arms,
the line of her nose, her strong jaw. When our hands brushed,
I pretended not to notice, but after the third time she said, 'Are

these accidents?' I blushed. She told me I had a 'nice blush'. I blushed more. I felt ridiculous and exhilarated. She laughed, took my hand, squeezed, let go. She gestured towards the sky, to the great round silhouette of the Prater Ferris Wheel. I could just make out the antique red cabins.

'Have you been up the Prater?' she asked, rolling the r. Prrrrrater.

'No, actually, I haven't.'

She bunched her fingers together, tips touching, and flung her hand into the air. I thought she was teasing, playing up to the Italian caricature, but I couldn't be sure. Her voice was louder than before, 'No! Why not?'

I decided to be honest. 'Because I'm not great with heights.'

She looked perplexed, like this wasn't a good enough reason to miss the spectacular *Prrrrrater* Ferris wheel. 'You must go.'

They say 'must' in German more than they do in English. Maybe it's the same in Italian. So much obligation! You **must** go here. I **must** write this email. One **must** submit their marital status along with their CV in order to be considered for a position in the Habsburg Philharmonic.

But **must** Josh come to Vienna?

No, no, no.

Let's stay in the past a little longer.

I felt her eyes on me as we walked. Occasionally, I glanced at her, too, and we held contact for a moment. We made jokes – silly, circular jokes – and our laughter skipped across the

Danube like stones. She told me a little about her upbringing in Naples – her mother the teacher, her father the artist, her childhood home covered in his paintings. Mostly everyday still lifes – fruit, flowers, cups, and jugs.

She twisted her key in her door, then paused and turned back to me with a half-smile, eyebrows raised. The dim entrance lights gave her red suit the darker, almost glossy, colour of ripe cherries. I remember how I fought back a sigh as she collapsed beside me on the couch. I remember we watched a video on her phone of a mutual acquaintance in London playing Bach, our bodies so close I could feel the heat rising off her skin. I could smell the harmonising scents of her perfume and shampoo. I knew if I turned towards her, we would kiss, but part of me wanted to delay that moment. It's fun to trick yourself into feeling in control of inevitability.

My eyes fly open as a woman crunches my toes with her heel. A hot pain spreads across my foot.

'*Entschuldigung*,' she shrugs, before walking away.

I guess I'm done reminiscing. I wiggle my reddening toes and wipe the sweat from my brow. This heat can't be normal for Vienna in May. It's the kind of sticky heat that renders everything erotic and sweaty and tense. Or maybe that's just me.

The tram stop is empty but for a woman in a white linen dress eating tomato soup out of a jar. The sound of the spoon on the glass is loud, intrusive. More a clang than a cling. Arhythmic. Annoying. That odd thought that sometimes visits is here again – how far away am I from someone who loves me?

I could call my sister, but I don't want to bother her at work. Plus, I can already imagine how the conversation would go.

Lisa: So what is it exactly that you're worried about?

Me: I'm worried about losing my mind again and not being able to play the violin.

Lisa: Okay, so then focus on what you can control.

Me: Lise, we've been through this. I don't think there's a binary between what you can control and what you can't! I could move to London and marry Josh. That's 'in my control' and—

Lisa: Maya, stop. That's obviously not what I mean and you're not helping anybody by arguing with me about this.

For a moment, I cover my ears with my hands, focusing on the rhythm of my breathing, my pumping blood. Then I wipe my eyes dry with my sleeve, adjust my earphones, and scroll my listening history until I find what I need. I know plenty of people who bristle at the idea that music has a consoling or healing 'power'. They call it *undignified, cheapening, demeaning* to treat music as a tool to manage emotion. But it's undeniable – music soothes you, distracts you, guides you, provides a wordless language you can use to engage with memory, pain, nostalgia. And I listen like this, sometimes, especially when I feel in-between emotions – when sadness is almost pleasurably exhausting, or aggression is contained, or joy feels ironic. You get it. Right now, I'm feeling a deep, jittery, thrilling dread.

If everything that's happened hadn't happened, I'd already be listening to Brahms. I'd have started with his *First Symphony*, the relentless, throbbing drum, the orchestration that fights gravity, soaring slowly. I miss being lost in his moody worlds. Wistful, blurry, blissful melancholy, with notes that rub together and produce not sparks, but deep indents. Music so full of heartbreak it makes you want to collapse. I'd move onto his violin sonatas – to that recording of the first sonata by Augustin Dumay and Maria João Pires, where you can hear how in love they are by the way they breathe together. But I can't touch Brahms' violin sonatas. I haven't been able to for nearly two years.

I opt for Strauss' *Metamorphosen for 23 Solo Strings* instead. An appropriate second choice. I was introduced to the piece by Mrs P when I was a teenager. 'Devastated', she told me from her usual place at the piano. Strauss was 'devastated' when he wrote his *Metamorphosen*. Opera houses were crumbling, falling like dominoes around him – first Munich, then Dresden. When Vienna was swallowed by flames, Strauss mourned through music.

Play.

Small, rich melodic fragments. If tears were music, they might sound like this. Not all tears – the specific kind that accompany slow breathing, closed eyes, the kind that slip from under lashes. This is what I need. My fingers move with the violins, travelling along imaginary strings. Pressing onto nothing. Then, crash. A series of waves, each breaking with more intensity than the one before. And—

A gust of wind and my hair is in my eyes and my mind is pulled from the melodies. I give in and check the time. I've got one minute until the tram arrives. I open my emails, pressing the inbox with my thumb and tugging down. I'm aware that this is more of a bid for dopamine than an actual email check. I do it anyway.

My inbox is empty except for a message from my weekly German course. I arrived in Austria with enough German to be able to answer 'how are you?' with 'good', 'tired', or 'hungry', which served me reasonably well. These days, I only speak casual, how-was-your-day-off German with a handful of people. Even then, I miss choosing words because they feel right, rather than because they're the only one I know. Oh, according to this email, next week we're studying 'the subjunctive', the tense that lets you imagine. It says here 'the subjunctive is the magical mood that will enrich your life. You'll learn how to express hypothetical situations, doubts, and wishes'. Great. Meanwhile, the very unhypothetical tram is finally here.

I'm about to put my phone away when it buzzes in defiance. A notification, a 'photo memory' – when did iPhones start doing this? – and my silly heart gasps because it's Josh. Did my phone notice his call? Is my phone meddling? Does my phone miss Josh? How do I tell my phone that I don't want to delete this photo, but I also don't want to look at it? I look at it. It's from our first anniversary – he's on the roof of the Tate Modern, almost silhouetted against the London sky. I say 'almost' because he's colourful, laughing. He's in that dark red jumper I loved, sleeves rolled up, facing slightly away from the camera.

I need to be alone in a practice room. My foot is tapping as if it will make this tram go faster. My violin sits beside me, looking forlorn. Neglected. I rest my palm on her case – a gentle caress – like we're lovers, holding hands, on our journey to work.

—

A teenager on Kärtnerstraße is playing a pretty decent version of the Blue Danube on an accordion while a very blonde woman and her very blonde baby waltz leisurely, ringlets blowing in the wind. The air is rich with chocolate, cinnamon, a hint of caramel. Glamorous, decadent Vienna. This feels better.

Then I'm face to face with the Staatsoper. On paper, this sturdy rectangular building should be dull. Beige bricks, curved copper roof. But it is magnificent. The scale! The way it rules the street, demanding attention like an architectural monarch. Mozart, Strauss, Beethoven, Schubert, Wagner, Verdi, Mahler have all stood here, where I'm standing. I breathe in the air, flavoured with history, and savour the sensation I sometimes experience when I think about the intersection of my present and the Grand Past. It's a thrilling, swelling feeling in my chest. Awe, gratitude. It's hard to imagine bombs and air raids annihilating such a powerful structure only decades ago.

'Maya! You're early too!' Elsa, a Swedish bassoonist, calls from the stage door. Her accent is melodic; there's a richness to her elongated vowels and something French about the light-touch consonants and gentle bounce of her voice. 5'9' with angelic, champagne-coloured curls, Elsa has the kind of bone structure that plastic surgeons try to replicate. She's dressed in her usual: no-nonsense black activewear with yellow neon rollerblades slung across her rucksack. I once heard one of the programme directors tell her she should dress more professionally. She reminded him that if she was paid what a highly-trained, award-winning instrumentalist should be, she wouldn't be forced to moonlight as a yoga instructor between rehearsals. She walks towards me.

'Hey! Yeah, I was up early and thought I might as well come in,' I lie.

She links her arm through mine, 'Come, let's get coffee.'

But I resist her pull, clutching my violin case, eyeing the entrance to the building.

'Actually, I thought I should practise a bit before rehearsal.'

She doesn't let go of me. That's when I notice something's off. Her mouth is tense, and her fingers are too tight around my arm.

'Can I buy you a pastry? There is something I need to talk to you about. I will take fifteen minutes of your time and you can use the rest of the hour to practise, I promise.'

Two things: firstly, I am still very hungry and probably should eat something more substantial before our three-hour rehearsal. Secondly, a 'theme' in therapy lately has been balancing being a **good musician** and being a **good person**. Tragic, I know, but true.

Another gentle tug.

'Okay, okay. Of course. Let's go.'

My violin and I are led away from the solace of the practice room.

We dodge the long and boisterous queue around the Mozart Café and duck into the Joseph Bäckerei next door. It looks more Scandinavian than Austrian – all whites and pale woods. The barista narrowly avoids whiplash, doing a double-take as Elsa approaches the counter. His hair is gelled in a frenetic, chaotic way, as if he's been electrocuted.

Him, stuttering mostly.

Her, German flowing, smile radiating.

'Oh, what pastry do you want, Maya?'

She orders me a five-euro almond croissant.

'You don't have to—'

'Don't be silly! Coffee?'

'No, no, I'm good, thank you.'

She asks for tap water and the waiter reddens, then tells her he will check with his colleague. Austrians love to boast about their superior tap water, but waiters seem completely appalled when you ask for it. His colleague denies us the privilege.

We take a table by the window overlooking the queuing tourists. A few of them are in deep discussion with Mozart (a tanned twenty-something in a long red robe and powdered wig – even from here, I can see the sweat on his cheeks and neck) about tickets to a tourist concert or the opera. I bite into my croissant. It is perfectly flaky and buttery, and crumbles all over the table.

'Let me text Lucia to tell her we're here,' Elsa says. She doesn't know Lucia and I are sleeping together. Lucia thinks I left to practise. Josh must be arriving soon. I should be in a practice room. Fuck's sake.

'She's on her way!' Elsa's face darkens as she places her phone face-down on the table. 'Okay, can I please talk to you about something private?'

'Of course. What's going on?'

'Okay,' she says again. I watch as she breathes through her nose, shoulders tensing, then releasing. 'I've never mentioned this before because I thought I could deal with it, but—'

She pauses. '—I think I have a problem with Davorin.'

Davorin, a very tall Slovakian percussionist who wears his hair in a headband, isn't my favourite orchestra member, but he has always seemed harmless to me. He's my age, 27, so one of the youngest, and strikes me as the kind of percussionist who might throw his mallets in the air after a particularly thrilling phrase.

'He is always staring at me in rehearsals, he will find any excuse to touch me, he keeps asking for my number, and my yoga colleague just told me that he came to the studio where I teach and asked for me.'

Had I noticed that Davorin fancied Elsa? Sure. Had I realised how much it bothered her? No. Honestly, no.

'Jesus. How long's it been like this?'

'Basically since we joined.'

She looks at me with furious grey eyes.

'Have you spoken to him about it? Like, did you tell him it was weird that he came to the yoga studio?' I ask. The colourful anti-harassment posters plastered around the opera house backstage say: *Kein Spielraum für sexuelle Belästigung.* In my beginner's German, this translates to the bizarre (but clear!) 'No play room for sexual harassment'.

'I have been very clear. I don't know. Maybe things are different in Slovakia.'

She's right, of course. In a career as international as music, you must adapt your expectation of harassment to each new place of work. At a competition in Budapest late last year – my first since the breakdown – an established conductor put his hand on my leg and promised he would help me 'make it big'. I didn't brush his hand away, but I made an excuse and left the room. When I wrote to the head of the competition, he told me that if I was uncomfortable, I was 'free to leave, of course'. Naturally, most young women in our industry have perfected the *yes-I'm-so-happy-to-be-here-but-don't-fucking-touch-me* smile.

'I told him he was making me feel uncomfortable,' Elsa says.

'Okay, and how'd he respond?'

'Oh, he just laughed and squeezed my arm. And then he walked away before I could say anything else.'

I can imagine this. I can picture the exact scene Elsa is describing, and I feel helpless on her behalf. I take another bite of my perfect crumbly croissant.

'So what do you think I should do?' Her face is unchanged, but her voice wobbles.

'Look, I hate to say this, but I don't think you can *do* anything until he does something reportable.'

She sighs.

'No, I know, you're right,' I say. 'It's ridiculous, maybe I'm wrong, let me think.'

Buzz.

JOSH:
Just touched down.
When/where should I meet you?

I don't reply. I've promised Elsa five more minutes of my attention, though I'm not sure how helpful I'm being.

'Do you want me to say something to him?' I ask, then spot Lucia through the window, dodging another Mozart as he skips towards the tourists, wig dancing in the wind.

'Maybe, but not right now. I think I just needed to tell someone about it, so I don't feel like I'm going crazy on my own.'

'Of course.'

I finish my croissant and try to give Elsa a reassuring nod. She clasps her hands together and the sound makes me jump, 'Okay, no more talk of harassment for the morning, yes?'

Lucia has pulled back her hair and changed into a red vest and black shorts. Her legs look longer, smoother, almost polished in the morning light. As she walks towards the café entrance, muscles carve lines in her calves and thighs. Thoughtless elegance. Last week in my German class, I learnt that you can make any adjective into a superlative pretty simply. I know we have this in English for some adjectives – we add 'est' (youngest, smartest) – but in German, they can do it with all adjectives. Like 'elegant'. Lucia's legs are the *elegant-est*.

'Ciao,' she sings. She kisses us both like she's seen neither of us naked and pulls a chair to our table.

'Hey! I was just about to practise when Elsa asked to talk to me,' I say too quickly. Lucia winks at me. Okay, she's not concerned that I ditched her to meet Elsa. We're *casual*.

'Lucia, *morgen*! I think you should wait for the *Warteschlange* to shrink before you order.'

'*Warteschlange?* Like "waiting snake"? Is that actually the word for "queue"?'

They both laugh at me.

'*Genau*! Exactly! You're picking up German very quickly, Maya.'

The compliment makes me glow, but I brush it off with a wave of my hand. Lucia leans forward, so that our fingers are almost touching.

'You know,' she purrs, 'when I first arrived in *Wien*, I told a waiter that I would like to *be* a glass of wine.' She leans back and I grieve our lost, almost-touching fingers. I can't believe that after over a decade as a sexually active adult (and having already had sex with Lucia. This morning, in fact), I am still so *thrilled* by incidental contact.

'Oh, classic. When I studied in Germany, I used to tell everyone that I was vegetarian,' Elsa adds.

'That seems fine?' I say.

She shakes her head, smiling, 'No, like, that I am physically vegetarian ... Meat free.'

Lucia looks thoughtful while she laughs, 'You know, I wonder if Germans have a more fixed idea of identity because of their grammar. Like *"Ich bin gut"* doesn't mean you feel good, it means you are a good person. Maybe they think people are less changeable.'

'Maybe,' I say. I really love the way her mind works.

Buzz.

JOSH:
Can catch the bus
into town and meet
you wherever :)

'So, what did you want to talk to Maya about?' Lucia asks Elsa.

'I was just saying that Davorin gives me the creeps.'

'Oh, he *is* a creep. I heard him say some fucked-up things at a few parties last year.'

Elsa shrugs, taking tobacco and rolling paper out of her bassoon case, 'I think I'm just going to have to deal with it.'

My phone is ringing. I give in. 'Fuck, sorry, I'm gonna take this outside.'

'Maya, hey! I thought I might have missed you!'

His voice has an immediate, absurd effect on my body. My heart rate quickens, heat rushes to my cheeks.

'Sorry,' I say, glancing back at Lucia and Elsa laughing

together through the *Bäckerei* window, 'I didn't have my phone on me.' More lying. It's not even 11 a.m. I wave off an eager approaching Mozart. This one looks Nordic – square jaw, long blonde hair barely concealed by his wig. His costume is dark with sweat.

'I'm just in the queue for passport control – it's taking way longer than usual.'

'Right.'

'Where should I head?'

'Well, I'm rehearsing at the opera house for the next few hours, but I can meet you after.' I sound annoyed. I *am* annoyed.

'Sure! Should I aim for the opera house then?'

The image of Josh and Lucia meeting at stage door.

'No, um, why don't I meet you at the Volksgarten? It's a really beautiful park nearby. I can probably be there just after two.'

'Cool' – pause – 'I guess I'll see you there, Maya?'

'Yeah, I guess you will.'

The fact that Josh is in Vienna makes me nauseous. But, fine, yes, I'm also excited. And I'm a little bit disgusted by my excitement. I gesture through the glass that I'm going to go and practise. Elsa waves and Lucia blows me a kiss. You know what? This isn't that big a deal. Everything's going to be fine.

—

The porter doesn't smile as he buzzes open the stage door. None of the smiley porters work on Fridays. I walk by the exhibition of headshots of opera singers past – from black, white, and serious, to colour, glamour, and smiles – and take the furthest staircase to the third floor.

An empty practice room, at last. My sweltering, window-less little sanctuary. I consider unbuttoning my shirt, but you can't lock these doors. I take my violin from her case and my tea-stained Mendelssohn score from my bag. Some people are precious about sheet music, but I like seeing the wear and tear. Music as living history, rather than sacred object.

'Let's start with scales,' my violin says, and I nod, turning us to face the door. I'm already sweating.

'Today, we want to focus on colour. I want to hear the spectrum of sounds we can produce within the scale.'

She's right. I heard the guest conductor observing today's rehearsal might be Lorenzo García. And I'm the concerto soloist. It's opportunities like these that make our programme so competitive, despite the pitiful stipend.

But Elsa is being harassed.

And Josh is probably already out of the airport.

And Lucia—

No.

I close my eyes.

'Give me a second,' I tell my violin, and she waits, her body resting against my shoulder.

At first, I concentrate on the sounds in the room – the whirring, useless aircon, my own even breathing. Then I extend the radius of focus, eyes still closed. The quiet patter of walking in the corridor, creaky elevator doors sliding open, the hum of the traffic outside. I do the same with my vision – starting small with a lightning-shaped crack in the wall, then expanding it to include both corners of the room, the gold stool by the door, the piano keyboard beside me, glinting in the sun.

'Ready?' asks my violin.

'Ready,' I say.

———

We start with scales. I slice the strings with my bow, over and over, until my anxiety turns to dust. Double stops – thirds, sixths, octaves. I bounce my bow off the strings, *spiccato*, ricocheting.

'Good, but you need to loosen some tension in your shoulders.'

She's right. I stretch my neck from side to side and begin again, bouncing, ricocheting. Good, better. *Colourful.*

I still practise with the exercises my professor taught me in my first year at the Royal Academy. Professor Forrest. And I still play the way she insisted upon: begin with first position, even if you're only there for a moment. *'Orient yourself, then fly wherever you need to go.'*

'Yes, but now let's find the drama in the scales,' says my violin. 'What does it *mean* to climb from note to note? What does it *feel* like to ascend? How can we make ascension sound sweet? Sorrowful? Full of desire? And when we get to the Mendelssohn, we need to find that same drama in the line. We need to cut deep into the music's melody. I want to taste the blood, Maya. Even if you still refuse to use the memory drawer.'

'Got it,' I say.

Professor Forrest introduced me to the concept of a 'memory drawer' on a walk we took together in Regent's Park. She used to talk about a 'fire' she heard in my audition for the Academy. The fire was out of control, she said, but she promised she'd teach me to tame it. And she did. For a while. We were sitting side by side on a bench facing the lake, watching young couples and families ride the cornflower-blue pedalos, like dodgem cars, on an October afternoon.

'I want to introduce you to an idea, Maya, that I think will be beneficial to you.'

'Okay,'

'The reason I think it will be beneficial is because of the fire I told you about, the one I hear when you play. It's special.'

'Okay.'

'I don't think you hear me. I think you have something special to say with your music, Maya. Something far deeper than most eighteen-year-olds.'

She looked at me, then, like she knew no one had called me special before.

'That doesn't mean to say you're brilliant,' she warned. 'You're good, yes, but you're far from brilliant. I hope I can help make you brilliant, but you're going to have to trust me.'

'I do trust you!' I blurted out, though it sounded like she had more to say. I was surprised because it felt true. I trusted this softly spoken fifty-something who I'd only met a handful of times before, who wore only black – trousers, shirt, scarf, coat – and smelled strongly of caramel. Next to her, I felt a new kind of calm. It was almost meditative. I grew aware of the pressure of my feet on the pavement, the piles of leaves nearby, and the gentle breeze on my neck. I could tune in and out of the chatter, splashes, and birdsong that surrounded us. When she spoke to me about music, I wanted to record and transcribe her ideas, word for word, print out the transcriptions and sleep with them under my pillow. I would have jumped into the dirty lake then and there if she'd told me to.

'Good. Here, have a biscuit,' she said suddenly, and pulled a half-empty box of Jaffa Cakes from her bag. I laughed as she put the whole biscuit in her mouth in one go. Then I did the same.

The memory drawer, I would learn, was a kind of mental storage unit where you store deeply personal and emotional memories to draw upon while you play. Professor Forrest recommended I 1) label them to make them easier to recall and 2) be very deliberate about choosing the right memory to fit a particular piece of music. Take this tea-stained Mendelssohn on my stand. To be honest, if I still used the memory drawer, I would have infused this Mendelssohn with the memory of Josh and my break-up.

Silent violin in hand, I imagine the way my temples would have pounded as I played, the melody growing fiercer with every stroke of my bow, like I was sharpening a knife with each note. I'd soar up to the high C, vicious, feral with emotion. Then I'd fall, gently, downward to an open G. I'd already be exhausted. The woodwinds would invite tranquillity. It would almost feel romantic. I'm more tempted to open the drawer now than I have been in months, but I know I shouldn't.

My therapist, Julie, made me lock it shut after a particularly bad panic attack, which ended in me lying, breathless, on a filthy Tube floor. I argued at first and said I needed the memory drawer to 'tame the fire in my playing' just like Professor Forrest taught me. Julie rebutted, 'But can't you project the fire without feeling the heat? And who is music for, anyway, player or audience?' She had a point. But so did my professor.

'It's difficult, maybe even impossible, to find a perfect balance between surrender and control,' Professor Forrest used to say. 'The trick is perfecting a push and pull between them.'

Okay, just for a few moments, I'll let myself indulge in the memory. Then I'll practise properly. *Safely.*

Memory: The Night We Broke Up
Even Though We Were Still In Love

I fiddled with the chain around my neck while he paced, hands in his curls, jerking them back and forth. He looked uncomfortable, unnatural, like he was following a stage direction he didn't understand. Our kettle finished boiling though neither of us dared to acknowledge this. I just stood there, watching him.

'I don't understand. You've never said any of this before. How can you not see that this isn't about us? It's about everything else that's happened. Everything with your professor, and—'

'Of course it's about us, Josh. It's about us wanting different things, and eventually … I don't know, we have to think what will be more painful in the long run.'

'Look, even if that's true, why do we have to prioritise the long run?'

I didn't know how to answer.

Then he stilled. He stared at the floor. His hands found his pockets in slow motion and I asked him to look at me. I thought, I truly believed, that when our eyes met a solution would present itself. His gaze rose slowly, caressing my body like his hands used to. He looked at me. His mouth quivered, then tightened. Then he shook his head, there is no solution.

'Look, if this is what you want … Then I think … I don't see how we can …'

His dark eyes were disbelieving, then vacant, then loving. Devastation. It ripped me open, tearing my skin, clutching my heart in its hands, squeezing and rubbing the valves together.

He walked towards me and pulled me into his body. I felt his lips on my hair, heard his sigh. Josh's tears trickled down my face, down my cheeks, catching my own on their way. We swayed from side to side like a last dance, his arms encircling me. But then he stepped away from me and I didn't recognise his expression. Resignation? It could be resignation. Anger, or fear, raced through me, waking every vein and vessel, until every part of me felt alive and hot and pulsing. Volcanic. He tried to soothe my erupting body with a kiss. It wasn't a passionate kiss. His lips were light on mine. They were tired lips or stoic lips or suffering lips. Then he turned away from me.

It would have been perfect, this memory, don't you think? But I don't play like that anymore.

'Come, let's begin,' my violin instructs. '*Violin Concerto in E Minor, Op. 64: 1 Allegro molto appassionato.* I'll count us in.'

———

I'm covered with sweat when Lucia swings open the practice room door.

'Oh, sorry, I thought this room was free!' she grins at me, 'But hi.'

She leans against the doorframe and my eyes climb from her sandals to her vest. Her red strap hangs loose on her shoulder.

'I see you,' she says.

'You see me?'

'Taking my clothes off with your eyes.'

I laugh. 'Am I that obvious?'

'Yes,' she tilts her head. 'But you should use your hands.'

And you know what? I do, grabbing her arm and pulling her inside the practice room.

She spins me around, so we're pressed together against the door, my fingers splayed on the wood. I can feel the contours of her breasts and hips against my back. Fuck. Her breath is playful on my neck as she slides her hands down my sides, pausing at my hips, grabbing.

'This door doesn't lock,' I whisper, as she slips her hand into my shorts.

'Why do you think I've pressed you up against it?'

Fuck.

She kisses my neck as she touches me – hot mouth, soft, slow fingers – and I bend my body to fit into hers. The concerto is still in the air.

Someone tries to open the door and we freeze. I turn and cover Lucia's open mouth with my hand. I feel her smile against my fingers.

'Won't be long,' I manage, 'just finishing up in here.'

Lucia raises her eyebrows. Her tongue grazes my palm. Fuck.

'The rehearsal will begin in ten minutes, yes?' says a voice I think I recognise as Neele's, the very serious, no-sex-in-practice-rooms Viennese harpist. That said, I did once see her file her nails behind her harp in rehearsal, so she's no angel.

'Yes! Great! See you then!'

Lucia sighs, or giggles, into my hand and I'm about to laugh, too, when she looks me dead in the eye and opens her mouth so that my fingers fall inside. She sucks and swirls her tongue. Fuck. Fuck. Then I'm kissing down her neck, drawing my lips from collarbone to collarbone. Her head rolls back. She grips the door-handle while I touch her and she hums with pleasure. Lucia's moans are usually communicative. They spell out desire. They ask for more. *Yes, just like that.* But this is different. She's moaning like she can't help it. And my God, it's hot. And just quiet enough that we should be undetectable. She holds her breath until I feel her shudder against my fingers.

—

Buzz.

JOSH:
Okay, I'm in town!
Going to take myself off to a museum.
See you just after 2!
Hope rehearsal goes well ☺

Excellent.

—

The orchestra members wait for the conductor outside the rehearsal room. In the corner is Stefan, a quiet, bald violist: the type who more than likely celebrates Bach's birthday. Standing beside him, the brass section all look hungover – crossed-arms and under-eye-bags. Especially the trombones. I'm not sure why trombonists are such heavy drinkers. I've heard it stems from some kind of competitive drinking culture – if you don't keep up, you won't pass your trials. Not in all orchestras, of course, *#notalltrombonists,* but often. Though today it's Jacobo, a Colombian hornist, who looks closest to keeling over.

Neele, the Viennese harpist who nearly walked in on Lucia and me, is standing by the window looking wary, or suspicious, or annoyed – I can't be sure. We've only really spoken once before, when she told me in German that life as a harpist was 'hard and beautiful', before declining my invitation for a drink at Golser after rehearsal. I've yet to meet a harpist who knows how to have fun, and Neele is no exception. She wouldn't last a day in the brass section. Then there's Davorin, whose white T-shirt is so tight I can see not only his nipples, but the outline of his chest hair suffocating against the fabric. He's gesticulating wildly, but I'm not quite sure who he's speaking to. A few of the Austrian woodwind players nod along, though I can see their eyes glazing over. Lucia squeezes my arm, then walks towards the rest of the cellists. It's an odd position, leading a section. Everyone behind you plays the same instrument, so you have to prove in every rehearsal that you're a leader worth following. Cellists and violinists are raised to be soloists, so in orchestral contexts, the dynamic can be tense. I've seen the men who sit behind Lucia exchange glances, occasionally roll their eyes. Blah.

Svetlomir, our resident conductor, arrives one minute before eleven and unlocks the door, leading us inside. It is sweltering in here, the kind of heat that coats you, sticky and thick, then swallows you whole. The floor-to-ceiling windows are locked. I should have brought a water bottle. Svetlomir takes his place at the front of the room and adjusts his music stand. His shirt is the colour of blueberries, with dark underarm stains that don't seem to bother him. Usually, he conducts with one pencil and keeps another behind his ear, though today he's brought a baton, and his ears are pencil-free.

Conductor Hair, in my experience, can come in a myriad of textures, colours, or lengths, but needs to be capable of its own momentum. It has to move with a jerk, flip, or twitch of the head. Some instrumentalists roll their eyes when conductors dance at their podiums, but I'm kind of into it. Svetlomir sports a buzzcut, so he lacks that dramatic, wild-hair-flicking effect so many conductors make careers out of. He gives clear downbeats and precise direction, and communicates the essence of his interpretation with his body, but nothing changes inside me when he enters a room.

I lift my violin from her case and check the tension of my bow. As I do, a tall, obscenely handsome man walks past me with a score under his arm. I know immediately that he's the guest conductor by the way he walks – his powerful shoulders and commanding eyes. He has my full attention. I feel my body respond to the tension and direction of his hands as he drags a chair to the corner by the locked window. He sits down and opens his score. He's in his early forties, maybe, in a loose black V-neck T-shirt. He runs his hands through his long curls without making eye contact with any of us. Yet we're all watching him.

A tuning cacophony takes over the room – loud swells of different colours, sustained notes, quick notes, arpeggios. Even after all these years, the messy sound makes me smile. I glance at Lucia, who is looking at Davorin, who is looking at Elsa, who is looking at the hot conductor in the corner, who is looking at – me? His eyes are fierce, but gentle. He nods once and I nod back. Within minutes of meeting an orchestra, a conductor must establish a sense of chemistry, intimacy, trust. It's a position full of paradoxes. A new conductor is top of the orchestral food chain, yet the only musician in the room whose competence is immediately in question. He has an uncontested musical will, yet is completely dependent on the players. The only musician in the room who makes no sound. I've never wanted to be a conductor, though I envy them their bird's-eye view. Learning to think about complete music is one of the most joyful parts of any musical training. It's something you relinquish as a player, accepting your line's purpose in the musical tapestry.

Oh, my D string is a little flat.

Svetlomir taps his music stand with his baton as the guest conductor stands and smiles. Of course his dimples are symmetrical.

'This is Maestro Lorenzo García,' says Svetlomir. I knew it. I wonder if he's speaking English for the Maestro's benefit. 'He's here as a guest and will be observing today's rehearsal. Maestro García studied through *El Sistema* in Venezuela before working under Barenboim in his West–Eastern Divan Orchestra. He now splits his time between Berlin and London. He's here in Vienna to conduct *Tosca*.' A few brass players clap and I join, tapping my bow on my stand. The men behind me follow.

'Thank you,' says Maestro García, in a sonorous baritone. 'It's very good to be here. For those of you who don't know, *El Sistema* is Venezuela's free classical music programme for social change. We have over 400 music centres and 700,000 participants on the programme. So, the education of young instrumentalists has always been very close to my heart.

With this in mind, as well as observing your rehearsal today, I would like to invite the entire violin and viola sections to an audition on Sunday before I leave Vienna. It will be very informal and will take place in one of the practice rooms here at the opera. I want you to play something that shows me who you are as a musician. I have some important projects coming up in Berlin and at the Salzburg Festival this summer, and I am looking for a few young soloists to join us. I don't want to take up any more of your rehearsal time, so thank you for hearing me, and I look forward to listening to your Mendelssohn.'

We clap again. Right. No pressure. I watch Lucia wipe her palms against her shorts and adjust the music on her stand. She isn't looking at me. She's focused. I close my eyes and centre myself. I imagine a silver string running from my head, through my entire body, down into the floor. Then I stand and ready my violin. The orchestra rumbles, a rich shimmering rumble, and I join them with Mendelssohn's melody and we're off.

—

The room is silent but I'm vibrating with the music we've made. Svetlomir wants to repeat the transitional passage. Fine. But God, it's hot in here. I wish someone would open the windows; I want Vienna to blow its powerful breath into our sticky rehearsal room. The street would welcome our Mendelssohn, I'm sure. I glance at Lucia, who is staring at me, and I feel my face flush. She mouths 'brava', and I watch her teeth bite down on the v. I breathe through my nose.

Oh, Svetlomir is waiting for a signal from me. I nod, yes, I'm ready, let's go again. I focus on my technique, attending to the piece's Bach-like precision. And the *legato*. And the *martele*, attacking each stroke with my wrist for a more severe articulation. Eventually, Elsa leads us into the calm second movement.

—

At exactly 2 p.m., Svetlomir thanks us for our work, slams his score shut, and leaves the room. A single bead of sweat slides down my calf. I haven't thought about Josh once since we started rehearsing. Music is magic. It's all going to be fine.

'Can we speak a moment?' Maestro García is standing beside me.

'Yes, of course,' I say and extend my hand. 'I'm Maya, by the way.'

'Lovely to meet you, Maya,' he shakes my hand, doesn't linger, thank God, 'Thank you for your Mendelssohn. Are you available to come for my little audition on Sunday?'

'Absolutely, yes.'

'*Bien.*' He pulls a white business card from his pocket and hands it to me. It's plainer than I expected – just his name, number, and email address. 'You know, Maya, when I first look at a score, I often think about the ways that composers make us feel awkward. Maybe they're not familiar with the instrument, so they challenge our perception of it. Or maybe they know the instrument too well, so they choreograph our relationship to that instrument for the maximum effect. Tell me, what do you think feels awkward about this piece?'

'What do I think feels awkward about Mendelssohn's E minor violin concerto?' I stall. Is this a test? 'I think there's tension in the violin part, which can be uncomfortable. Or awkward, I guess. But you need to not feel shame around discomfort. You just have to harness it.' I parrot Professor Forrest. I can almost hear her inflections in my voice.

'Yes, *sí*, exactly!' he beams at me. 'And I heard this in your playing! It was very beautiful. Congratulations!'

'Thank you,' I say as he continues.

'But—' He pauses.

But?

'—I'm going to be very honest with you. There were moments of light in your playing that felt like the sun, but then the light would dim and I was in the dark. It made me wonder if the tension in this piece was frightening to you. But it sounds like you are not scared of tension. So I have to ask you, why are you holding back?'

His curls are shiny with sweat, reflecting the light above.

'Oh,' I say, 'I—'

'Maybe you don't have to answer right away.' He grins and wipes his brow. He has a boyish smile. 'Maybe something to think about before your little audition. Okay, I will leave you to the rest of your day. *Hasta pronto.*'

He taps my music stand twice with his palm and walks away.

Panic. I can feel it building in the base of my stomach. No one has spoken to me like this about my playing since I moved here. I thought no one could hear the change. This audition matters. Impressing Maestro García on Sunday is vital.

But Josh is in Vienna. He's here right now. And I'm sleeping with a colleague. And I'm watching her during rehearsal. What am I *doing*? I feel the panic spreading down my thighs, locking my knees, gripping my ankles. No. I cannot afford to fall back into last year's paralysis. Not now. Not ever. I am strong enough to deal with all of this. I am in control. The audition is informal and he's already heard me play. I just need to stay focused, find time to practise. Chill out. No coffee. No alcohol. It'll be fine.

I smile at the Maestro's back and return my violin to her case.

———

The first time I used the memory drawer, Professor Forrest brought two hot chocolates to my lesson. We spoke for fifteen minutes before I even touched my violin – about our childhoods, how we found music, what it meant to us. Then she asked me to think of a memory, any strong memory, and improvise a five-note melody.

'And how would you describe what you just played?' she asked, using her finger to collect chocolatey foam from the rim of her takeaway cup.

'It was a bit sad, wasn't it?' I said, readying my violin to try again.

'No need to try another. Let's stick with this one for now. Yes, it was a bit sad. But it wasn't just sad. It was deeper than sad. I heard longing.'

'Yeah, okay, maybe there was longing, too.'

'What else?'

'I thought it sounded kind of peaceful, actually?' I asked.

'Peaceful sadness. Peaceful longing,' she repeated, playing my five-note melody on the piano. 'Who composes peaceful sadness?'

I thought for a moment. 'Maybe Brahms?'

'Definitely Brahms. Definitely, definitely Brahms, very good. Now, you don't have to tell me what you were thinking of, but I want you to label that memory with a title. Do you have a title in mind?'

I did. I'd been thinking of a faraway memory of Mum standing in the bedroom I shared with my sister. She was watching us sleep, but she didn't know that I was awake, that I could see her. I called the memory, <u>Mum in the Dark</u>. But the picture is hazy. I've always wondered whether I made it up.

'I'm not sure it's entirely true,' I admitted to Professor Forrest, fiddling with my bow, 'the memory, I mean.'

She calmed my hand with hers and said, 'That doesn't matter. Recollection isn't remembering something in its entirety. It's re-collecting. Scattered moments. Pieces. And we're not really trying to recall what happened anyway; we're trying to recall what it *felt* like.'

We tried again, again, again, until I wasn't in the room anymore. My violin and I were flying through time, riding memories like waves. Through living rooms and restaurants, landing on unmade beds and scratchy grass.

By the end of the lesson, I felt drained, dizzy, like I'd just given blood. But completely blissful.

'So something like that?' I said as I packed up. I could hear the pleading in my voice.

'Something exactly like that,' Professor Forrest smiled. No, beamed. Her lip twitched, I remember. For a second I thought she was going to laugh, but then she said, 'This is exciting, Maya. I'm excited!'

———

Elsa swishes towards the string section, earrings like tiny chandeliers catching the light. She waits with folded arms while I pack up my music. Dozens of male eyes press against our backs as we leave together. Lucia is waiting for us in the corridor.

'Well, that was good,' Elsa claps her hands together in the lift. 'You really go for it, don't you, Maya?'

'She really does,' Lucia says, leaning against the mirror. When I look at her, I see both our faces staring back. Mine is redder than I expected. Lucia drapes her arm around the neck of her cello case and grins at me. She can't hear when the light dims, can she?

'What did the Maestro want to talk to you about?' Elsa asks as we walk towards the stage door.

'Oh, just logistics about the audition this weekend,' I sound nonchalant. Good.

We 'Tschüss!' the not-smiley porter as we leave the opera house. I've started sing-songing my goodbye like the rest of the group, promoting Tschüss to two syllables.

Tschü-üss!

A horse pulls a carriage down the expansive boulevard, pausing by the sea of motorbikes at the stage door. Men in black
Technik shirts smoke by the pillars.

'What do you think you'll play in the audition?' Elsa asks
me. 'I think Maestro García is a Mahler specialist, but it
would be dumb to play a conductor's favourite repertoire at
an audition.'

I'm about to respond when Davorin stumbles into our
triangle, adjusting his headband, 'Hey, wait!'

He smells of soap, peanut butter, and cigarettes. He ignores
Lucia, and looks me up and down with pale eyes. His attention is so short-lived, I feel more a victim of the male glance
than the male gaze.

'Do you want to go get a coffee?' he asks Elsa.

'No, thank you.'

I wait for her to say something else – to give an excuse,
even reproach him – but she stays quiet. He tries again,
almost as if conviction, or reshuffled grammar, will produce
a different result, 'I would like to get a coffee with you.'

'I would not like to get a coffee with you.'

'Okay. We will do it another time.' He smiles at us and
walks away. We don't smile back.

'Jesus,' I say loud enough for him to hear. 'Are you
alright?'

'Fine. I'm fine,' Elsa brushes me off. 'I just have to ignore it.'

I check my phone while Lucia and Elsa discuss the availa-
bility of practice rooms on the Mariahilfestraße. I should be
practising too, not meeting with –

JOSH:
Hope it was a good rehearsal!
I'll be at the garden at 2.15pm
hope that's okay.

Lucia is close to me – when did she get so close to me? – close enough to read my phone, or at least to glimpse a name in CAPS.

'Everything alright?'

'Yes. Sorry, ah. Josh, a guy from London, is in Vienna. We're going to meet—'

'Oh. Is that who you called this morning?' There's a line forming between her brows, the same one that deepens when she plays the cello. I would give anything to be back in her cool living room, lying half-dressed on her couch, listening to *Tuono della Vita* . . .

'You coming, Lucia?' Elsa calls from a few metres away, already walking towards practice rooms, peace, better choices. She hums my Mendelssohn melody.

'Yes, he called this morning. I'm just going to meet him in the Volksgarten, but I'll call you after?'

Lucia smiles, shrugs, and kisses me slowly on both cheeks. My stomach twists with abrupt, urgent lust. *Desire is strange.*

But I swear she frowns as she walks away.

I lean on the nearest pillar, close my eyes, and exhale sharply – loud enough that a few of the *Technik* men look my way. Then my phone buzzes. Josh? No, Georgia.

Georgia:
We still on for tonight babe?
x x x

Oh, of course. Georgia was meant to come over tonight for 'an evening of painting and prosecco' – obviously not my idea. I have told her that I'm a terrible painter and she has reassured me that it doesn't matter. Georgia is an Australian writer, currently working on her second novel, though she never talks about her work. We met by chance on the number 49 tram just after I moved to Vienna. I liked the way her eyes drooped a little at the sides making her look perpetually sad. She would probably describe them as 'seductive'. Georgia ends each day asking what percentage of her waking hours were spent doing what she wants to do. Anything below 80% is considered a failure. Though she spent three and a half hours waiting with me for my residency permit appointment, so maybe this is bullshit. Georgia wears mismatched earrings (feathers often feature) and says things like: 'For me, dating is all about wondering why someone is single, then finding out the answer'. She strikes me as someone who is very good at painting. She picks up on the third ring.

'You know, replying to a text with a call is very *my* generation of you.'

'You're four years older than me, Georgia.'

'I'm clearly not the one who needs reminding!'

My laughter is slightly more hysterical than I intended.

'Righto, what's up with you?'

I check to see no one from my orchestra is lurking by the stage door and whisper,

'Okay, so I have kind of been seeing someone from work. Very casually.'

Georgia's dramatic inhale whooshes through my earphones. She separates each word with a small pause. 'This. Is. Huge.'

I roll my eyes.

'Why am I only hearing about this NOW?' She sounds EXASPERATED.

On one of our earlier friend-dates at a tiny, expensive 'speakeasy' in the First District, Georgia said that the conversation topic she couldn't live without was 'romance'. She said it whilst swaying to a French rendition of 'Dream a Little Dream'. Then she told me she'd never been in love. Liar. She doesn't know that I read her first novel – a love story set at a university campus in Canberra that rings a little too true. Each page is laced with heartache. And she has an Ocean Vuong quote tattooed on her ankle. 'Maya, who are they?! Have I met them?!'

When I first told Georgia I was bisexual, she nodded and gravely asked me what I thought of the way-too-explicit sex scenes in *Blue is the Warmest Colour* and whether I followed the 'Dyke Blanchett' account on Instagram. Georgia may be straight, but I am definitely not her first queer friend.

'Her name is Lucia. She's an Italian cellist in my orchestra. She's amazing.'

'Yeah, sure, this sounds suuuuuuper lowkey. Okay, obviously tell me more about her.'

'That's not why I called.'

I explain my Josh situation in short, breathless sentences.

'Um I'm sorry what the fuck? This is mad? Josh as in your Big Ex in London?! When is he coming?! What are you going to do?! Can I use this in my novel?! Are you okay?!'

'It's all very confusing. I'm very confused.'

'I think "confusion" is a fair response to most things in this silly world. You didn't stay friends, did you? You've never mentioned— '

'—No, that would have been bizarre . . .'

'For sure. No, yeah, it's always such a patronising conversation – when an ex says they're ready to be friends, what they're really saying is "Ha! I'm over you!"'

'Right,' I say as a few *Technik* men pass me on their way back into the opera house.

'I think you should see if your therapist has some time free to chat? Tell her it's an emergency?'

Am I really going to outsource my stress?

'Maybe,' I say, 'but anyway, I'm going to tell Josh he can't stay with me. I have an audition on Sunday. It's very informal, but still, I shouldn't—'

'God, you are so disciplined!'

I flinch. I don't like being called disciplined. It makes me feel robotic. Yet you can't be a professional musician without discipline.

'Is that what you really want? For him to leave?'

Someone taps my shoulder and I jump. Josh? No, it's Davorin.

'Okay, I'm sorry, I've got to go.'

'Wait! I'll see you tonight then, yes? I'll still come over at six? And you can tell me all about your afternoon with your love-of-your-life ex. I'll bring the popcorn.'

'Yes, do, okay, but it can't be too late a night! And I won't be drinking.'

'Killjoy, fine, more for me, bye, bye, byeeeeee.'

'Hey Maya, what's up?' Davorin asks with a slight American twang.

I text my therapist as I answer.

Me:
Hi Julie,
Hope you're well!
You don't happen to have time to see me
tonight or on Saturday, do you?
Sorry for late notice! No worries if not!
M

'Not much.' I don't think we've ever spoken one on one before. 'Why are you still hanging around?' I delete *No worries if not!* and click send.

He ignores me. 'Can I ask you a favour? I'm meeting a photographer any minute to take some new photos for my website. Can I borrow your phone to check my hair?'

'Sure, I guess,' I shrug, handing him my unlocked phone.

Davorin's laugh bounces off the pillars.

'I can't believe you fell for that!' he says, scrolling through my phone, holding it way above my head.

'Fell for what? Davorin! What are you doing!'

'I only need a minute,' he says, still grinning.

'Davorin, what the fuck?' I look desperately to the remaining *Technik* men, but they aren't paying us any attention.

'Done! Sorry, but I want Elsa's number and it's not on the orchestra contact list.'

Anger burns my cheeks. This is absurd. 'You can't just—'

'It's done, Maya. Let it go. And someone called Josh is calling.'

—

On our first date, Josh drew me flowers on the back of a napkin in a corner of a wine bar, the candlelight casting a sepia filter over our evening. The colours came from our conversation. When he excused himself to the loo, I took a photo of his blurry figure walking away from me. The act felt instinctual, like my body wanted me to remember this moment. Meeting Josh? Or Josh walking away from me? I don't know. I saved the picture as his contact photo on my phone and I'm looking at it now, in Davorin's meaty fingers, as he rings.

—

I've told Josh to meet me by the Mozart statue in the Volksgarten. The air is thick with sunshine and the occasional earthy waft of pot and tobacco. A sweaty fitness group stretch their necks in unison. Beside them, an older couple hit a ball back and forth, using a hedge as a net.

I perch with my violin under a tree, near a group of teenagers speaking a mixture of English and German. They're sitting in a circle, evenly spaced, though their bodies are angled so that you can tell who is dating whom. A girl in a crop top and black shorts holds a cigarette in one hand, an iPhone in the other. 'We're sitting next to Mozart,' she says. 'He is pointing at us.' I look up at the grand, white statue of Mozart, whose finger extends towards this group of teenagers as if to say 'Yes, she's right! Your friends are here!' Beneath him, red flowers swirl into a perfect treble clef. Polished Vienna, glamorous Vienna. I debate calling Lisa before Josh gets here – maybe I need someone to tell me this is a bad idea. Maybe I need someone to tell me to run to a practice room far away from Mozart and all these roses. There are so many roses!

But Lisa is smack bang in the middle of her workday, and what would I say? *Hey Lise. I'm calling because Josh is here in Vienna. Do you remember when we broke up and you were so worried all my crying would dehydrate me, you left two glasses of water next to my bed every night?*

Music, more music. I scroll Spotify for Lucia's album of cello pieces by French female composers. *Lucia Rizzo – Découvert.* My favourite is the *Boulanger – 3 pieces for Cello and Piano.* I once touched myself while listening to this recording. I'm in the mood for *No. 3 – Vite et Nerveusement* – obviously. There's something entrancing about a motif that quickly climbs, then crashes, only to climb again. Like a musical Sisyphus on speed. I'm waiting for the shift in metre in the cello – the one that leaves you unbalanced. 2/4 to 5/8. Yes, yes, yes, there it is. As if Sisyphus suddenly decided to drop the rock and dance, running his exhausted hands through his hair, rolling his shoulders, face to the sky.

'Hey Maya,' His voice makes me jump. I swivel violently to face him, ripping the headphones from my ears. His shoes are scuffed. My eyes climb the dark denim of his jeans. He's standing beside me, phone in one hand, the other in his pocket. His T-shirt is pulled tight across his chest and tucked into his trousers. *I know how those shoulders taste.* I reach his eyes, and trace the outline of his contacts around the rich brown. I feel dizzy, hot. I'm 22 again and freefalling. I manage a 'Hi Josh' and stand. Hover. Unsteady. I think he might look away, but he is transfixed by me like I am transfixed by him.

'Hey Maya,' he says again, laughing a little. Our names float in the air between us. I wonder how many times he's said my name since our break-up. Maybe he's met another Maya. Maybe his parents still ask after me. Maybe his best friend Aden forbade my name. *£1 in the break-up jar, it's for your own good, Josh.* Something in my chest feels frenetic, unhinged, and I almost laugh out loud too. I feel my heart thumping stupidly against my ribcage, like a prisoner, like it can't wait to throw its arms around Josh and kiss him sloppily. I feel—

'Do you want to sit?' one of us says. We don't sit. I don't know how close we should sit. Everything feels stilted, awkward, unnatural. Even my shadow looks tense. I roll my shoulders, willing myself to relax.

'I promise I will explain everything soon, I just need to— I don't know, how are you?'

Josh's voice is like hot butter, or melting sugar, or that moment just before they turn to caramel. It's been a year since I've seen him in three dimensions: the texture of his hair, his fidgeting fingers, the lightest of lines on his forehead that cameras don't yet capture. I'm staring at this man I spent so long loving, realising how much of his face I've already forgotten. I know the outfit I wore the first time we had sex, the black skirt I can't wear anymore or throw out, but I've forgotten the v-shaped crinkle between his brows, the exact pink of his lips, his slightly crooked bottom teeth. Damn it, and I've forgotten how he moves.

Wait, I think the line between his brows is deeper, a little more fixed.

Oh, there are dark bags under his eyes. He looks exhausted.

'I'm fine,' I say. 'Josh, what's going on? Are you alright?'

'I'm okay, yeah.'

We face one another for a moment before he sits cross-legged on the dry grass. I realise he's carrying his old, broken black backpack. It looks overpacked. *How long are you staying Josh? And where?* I sit opposite him, as far away as I can manage without it seeming weird. I feel unsettled. I feel ridiculous.

'I didn't expect there to be so many teenagers here, you know? When I think of Vienna, I tend to think of older people.' He gestures to the group next to Mozart, who have broken off into even kissing pairs. His smile is playful. I remember that smile – laughing at an underground comedy gig, lounging in the sunlight on Brighton beach. Then I see something leave his eyes. They're darker, deeper. He's not just tired; it's something else I can't place. Josh. Josh, who I spent so much time loving and then locking away.

'So how long have you been living here?'

'A few months now. I've got a job here with the Habsburg Phil.'

'First violin?'

'You know it.' I smile.

'So you're living the life.'

The life he didn't want. The childless, adventurous, quasi-nomadic life I left him for. Or he left *me* because of? I watch his eyes watching me as I lean back in the grass and stretch my legs. I consider whether alcohol might untie the knot that is my stomach. No, I still have to practise more today. And for God's sake, I am an adult who can deal with 2.30 p.m. discomfort sober. Josh openly studies me. Has much changed about me in the last year? I'm at an age when I don't know whether a year is a long time. I'd stopped myself from making any rash, body-altering decisions after our break-up. No new piercings, no tattoos, hardly even a haircut, just my usual bisexual bob.

'I guess I am!' I say. 'And now you're here! How was the flight?'

It feels like the right thing to say until it doesn't.

'You know me, I hate flying.'

Josh drank three G&Ts on the flight to Rome for our two-year anniversary. That was the same trip where I almost crashed the rental Vespa into a van. I trace the perimeter of my round ankle scar, the same one Lucia touched this morning. I remember the shock I felt that evening – a kind of calm, peaceful shock, unaware of colours, sounds, pressures, momentum. Josh, who'd been driving the scooter behind me, made sure our Vespas were collected from the side of the road. He bought me burn cream and a colourful three-scoop gelato – 'You need sugar!' – and wrapped my ankle in a bandage in our little hotel room. His fingers smelt of ointment all of the following day.

Present-day Josh shows me a picture he took from the plane window.

'Lame, I know, but I haven't been on a plane in forever.'

I look at the device, which holds the secrets of his last eleven months, and I want to grab it and run. I want to read all his notes, messages, emails, flick through his photos. I want to study his social media and his dating apps. Dating apps. Is he single? Does that matter? I realise his phone probably knows more about him than I do. Wonderful.

His mismatched socks. The way he blinks more when he's nervous. The tiny infinity tattoo on his calf he got as a dare at university.

After he left – after I told him he had to leave – I curled into our sofa and tried to disappear, drowning in the cushions. Eventually, I dragged myself into the bath. As the room grew steamy, breathing became harder. My face was covered in salt and sweat and snot and I gulped in the hot damp air and sank deep into the water. Then I wrapped myself in his fluffy grey gown and sat in a ball on our closed toilet, longing for him to come home.

'You know what, why don't we go for a walk around the park?'

'Sure!' He stands, hoisting his bag onto his back. I brush the grass from my hands and scoop up my violin.

'I don't know where to start,' I say, as we pass Mozart and the teenagers. 'Conversationally, I mean.'

'Me neither.' I can feel his eyes on me.

'Let's start with work. How is work?'

Josh tells me 'work is good, work is work'. His Year 9s are much easier than his Year 11s, but 'they're good kids, they're good kids'. Sure, 'work is work', but I know it means more to him than he lets on. Josh took online courses in child psychology and neurodivergence so he could be more flexible in his teaching style. He never mentioned this to his colleagues or his friends. He probably wouldn't have told me if we weren't already living together and I hadn't seen the textbooks on his bedside table, next to all the 'Thank you for everything Mr Greenberg' cards. Just like he never spoke about how quickly he was promoted to Head of English. It was strange, as a musician, to be around someone who didn't need to advertise his success.

We arrive at a sea of rosebushes.

'This city is fucking weird,' Josh says. There's a violence in the way he says 'fucking' that seems too severe for the sentence.

'Weird?' I ask, admiring the spiralling petals and lush greenery. Each rosebush comes with a dedication – lover, family, friend.

He shakes his head, 'Sorry. It just feels kind of weird walking around here. Everything is so ... pretty?'

'Oh,' I say stupidly, 'of course.'

'Can we go have a look at that Art Nouveau building?' he points to the Palmenhaus, eyes scaling the intricate wrought-iron framework.

'Sure.'

I nearly walk into a woman with a pram, suddenly reminded that the park is full of people going places. This surprises me because I've forgotten that other people exist, that mere metres from us strangers walk with thoughts and bodies and dramas all of their own.

Beside the Palmenhaus café, two groups have formed – one dancing salsa, the other waltz. The juxtaposition of styles is startling. There is something severe, almost royal, about the waltzing couples. They dance like brother and sister, lips far apart, hands safely placed on backs and shoulders. Their postures are straight, their necks are long, their movements swift and expansive. They glide over the stone floor like powerful, musical ghosts. Next to them, the salseros' hips seem scandalous. As though each spin, each touch, could set fire to the pair; yet it's a risk worth taking for the heat of every spark.

'Surely it's too hot to dance,' says Josh, wiping his neck.

His watch is upside-down. I don't point this out. He's

wearing a beaded bracelet I recognise as his mother's. She wore dozens of these colourful, South African bracelets around her wrist. 'They remind me of home in Joburg,' she told me once over coffee in her chaotic kitchen. The bracelets looked garish and loud next to her otherwise simple fashion. There are smudges on Josh's left hand. I wonder what he's been writing. Maybe he wrote in his journal at the airport, while I – completely unaware that Josh, *the* Josh, JOSH, would soon be standing beside me – was listening to Lucia play the cello in her living room. Lucia. I need to tell Josh he can't stay with me.

'Coffee?' he asks, already walking towards an empty table for two. I try not to think about how much this will cost. We sit opposite one another, Josh's backpack and my violin catching up on the seat between us. Beside us, a couple drink iced coffees in silence and play with each other's fingers. A waiter arrives, a twenty-something with reddish stubble and thin-rimmed glasses, '*Haben Sie sich schon entschieden?*'

'Have we decided what we want to drink?'

Josh grins and raises his eyebrows. I didn't speak a word of German when he knew me.

I smile at the waiter, '*Ich hätte gerne einen schwarzen Kaffee ohne Koffein, bitte.*' I pretend not to know what Josh will order.

He points to himself, 'Latte, *bitte.*' I haven't heard someone ask for a 'latte' in months. They say *mélange*, here. Never did I think the word 'latte' would inspire nostalgia. The waiter nods and leaves. We must just look like any other ordinary expat couple ordering ordinary expat coffees.

'So,' he leans forward, resting his chin in his hands.

'So,' I repeat, but they sound like different words.

'What do *you* think of Vienna?'

'I love it here,' I answer honestly. 'It's safe and beautiful and filled with music. You know what everybody says about LA, that every waiter you meet is an actor wannabe? Here it's the same, but all the waiters are classical musicians.'

'Really?' Josh gestures to our red-bearded waiter. 'What instrument do you think he plays?'

'Oh, he seems cool, chilled, friendly. Double bassist for sure. He lives for that epic moment in Shostakovich's chamber symphony, when the double basses play a low C in the first movement and the world splits open.'

Josh has no idea what I'm talking about, but laughs heartily. Okay, we've relaxed. Finally.

'Double bass!' he echoes. The couple on our other side look up at us from their menus. Wry smiles. The double bassist arrives with our coffees and two tall glasses of water.

'Okay, Josh, you need to tell me what you're doing in Vienna.'

Josh's eyes drop to his mug. His mouth twitches.

'I'm sorry. I promise we can talk about it, but can you give me an hour to build up to it?'

I don't understand and I almost push it, but then he looks at me with a face I hardly recognise. A pleading face, maybe. Vulnerability scribbled over every inch of him. I nod. This is so unlike him. The couples on either side of us have started making out. Why is everyone making out today? I sip my bitter decaf coffee.

'Oh, shit, I forgot, I bought you something. Well, it's hardly a thing, but I think you'll like it.'

Josh pulls a deformed Terry's Chocolate Orange from his backpack. My mouth waters. Did he choose orange chocolate on purpose?

'Oh, thank you, that's—'

'Shit, I think it's completely melted in this heat.' He presses the ball of chocolate, which immediately yields to his touch.

'Don't worry about it, it just needs a few minutes in the fridge. Déjà vu, huh?'

He smiles sheepishly, then asks me more about my orchestra. It feels good to share a few anecdotes, to caricature a few colleagues. I haven't really spoken to anyone at home about my new job. Most of my friends are musicians and 'work' is a sensitive topic. The arts scene in the UK is on fire. The mood is pretty bleak. I tell Josh about the Mendelssohn we're rehearsing, and about the visiting conductor and the audition. There's a reverence in his eyes I can't ignore and fine, fine, fine, I fucking love it. The deflated chocolate orange sits on the table between us.

Josh excuses himself to the bathroom. A woman and her two shrieking children take a table nearby. I don't want her to see me grimace – it's not her fault they're screaming – but the pitch of the screams is under my skin, pushing the buried Josh-is-in-Vienna panic to the surface. I want to put my hands on my ears. Please stop, please stop, please stop. Okay. I allow myself fifteen seconds to panic. I count them on my fingers. I'm panicking because this is overwhelming and because I don't have all the information. I'm panicking because he's here and because we're not together and because

I should be practising and because these screams are inside me and because Lucia frowned as she walked away, and I'm back in the bathroom, clutching his fluffy grey gown, on the day he left and didn't come back *thirteen, fourteen, fifteen*. I stop panicking.

Fuck it, I'm going to call Lisa as soon as I have a moment to myself.

No, no I'm not. I'm going to concentrate on something else.

A boy, a student, I guess, cycles past me with his arms folded. He looks bored. From the waist up, he looks like he could be waiting for a tube. The Tube – would I have made this link had Josh not suddenly arrived? Josh, who is standing beside our table.

'I paid. Do you wanna get out of here?'

'Oh, no, how much was—'

'Honestly, don't worry about it, seriously.' He smiles at me, and I imagine taking off his shirt. *What is wrong with me?* The thought I've been ignoring thrashes around my head, beats against my skull, possessed, angry. 'Engage with me!' it's screaming. Fine. I let myself think it just once:

Is he here for me?

———

Lucia:
Ciao cara!
The violinist in my gig
tomorrow afternoon has
just pulled out.

Are you free? 300 euros?
Do you know the Schubert
Piano trio? Op. 100?
Can I come over now with
the pianist to rehearse?
Baci

Georgia:
Triiiiiiiple checking we're
on for tonight?
Hope you're having fun! ;)
x x x

Julie (therapist):
Hi Maya.
I have a slot early on
Saturday morning?
9.a.m. your time?
Julie

I type while we walk.

Me:
Sure! Sounds fun!
Come over in half an hour?

Me:
Thanks so much, Julie.
That's perfect. See you then.

I'll write to Georgia later.

———

There are a few electric-green e-scooters parked by the Volksgarten entrance. Josh follows my gaze and says, 'Great idea!'

I point in the general direction of my flat. 'We're heading that way.'

We pass tiny gallery after tiny gallery as we ride. This one has a 3D sculpture of block-shaped people handing each other bits of technology. The next has a unicorn head jutting out of the wall, like a deer in an old English pub. The building to our right has a big glass cylinder sticking into its roof, like a straw. Ahead of me, Josh whoops at semi-regular intervals. I imagine scootering down these streets is the art-lovers' equivalent of always having Mozart in your ears, or chocolate in your mouth.

I once kissed Josh in bed with a slice of Terry's Chocolate Orange in my mouth, passing him the chocolate with my tongue. After he swallowed, he looked at me seriously and said, 'This is how I'd like to die'. I used this memory when I played the Dvořák Serenade for Strings. I named it Death by Chocolate Orange and it was *perfect*. Tender and lush and shimmering without ever straying into gushy sentimentality. God, the scoring of that piece is miraculous, isn't it? Otherworldly. So disarmingly delicate, so beautifully voiced that the chords glisten.

But I should be thinking about the Schubert piano trio Lucia and I are about to rehearse. I've played the Trio once before, a few years ago in concert at the Royal Academy. Once I'd automated the technique and memorised the notes, Professor Forrest made me play it over and over with different memories from the drawer. The second movement was the trickiest to set.

The memory of eating dinner with Lisa at Trinity Dublin after she'd left to study was *almost* a good fit, but the one we settled on started naked in bed one night when Josh read me a line from the book he was reading – Ben Lerner's *10:04*. 'Since the world is ending ... Why not let the children touch the paintings?' Without any context, this line resonated with me like music resonated with me. I was struck and confused by our strange desire to preserve, when time only moves in one direction. (I am now a little obsessed with stalling time.) I was touched by the innocence of children. (I am now jealous of the innocence of children.) I imagined a life without conse- quence – since the world is ending. (I now think, constantly, of consequence and the weight of Choice.) I was reminded of, and frightened by, my mortality. (This fear persists.) And the world's mortality. (This fear increases day by day.) But it wasn't some kind of nihilistic slap across my transient, aging, fleeting, fading face. I fell into those words like I fall into music.

Then Josh asked me to share a piece of music 'in exchange', so I played him Schubert's *String Quartet in G Major D887*. When he asked me what to listen out for, I told him to listen to it while drinking hot chocolate. I told him the quartet was indecisive but without negative connotations. I told him when I listen to this piece, I feel like I'm walking around a grand old house. Different sections are different rooms. You start in the ornate hallway, move to a little study, and back again. The garden has sharp, trimmed hedges at first, but the deeper in you go, the wilder it becomes.

Then he told me he loved me, words packaged in poetry and chamber music, his warm hand on my cheek.

And that was the memory we went with.

When I played the Schubert with that memory in mind, Professor Forrest stood up and slapped the wall. 'That's the one! That's the one!' she sang and started to laugh. We celebrated with sweet coffee from the machine in her office – she only ever had vanilla and caramel flavoured pods. And she came to the concert later that week with a bouquet of yellow roses, a box of Jaffa Cakes, and a tiny card with the words 'Brilliant, truly' written inside. That card is still in my wallet.

—

Josh studies my little basement flat, the mostly-underground box I've started to call home – the messy stack of books (mostly scores) next to my speaker, my cheap keyboard, the colourful empty vases. The flat consists of an open-plan kitchen/living room/study/studio space, and a small bedroom. The long tilted rectangular windows try their best to capture as much natural light as possible, but, at half-below ground, most of the light comes from my golden eco-friendly bulbs and mismatched lamps from Facebook Marketplace.

Josh is the first person to enter my flat without taking off his shoes. I put the melted chocolate orange in the fridge while he looks around. I need to keep my head screwed on until Lucia leaves, then I will find out what's going on with Josh. Easy.

'Wait, is that me?' He points to a long, framed photograph on the wall by my bedroom door – the back of a man's head in a bar. Oh God. My stomach seizes. It didn't occur to me to remove traces of Josh/heartbreak before we descended the crooked little staircase into my flat. Yes, I do realise that it's strange to hang a picture of your ex on your wall, but I really just like the aesthetic, truly, and you can't even tell it's Josh. Quick scan. There are no other visible relationship relics.

'It *is* you, yeah,' I say, because what else is there to say.

'Right.'

'It's from that pub in Kilburn we went to after we saw *White Teeth* at the theatre,' I continue, as though explaining the origins of the photo will also explain its hanging on my wall.

'I haven't seen this photo before, have I?'

'No, I don't think you have.'

'It's a really beautiful photo.'

I hadn't expected him to say this, though he's right. I love its textures: Josh's smooth white jumper, lush dark curls, hundreds of etchings in the bar, mismatched bottles and glasses that glisten as much as the black and white print allows.

'Yeah, I think so too. Obviously.'

'I still can't believe they made *White Teeth* into a musical,' he grins. He doesn't ask me why he's hanging on my wall.

I offer Josh more coffee, something to do before Lucia arrives, and pop one of the capsules into the machine. We're quiet while it roars. But I lose my grip on the mug. It falls, crashing, shattering spectacularly. Josh jumps, then hurries over to me. We are shrouded in a foreign, nervous energy as we collect the shards, acutely aware as to avoid touch. He's clumsy with the fragments, slices his finger, keeps on cleaning, dripping blood. The amount of blood is disproportionate to the tiny cut, gushing in stark, jagged lines. It's like performance art: this handsome, nervous man, blood and coffee streaks on a wooden floor. I can see the title: *Awkward Choreography Between Familiar Strangers*. Then he starts to laugh, shaking his head.

'We're a mess, aren't we? Maybe coffee was a bad idea.'

But I'm not laughing. Are my hands shaking? Is that why I dropped the mug? I cannot deal with shaky hands. That's how it started last time. First shaky hands, then the insomnia, then the panic attacks. A violinist needs still hands and sleep and composure. Maybe I should just tell him to leave.

'Hey, don't you like to refamiliarise yourself with music before you rehearse? I don't mind cleaning the rest of this up if you need to work.'

I hesitate. He's right. I haven't played this Schubert in years. 'Are you sure?'

'More than,' Josh smiles at me from the tap as he rinses his bleeding finger.

Okay.

Work mode. I plug in. I'm in the *zone*. I let the notes unfold in my mind, lyrical and aching. But as the piano takes the theme in octaves, all I can do is stare at the back of Josh's head on my wall, willing it to turn around and tell me what he wants.

The doorbell. I jump. I yell, 'It's open!', and Lucia lets herself in. She's changed into white linen trousers and a navy striped shirt. Loose and relaxed and low-cut. I'm still in yesterday's clothes.

'Hi,' I say as she manoeuvres her body and her cello down the stairs. She slides off her sandals and steps forward to kiss me on both cheeks. I feel my shoulders tense. Presumably she feels this, too. Josh hangs back, watching us.

'This is Josh.' I say his name meaningfully, like she's heard lots about him, though, of course, she has not. Josh smiles, waves, and shoves his hands in his pockets. Josh always puts his hands in his pockets when he meets someone new. The familiarity of this, him, is painful. Fantasy Josh is trying to break into my memory drawer, fiddling with the lock, banging at the handle, beckoning me to join him. Real Josh looks surprised when Lucia kisses him too.

'Please don't let me get in your way,' he raises both hands, like he's asking for a double high five, or being arrested. Lucia looks at me, then back at Josh. I can't tell what she's thinking. She's brought her own music stand and adjusts its height while she tells me about the gig.

'It is for the couple whose apartment I live in.'

She explains that they throw these soirées a few times

a year. The conductor and soprano are very proud of the musical history of their home – the renowned musicians who've lived there over the last century, the frequent visits by Mahler, Zemlinsky, Puccini ... Musical soirées were regular occurrences, and these latest tenants intend to keep tradition. 'And they like the idea of supporting young musicians,' she concludes, checking her phone.

I breathe out, pushing the air and shaky-hands energy away in an audible whoosh. Josh raises an eyebrow at me.

'Oh *merda*, Sergei cannot come to rehearse with us. He is stuck playing piano for auditions. How annoying.' She smiles at Josh, 'Do you play the piano, Josh?' His name sounds foreign in her voice.

'Afraid not,' Josh moves out of Lucia's way, brushing past me. I feel his hand on my back. I flinch. Lucia's eyes dart to his touch, then to me. I step forward.

'Are you both sure you don't mind me hanging around while you rehearse? I'm happy to take myself off for a walk or something.'

'Whatever you like,' I say. 'No pressure to stay or go.'

'I'd love to hear you play again,' Josh smiles at me.

'Stay, Josh!' Lucia says. 'It will be great to practise in front of an audience!'

I can't read her expression. Fuck me. This is objectively stressful, right? Not just me being anxious? Okay, I just need to survive this rehearsal, then I'll be able to sort my head out.

Josh lies down on the couch and closes his eyes. He has his hands on his stomach, and I watch them rise and fall, just for a moment. Lucia hands me a copy of the Schubert Piano Trio.

'Are we playing the whole thing?' I ask her.

'No, no, just the Second Movement.' She studies the score, swaying to the music in her mind, clicking the tempo, while I set up my own music stand.

Lucia sits and spreads her legs; her cello slides between them. I want to take her photo. *Why don't I hang it up next to the one of Josh on my wall? Candid shots of people I've slept with who aren't supposed to meet! Super! Though I'm sure that exhibition already exists in Shoreditch.*

Focus.

I like the way she breathes when she plays Schubert, the way she makes dark music glisten. Despite everything, her playing is calming. Small beads of peace drip down my face, soothing my tense forehead, mouth, jaw. More droplets. Soon I am wet with serenity. So much so, I don't even question this weird metaphor. Instead, I relax into her rich melody. I pretend to study the music while she plays, but, really, I'm watching her. Her eyes are closed tight. Her mouth is tense, too, but the tension seems passionate, powerful, and I feel my own breathing deepen. There is something sensual about her vibrato, like it's desire that's making her hand shake. The musical effect is startling, flooded with emotion. She leans into a long low note, and then, without warning, opens her eyes, staring straight at me. She repeats the low note, eyes locked on mine. We stay like this as the melody develops, and I join her with short accompanimental notes.

'Then the piano takes over the theme,' she interrupts my trance. 'Sergei wants us to play *sotto voce* here.' She sings the pianist's line over our quiet playing. Her voice is warm, *legato*. 'We can get louder with the swells.' She instructs. I obey. 'Exactly.' The melody is mine. I feel my own sound fill the room, and she joins me. I can see our notes in the air between us, dashes and swirls, clashing together, grasping at each other, forced apart.

—

Lucia and Josh are sitting opposite one another at my table. Lucia is fanning herself with her sheet music as Josh tells her, 'That piece was very beautiful. Who was it by again?'

'That was Schubert. And yes, violinists and cellists have the best repertoire in the world. The problem is, we know it.' I laugh from inside the freezer, where I'm digging for a bag of grapes. I wonder if Josh remembers that his family introduced me to frozen grapes at a Passover dinner a hundred years ago.

It was one of those classic London nights – beautiful, filthy, starless. Josh's entire extended family – I swear there must have been fifteen people present – sat around a long plastic table in his parents' house, talking about how hungry they were. The living room was chaotic and cosy, every surface covered with some appliance or ornament. In the kitchen, I spotted at least six different kinds of oils beneath a row of hanging pans. Ruth is a passionate, dramatic cook. She tosses salt and spices over her pan like she's dancing. No surface is spared from discarded potato peels, pepper seeds, flicks of tahini or balsamic. And that Passover dinner was no exception.

There was some rule, like, you couldn't eat until you'd finished reading from a book, and each family member took turns to read a paragraph as quickly as they could. It became a game – who could read the fastest? Consonants were sacrificed. Laughter mingled with the leftover vowels. I could barely follow the story. Eventually we ate – white fish cooked in a sweet, tangy cocktail sauce; alcoholic diced apples and walnuts on crackers; soft, nutty dumplings in an aromatic broth. I watched Josh's little cousin, still in her karate uniform, eat five, maybe six of these, and then refuse to eat anything else all evening. Not even the icy grapes they served with dessert. I didn't say much that night. I let the unfamiliar, big-family joy wash over me. I listened to Josh's Hungarian grandma tell stories. I loved the deep, raspy colour of her voice and the melody of her accent. They'd hidden a cracker somewhere in the living room for us to find, and the whole family cheered when I pulled it out of an empty Elvis Costello vinyl case. Josh's dad awarded me a box of Guylian chocolates. His grandma kissed me on both cheeks and my forehead, leaving a trail of thick mauve lipstick behind.

It used to be in my memory drawer, this evening. I'd labelled it: <u>Passover Dinner, or, Another Life.</u> It suited a particular kind of pure, Mozartian joy. Delight. Uncomplicated bliss.

—

'So, what is your life, Josh?' Lucia takes the frozen grapes from the bunch one at a time, touches them to her lips, and sucks so that they shoot into her mouth. Each grape is an event. Josh lifts a full stalk to his mouth and bites the grapes free. I shiver as they chew.

'What is my life? What a question! My life is London, books, the school I teach at, art, adventure. It's pretty simple, actually. I used to think the secret to happiness was dancing in the shower—'

'You don't think this anymore?'

'It's been a weird month.'

'No dancing in the shower?' Lucia presses her leg against mine under the table without looking at me.

'No,' he says, 'sadly not.'

Lucia nods. It doesn't look like she'll ask a follow-up question. I press back.

'What is *your* secret to happiness, then?' Josh returns. I've always loved this – his gentle way of reciprocating in conversation without just repeating someone's question back at them.

'I don't know if I seek happiness.'

'What do you seek?'

'Emotion,' Lucia sucks another grape.

'*All* emotion?' Josh reaches for another stalk.

'Sì.'

'And how do you seek emotion?' Josh asks.

'Through music, mostly.'

'Interesting. But is it, like, abstract? Or do you relate it to real life?'

'It *is* real life,' she says.

Josh turns to me, broad grin, 'Maya thinks about real events from her life when she plays the violin.'

'Used to,' I correct and he looks puzzled, then wounded.

'I love the way she plays,' Lucia says, turning to Josh. 'You must know each other well.'

'Very well,' Josh replies, though he's still looking at me. 'We go way back.'

'Josh,' Lucia sounds serious, 'is this your head in the photo?'

She's pointing at the photo of Josh's head. I reach for the grapes and pop two in my mouth at once.

'It sure looks like it, hey?' he replies, biting at another stalk.

'It is a good photo.' Lucia checks her watch, then clasps her hands together. 'Okay, I must leave. Maya, I will see you at the soirée tomorrow? I will text you the address.'

Does she sense that something is going on?

Nothing is going on!

'Sure,' I say, 'thanks again for thinking of me for the soirée.' I sound too formal, but it's too late to correct myself.

'*Prego.*'

Lucia packs her cello back into its case while Josh throws the grape stalks in the bin.

Please look at me like you looked at me this morning, I want to say to Lucia. *I'm going to tell him he can't stay.*

But there's another knock at the door. Lucia and Josh turn to me, expectantly.

'*Wer ist das?*'

'Meeeeeee'. The door swings open, skidding against the gravel road outside. The sound makes me wince. Lucia winces, too. Josh doesn't.

Leather flip flops, artistically chipped toenails, like tiny colourful mosaics, 'You didn't reply to my text, so I figured—'

Georgia is dressed in a black short/vest/jumpsuit thing that showcases the artistic splash of freckles on her chest. I can't tell whether her outfit is fashionable or pyjama-like. Or both? She's tied her ginger hair back in a tight ponytail. She ducks as she descends my crooked little staircase, carrying two giant canvases and a paper bag. She looks from me to Josh to Lucia, back to me.

'Oh, hi! Sorry to interrupt.' She does not sound sorry.

'Don't be,' I say, 'I must have lost track of time.'

Georgia kicks off her shoes and slips into the blue rubber *Hausschuhe* that came with the apartment. They fit her better than they fit me, though they look ridiculous with her outfit. She balances the canvases against the wall.

'I'm Georgia, how are you going?'

'Georgia, this is Lucia from my orchestra, and Josh from—' *from?* '—London.'

'Well HO LY shit' – she says 'holy' like it's two words – 'am I glad I came by early!'

She pushes her sunglasses back on her head and kisses Josh on both cheeks, then Lucia. She squeezes my shoulder, asking 'It's okay if I stay?' Actually, it's more of a statement.

Lucia carries her cello towards the stairs, but Georgia

interrupts, 'Oh, please hang around, just for a bit. Maya's told me *so* much about you . . .'

'Oh, has she?' Lucia turns back to me, flashing one of her dazzling soloist smiles. Josh clears his throat.

'I can stay for ten minutes, maybe, but then I must go practise,' Lucia smiles at Georgia and leaves her cello by my staircase.

Georgia takes my seat next to Lucia while I make iced coffees for the group.

'Don't worry, Josh, I know lots about you, too,' Georgia purrs. I worry she might whip out a notebook. Josh's laugh is carefree, though it doesn't sound like his laugh.

'What an entrance!' he says. The coffee smells deliciously smoky and nutty. God, I love real, caffeinated coffee, but I can't drink it when I feel even the smallest trace of anxiety – it disturbs my playing, makes my body feel like it belongs to someone else. I inhale the steam like it's a drug, catching snippets of conversation over the roaring machine.

'On a tram of all places!'

'Yeah, I arrived earlier today.'

The milk is silky as I pour. The golden crema stretches across the mug's surface, it's almost Guinness-like. I add a handful of ice to each cup, taking a few extra seconds to cool my face in the freezer. Then I pass out the iced coffees and take the seat next to Josh. Georgia laughs, clasping her hands together, 'Thank you! Brilliant! So what were you rehearsing?'

'Schubert,' I answer, deciding to play a more active role in this conversation. I fear if I don't steer this ship, we'll hit the iceberg sooner. 'Lucia and I are playing together in a soirée tomorrow.' *Together* feels like a loaded word.

'And how'd the rehearsal go?' Georgia asks. She sounds sweet and polite and un-Georgia-like.

'*Molto bene*. When I play with Maya I feel the blood in my throat,' Lucia says. Josh's eyes widen.

'Of course you do,' Georgia replies, beaming. 'Can I come watch the show tomorrow?'

Since we met, Georgia has not missed one of my concerts, despite having no obvious interest in classical music.

'I think it's a closed soirée,' I say, and Lucia nods.

'Fine, fine, you'll just have to tell me all about it. And Josh!' Georgia flicks her eyes towards him, 'I'm sorry if this comes across the wrong way, but I have to ask, why are you here?'

I don't know if she's asking as my friend or as a writer, but right now, I don't care. He might answer.

'Oh,' his face is blank, then pained, 'Well, I'm here because there was kind of a family emergency in London—'

'What?' I interrupt, sounding angry rather than concerned. The faces of Josh's entire extended family whizz through my mind. 'Is everyone alright?'

Georgia and Lucia exchange a worried glance like old friends.

'Yes. Sorry, no, it's more like family drama. Kind of. And I freaked out, packed a bag, and booked a ticket to Vienna.' He forces a smile and sips his coffee. 'As you do,' he adds.

'Fuck, I'm sorry,' Georgia looks at me, wide eyes saying 'fuck' louder than her mouth did. Lucia reaches across the table for Josh's hand. Either he doesn't notice or chooses not to offer it to her. She leaves her hand like that, vulnerable, extended across the table.

'*Condoglianze.*'

I'm surprised by the reflex to take her hand in mine.

Josh repeats the word, '*Condoglianze.*'

'It is *con*, with, and *doglianze*, lament. Like the music.'

'Thank you,' he says, another fake smile, 'but it's really not that big a deal. Well, I don't know, but you don't have to lament or anything. I don't want to bore you all with my family stuff.'

'I once panicked and booked a holiday after I saw someone get stabbed,' Lucia says. 'As soon as the police let me go, I booked a flight to France to see my sister,'

We all look at her. She shrugs. 'I worked at a bar while I was studying at the music *conservatorio* in Napoli and a man was stabbed with a kitchen knife and I spent the whole night in the police station. I still don't know what happened to the man.'

No one speaks. Georgia slurps her coffee loudly. 'Go on! Go on!' she says.

'There is not much more to say,' Lucia continues. 'In between the interviews I listened to ABBA. I do not think that most people have such *morbose* experiences with ABBA.'

Lucia starts to sing, her Italian accent adding melody to the lyrics, 'The winner takes it all!'

Josh laughs first, his real laugh. Lucia is still singing and soon Georgia and I are laughing too. Everything about this scene is absurd. You know what? I might as well lean in.

'Chiquitita, tell me what's wrong?'

Georgia knocks a beat on the table and the coffees wobble. When Lucia sings 'Mamma Mia', she exaggerates her accent.

I'm sure it's you-had-to-be-there funny, but I can hardly breathe.

The textures of our laughters rub together, building a new sound, like a chord. It's the first time my apartment has filled with chords of laughter. *Morboso* giggling.

Lucia is finally looking at me the way I want her to look at me – with easy familiarity and uncensored desire. In this instant, I'm too relieved to care if Josh sees. Lucia wipes her eyes with the tips of her fingers, *'Amici,* I must really go,' she takes her mug to the sink. *'Grazie,* Maya, and nice to meet you both. I hope things get better, Josh, and you dance again in the shower soon.'

I follow Lucia and her cello up my staircase onto the empty street. I lean in to hug her goodbye, but she places her hand on my cheek, the tips of her fingers brushing my temples, and kisses me on the mouth. I feel her lips smile just before she pulls away.

'Ciao, Maya!' she says, and turns away from me.

I feel my face transit through various emotions as I climb down to my flat.

'So, Josh, are you going to join us with our painting?' Georgia takes her and Josh's mugs to the sink.

—

I am hovering, floating, between table and sink. Georgia is holding a bottle of prosecco, undeterred by my paralysis. She's telling Josh it's the only alcohol that doesn't give her a hangover, insisting that a mostly-prosecco drinking plan has been an excellent decision – 'hangover free and constantly celebrating'. I doubt this. Prosecco is full of sugar. I say nothing. Georgia helps herself to three champagne flutes from my cupboard. She has told me before that she finds my champagne flutes very stylish as the bases are tinted navy blue. I bought them at Sainsbury's when Josh and I moved in together. He never liked them.

'So, what are *you* celebrating?' she tilts the glass towards him while she pours. Thousands of tiny gold bubbles rush to the surface.

'Spontaneous trips abroad?' Josh doesn't raise his glass. Georgia laughs and reaches for his shoulder.

'And what about you?' he asks her.

'I've finally made some progress on the book I've been writing!'

'That. Is. Huge,' I say, joining them. Georgia's dramatic pauses sound ridiculous in my voice. She offers me a glass, but I shake my head.

'Fuck yeah it is!' Josh adds. Neither of us sound like ourselves. 'What is your book about, then?'

'Hedonism,' she says. This is already more information than she's ever shared with me. 'But it's still early days. Second novels are hard.'

'Can you say more about it?' Josh asks.

'That's a no from me.'

'Superstition or distrust?'

'Superstition and distrust are anything but mutually exclusive, babe.'

I excuse myself to the bedroom to practise and tell them to get started on the painting if they'd like to. I don't mind leaving

them alone together. They seem to get on well. Through the
door, I hear Georgia toast, 'Well, to the success of your spontaneous holiday and my novel, then!'

One thousand thoughts attack, but I won't engage with them.
I'm back in work mode. I wear noise-cancelling headphones
while I consider what to play in my audition with Maestro
García on Sunday. My first thought is the *Carmen Fantasy*
by Pablo de Sarasate. It's a technical party piece spun out of
themes of Bizet's opera, *Carmen*, and it's served me well in
competitions. I tend to play the piece faster than the opera –
more of a mood than a tempo – but it doesn't really show off
my 'musical personality'. Just technical virtuosity. What *would*
show off my personality? Yes, yes, I know, there's the obvious
answer – Brahms. Professor Forrest told me Brahms was 'my
composer' because of the way I make my violin sing. It was the
only time I thought she might be lying to me. Really, I think
she could hear that I understood the darkness in his music –
the grief and misery, loneliness, shame, desperation. Even the
anger. People say Brahms is nostalgic, but they're wrong. He
doesn't look backwards. He lives in the space between – major
and minor, triple and duple time, modernism and classicism,
control and surrender, longing and belonging. Nothing is
ever just one way or another. There are moments in his works
where the entire tonal system is hanging by a thread. And do
you want to know the trick to playing Brahms? When you feel
that abyss opening underneath tonality, you need to lean into
it. You need to submit and let yourself fall.

Brahms was madly in love with Clara Schumann. And he was very good friends with her husband. When Robert Schumann attempted suicide and asked to be admitted to a mental hospital, Brahms wrote music and played for Clara to distract her. He visited Robert in hospital over and over and eventually moved into his home to 'help out'. Supposedly, living with Clara, but sleeping in separate rooms, caused him to go mad. We know he wrote letters to her. One said: *'I can do nothing but think of you ... What have you done to me? Can't you remove the spell you have cast over me?'*

But nothing ever happened between Brahms and Clara Schumann. Even when Robert passed away. They both travelled, performed, composed. Separately. When Clara died of a stroke forty years later, she was buried next to her husband. Brahms only lasted another year. He was buried in Vienna. Alone. Not too far from here.

Do you know what? I'm going to go with the *Carmen Fantasy.*

—

Josh and Georgia have moved the sofa to the side of my living room and covered the floor with bin bags and glasses of water. They are sitting close to one another at the base of the sofa, fiddling with empty glasses. There's sandalwood incense burning. Georgia must have brought this with her. Two oversized canvases sit side by side, untouched, in the middle of the floor, surrounded by bags of paints and brushes. I feel infinitely calmer having prepped for this audition. And I'm making 300 euros tomorrow. I'm going to concentrate on relaxing this evening. Relaxing increases productivity, anyway.

'Mayaaaaaa! I was just telling Josh how much I hate Schiele,' Georgia says, pressing her empty glass against her cheek.

'You don't like Schiele?' I ask her, filling a flute with tap water. Schiele is exactly the kind of artist I'd expect Georgia to *adore*.

'I think I know too much about him as a person to like his art. You know he was probably involved with his younger sister, right? And he was arrested for seducing a thirteen-year-old girl?'

'You're kidding,' I say.

'Was he charged?' Josh asks.

Georgia shakes her head. 'I'm not sure that's the most important question,' she chides.

'I don't know if I like Schiele,' I say, sipping my water, 'but I do think it's important to separate the art from the artist. Like, a lot of composers were horrible people, but I can still play and enjoy their music.'

'Like Wagner,' Josh joins in, smiling at me.

'I'm not sure that's the same, though,' Georgia contests, refilling her and Josh's glasses. 'Music can be much more abstract than visual art, right? Like, if Wagner wrote an opera that was explicitly antisemitic, surely you'd think differently?'

Josh is quiet. I don't know much about Wagner's operas, but I'm pretty sure some of them *are* explicitly antisemitic.

'Like, Schiele painted nude children *and* he was accused of paedophilia,' she shudders. 'Which is just gross.'

'Maybe it's important to include information like that in galleries, but still show the work?' I say.

'What about books?' Josh asks. 'Is it important to know about an author before you read their novel?'

'Take it easy there, Roland Barthes,' Georgia leans closer to Josh. 'Look, in my experience, people definitely seem to care about whether there is truth to fiction.'

'Surely that's different, though,' I say. 'That seems to come more from curiosity than any sense of morality.'

'Right!' Josh grins at me. Not gonna lie, it feels good to have a conversational teammate again.

'I often read books and wonder whether the author is basing a story on their own life, but definitely just out of curiosity,' he says, still smiling at me.

'Especially if that author is a woman, right?' Georgia stares at Josh.

'How do you mean?'

'It just comes up a lot more with female authors. I've always felt like readers are trying to disprove the creativity of women. Like, "she couldn't possibly have made this up!"'

'Yes, okay, maybe you're right,' says Josh, 'but for me, I think I just want to know more about the author. And maybe I'm so invested in a story, I want it to be true?'

'I think the way people engage with fiction vs non-fiction makes a difference here,' I say, thinking of my memory drawer. 'Like, I tend to engage with stories kind of reflectively, or passively, but the minute I find out something is non-fiction, the stakes seem so much higher.'

Josh beams at me. 'That's what Rachel Cusk says, too! That

non-fiction directly accesses our shit – fears, anger, envy, sympathy – I was discussing this with my Year 13s a few weeks ago!'

I've forgotten how much I loved the rhythm of our conversations. How, occasionally, they felt almost predetermined, like we were reading off a score. Georgia stares at us. I don't know what she's thinking. Finally she shrugs, 'Sure. It just annoys me that it seems to happen so much more frequently with women, right?'

'Fair,' Josh nods.

'Right, should we get started?' Georgia asks. 'Are you two okay to share a canvas?'

'Sure.'

I sit beside Josh and watch Georgia's eyes dart around my apartment.

'You know, this apartment always makes me think of an escape room.'

Not what I expected her to say.

'I mean there's a kind of mysterious energy in here.'

I don't feel that my flat boasts any particularly mysterious energy, so I wonder the obvious. 'Do you ... want to escape?'

Josh laughs and fiddles with a tube of paint.

'No, no, it's not that! Maybe it's the way you've decorated? A bit eclectic?'

'Yes, yes, I know, I'm not very *visual*,' I say with mock shame.

'She's amazing at literally everything else, though.' Josh smiles at me.

Georgia looks from Josh to me, back to Josh, back to me, so fast, it looks like she's disagreeing.

'I don't really get escape rooms,' I move the subject away from myself. 'We pay money to be trapped with others and then we try to escape?'

'Sounds like twenty-first century dating,' Georgia quips, gulping down prosecco.

'I think it's more about the puzzles than the actual escape,' Josh offers. Both canvases are blank.

Georgia gestures to the photo of Josh's head hanging on the wall behind us. I brace. I've been waiting for this. I'm surprised it didn't happen sooner. 'Maya, I've always wanted to ask,' *Here we go,* 'did you take that photo yourself?'

Interesting.

Surely she knows it's Josh? Even Lucia could tell.

Lucia.

Should I message her? Reassure her?

'I did.' I sound nervous.

'I like it. I don't think I've ever told you that before. I like it a lot.'

That's all?

Georgia is the first to paint – a curved red line at the top of her canvas.

'Did you ever read that Susan Sontag essay, "Plato's Cave"?' she asks, not looking up.

'No' / 'Yeah' Josh and I duet. Georgia smiles at our dissonance.

'Susan says photography is as widely practiced an

amusement as sex and dancing, and I think she's right? Like, I have thirty thousand photos on my phone, but I've never printed and displayed any of them like you have. Have you framed any others?' Georgia's eyes don't leave her canvas.

'No, I haven't,' I admit.

Georgia shakes her brush in a glass of water. I watch the red melt away, dyeing the liquid a dull pink. 'Susan says photographs give people a fake possession of an unreal past.'

'Or just a long-ago past,' I tell the back and front of Josh's head. He winces. I think. One of us needs to paint something. I splatter yellow onto our shared canvas in erratic flicks.

'Are you dating anyone, then?' Josh asks Georgia. She looks him up and down. 'You said dating felt like an escape room before!' he adds quickly.

Georgia returns her attention to her painting, 'Not seriously. I'd rather be wet from orgasms than tears.'

Josh chokes on his prosecco. Georgia laughs, a few strands of ginger hair coming loose from her ponytail. I add a thick purple slash to our canvas.

'Is it hard, then? Dating in a German-speaking country?' Josh asks Georgia, reaching across me to connect my yellow splashes with an orange line. He's sitting a little closer than before.

'I actually used to date to practise my German,' Georgia says. 'Then it became about meeting new people. And I guess now it's just part of my routine. I go on one app date per week. If I want to see the man again, they count as the next week's date. But that's never happened.' She doesn't tell Josh that she uses a fake name – Sasha.

'How was this week's date, then?' I ask, adding a navy shadow under my purple slash. I look down. I realise I'm holding my brush like it's my bow. I used to play with the Russian bow grip – fingers together, wrist up – before I met Professor Forrest. She taught me to play with spaces between my index, second, third, and fourth fingers. Second finger opposite my thumb. I like the accentuated pressure and the freedom this grip allows. Not that these two would notice. Not that this helps my painting.

'Well, two nights ago I met up with a guy who had a face like an owl. It was actually spooky how much he looked like an owl, but it's also the reason I swiped right. His huge round eyes, beaky little mouth—'

'Not to mention the wings and feathers!' I add and Josh's laughter knocks his red border askew.

'Also I thought he sounded interesting – he's a professional chocolatier. I know. So "Vienna". It takes a certain kind of person to dust truffles while the world burns, I reckon. Anyway, blah blah blah, pretty early on he said he was pro-life, so I left while he was in the bathroom.'

'Fair.'

Georgia explains to Josh that she sometimes likes to slip in and out of formal and informal German grammar to 'be playful with power dynamics', though she knows they probably just assume she is less grammatically competent than she is (I've heard all this before).

'So, like, I might ask *"Wie geht's dir?"*, which is a casual way of saying how are you?' She locks eyes with me, continuing, 'But then later in the evening, I might switch to more respectful, conservative grammar and say, "*Ich möchte, dass Sie meinen Hals küssen*"'

'And what does that mean?' Josh asks. He seems enthralled. Georgia nods at me. She wants me to translate. I stare at her for a moment, then turn to Josh.

'It means, "I would like you to kiss my neck" but as if you're speaking to a stranger or someone who is your superior,' I say. I watch Josh's throat as he swallows.

'Oh, I completely forgot,' Georgia smiles like she hasn't just composed symphonic sexual energy. 'I brought us some popcorn. To soak up the alcohol.'

'I didn't realise popcorn was especially alcohol absorbent,' Josh says, while Georgia grabs a packet of microwavable popcorn from her tote and flings it towards him. He doesn't catch it because he has a glass in one hand and paintbrush in the other. Instead, he spills a few drops of prosecco as the packet slides along our canvas leaving a blurry trail.

'Shit, shit! I'm sorry,' Georgia sounds genuinely apologetic, hands flailing.

'It's fine! It adds to the texture. It's like a collage of our evening,' I say as I peel the plastic from the paint. Look at me being the calmest person in the room! The prosecco drops have infected my slashes, spreading like a fizzy virus.

'*Puffmais?*' Josh reads from the packet with a terrible accent, 'It's like they've robbed the word of onomatopoeia!'

I laugh but stop short of leaning into him. On my way to the microwave, I pass Georgia's painting, which looks a little like—

'Georgia, are you painting Josh?'

'Maaaaaybe.'

Georgia is generally more into the stories surrounding art than the art itself. She has a black-and-white sketch of a naked woman hanging above her bed – naked Georgia, apparently – drawn by a one-night stand. *Provocative.* She is so *provocative.* The popcorn plays an erratic beat in my microwave, like a toddler in front of a drum kit. Gradually, the beats slow.

'How would you describe your attachment type, Josh? I'm trying to choose a colour for your hair in my painting,' Georgia asks. She's explained attachment theory to me before. Three categories: anxious, avoidant, secure. According to Georgia, I am avoidant (lol), she is anxious dressed up in avoidant clothes, and secure people are wonderfully, perfectly boring, brilliant, and rare. Obviously, Josh has no idea what she's talking about.

'I know you'll probably find this dull, but I think I'm secure,' he says, biting the edge of his paintbrush. *How on earth does Josh know about attachment theory?*

'I don't find that dull,' Georgia lies, 'I find that admirable. I swing aggressively between the other two. Blue it is!'

Ding!

I empty the popcorn into a bowl and fill their glasses with the final few drops of the prosecco. The last time I had popcorn, I was sitting in the bath at my mum's house. Lisa had tried to stuff as many comforts as possible into the tiny space – candles, wine, music, popcorn. I dropped a piece into the water. I watched it grow soggy in the candlelight. Tonight, the popcorn is overly salted and my hands are covered in greasy butter. I check the time – it's already eight o'clock. I'm not going to be able to practise again tonight, but that's okay. I know the piece inside out. Plus, the audition is informal and I'll go through it again tomorrow.

Georgia excuses herself and I check my phone. No new messages. From my bathroom, Georgia yells that 'Days that are so busy you forget to change your tampon are good days!'

'While you were practising earlier, she told me she was considering buying tampons infused with CBD,' Josh whispers. 'Apparently they're meant to help with cramps.'

'They sound expensive,' I whisper back.

When she returns, Georgia stands over my shoulder, arms folded, looking at our canvas – now a kaleidoscopic series of slashes, dashes, splodges, prosecco, popcorn tracks. I quite like it.

'We decided to go abstract,' I tell her, as if this isn't obvious.

'Why?' she asks, rubbing orange paint onto her cheek.

'Because I can't paint and Josh joined me at my level so as not to embarrass me.'

Josh tries to contest, but Georgia interrupts, 'But there's a joy to amateurism, isn't there?' she says. 'Doing something just because it's pleasurable?'

'I'm enjoying myself,' I reassure her. *Though who the fuck finds amateurism enjoyable?*

Somehow, Georgia's canvas has transformed into a Cubist interpretation of the back of Josh's head. It's very impressive. She says she'll hang it in her living room 'so that we match'.

Josh is next to use the loo and as soon as he closes the door, Georgia bum-shuffles towards me, popcorn bowl balancing precariously on her lap.

'Right, mate, what's the deal with you two?'

'There is no deal,' I say. 'He still hasn't bloody told me what happened in London that made him book a ticket here.'

The smell of alcohol on her breath isn't even unpleasant. I love prosecco.

'Promise you'll tell me as. soon. as. you. know. more.'

'I'm obviously not going to promise that.'

'I've always found tiny lights quite emotional,' Georgia says suddenly, drunkenly, staring at the fairy lights above my keyboard. 'Something about their innocence.' I can hear the alcohol blunting her consonants. Josh returns from the bathroom and raises his eyebrows at me. Then Georgia laughs and stands, 'Right, I think that's my cue to leave, actually. Josh, what are you doing while Maya plays in this soirée tomorrow? Can I show you some of Tourist Vienna?'

Josh and I stand, too.

'That'd be great! I'd love to see St Stephen's Cathedral, actually. I studied it when I wanted to be an architect, before I went down the teaching route.'

Georgia's eyes blaze. Perhaps she just finds him charming. This is becoming clearer.

'Or we could all three go to a sauna together after the soirée!'

'Absolutely not,' I say quickly. I can't tell if she's joking.

Josh puts his hands in his pockets and turns to me. This feeling, the craving in me right now, is not a nostalgic one. It's present, living. I swallow.

'The soirée's at two,' I say. 'We'll meet you at one in front of the opera.'

Georgia gathers her things. Josh does not. Obviously.

Why do we agonise over decisions we've already made? I knew from the moment Josh called that he'd stay here. I assume you did too.

When Georgia kisses me goodbye, she whispers, 'The best way to approach inevitability is to enjoy it.'

—

'Right,' says Josh, leaning against my staircase, arms interlaced in the railing. This could be a photoshoot. Though if he knew his stance might be considered 'posing', he would be appalled.

'Do you want to go out for a late dinner? It smells like paint in here anyway and—' I pause. *And ... I don't know. And you need to tell me why you're here. And we obviously need to discuss Lucia '*—and my fridge is empty and we haven't eaten enough.'

—

The evening wind bites despite the thick heat. We walk close to one another, arms folded across our chests.

'It's funny seeing you like this,' he says.

'Like what?'

'So relaxed walking the streets this late. You haven't once looked over your shoulder.'

It's true. I can't remember when I shed the fear of walking at night.

'DoyoupreferViennatoLondonthen?' His tone is almost casual, but the speed gives him away.

'Parts of it,' I say stupidly.

Josh crosses the street without waiting for the green women to flash. I don't have 70 spare euros to spend on a jaywalking fine. One morning about a month ago, I forgot to set an alarm and was running late for work, so didn't wait for the lights to change. A policeman jumped out from behind a bin and booked me on the spot while an elderly lady shouted at me about endangering children. There were no children present, of course. And the fine was more than I made that day.

'You're really set up here. Good job, cool basement flat, social life. I liked Georgia, even if she was a bit . . .' He trails off. *A bit what? Strange? Abrasive? Sexy?* 'What have you told her about me?' He senses my surprise, 'I mean, I wouldn't want to tell her anything you've chosen to omit.'

Yes, okay, this sounds more 'Josh'.

'She knows you are my ex.'

A group of rollerbladers overtake us on both sides, leaping over the tram lines.

'Okay,' Josh says.

I feel my cheeks blaze as I think back to all the conversations I've had with Georgia about Josh and how likely she is to share these with him.

'What's up?' he asks.

'Okay, I'm only telling you this because she'll probably bring it up.' I pause, weighing up the imminent embarrassment with the odds of this actually happening. A woman brushes past us holding an upside-down chihuahua in one hand and an overflowing ice-cream cone in another. She's walking with my neighbour, whose barrel-shaped body bounces as he tries to match her pace. His piercing yellow eyes gloss over me without recognition.

'When we first met, she asked me whether I thought I'd ever crash a wedding.'

Josh smirks, 'I see.'

Despite my obvious discomfort, I enjoy the way his dark eyes crinkle and catch the streetlight.

'Yes, well, I told her that—' I shudder at the memory, with increasing certainty that Georgia will bring this up. Josh watches me as we walk, clearly amused by my embarrassment.

'I told her that I think everyone has a past love that might crash their wedding and that I am probably yours.'

'Well,' he says, 'for what it's worth, I am definitely also your wedding-crasher past love'.

We pass an outdoor ice-cream parlour full of happy couples sharing extravagant, cherry-topped sundaes. Swirls of cream, rivers of chocolate sauce, freckled with colourful hundreds and thousands.

Four buzzes.

> **Georgia:**
> **F. Scott Fitzgerald: intelligence is holding**
> **two opposite opinions in your head**
> **at the same time. Maybe also two people.**
> **See you tomorrow x x**

> **Georgia:**
> **PS – Find out why he's here.**

> **Georgia:**
> **PPS – then tell me!**

> **Georgia:**
> **PPPS – Obviously here if you need me**

My voice sounds weird, all breathy and unsure, 'Josh, you need to tell me why you're here.'

He's psyching himself up, bouncing on his toes like a tennis player about to serve. He looks away from me, at the stupidly romantic swirl of stars above us, like a faraway chandelier. Then he reaches into his pocket and hands me a beige envelope.

'What is this?'

'Please, just read it. Then we can talk.'

'You've had this in your pocket the whole time? You are

so dramatic!' I try to tease, but he isn't smiling and, actually, neither am I.

We stop walking metres from the entrance to Miznon Restaurant. I turn the letter over in my hand. Familiar, messy scrawl:

MAYA EVANS

SOMEWHERE IN VIENNA

—

The first time I told Josh I loved him, I wrote it in a letter. I had it in my wallet for days before I gave it to him. I wrote it at his desk with the pen he used to write in his diary, which felt thrilling, almost erotic. I don't remember what the letter said besides I love you, but I know that it was full of dashes and commas. I was 23 and I wanted to use punctuation like Beethoven, to make, the letter, seem, breathless. I gave it to Josh over breakfast one morning, slid it across the table. The letter told him I wanted him so severely – so completely – that it must be love. I remember he punctured his poached egg as he read. I remember how it oozed yellow.

Josh has dated this letter like he dates all his letters. Top right corner. Underlined as if with a ruler.

24 May

Dear Maya,

_Hi._

Presumably, if you're reading this, I have made it to Vienna and you haven't yet slammed the door in my face (which would

have been totally acceptable behaviour! So you know!).
I'm sorry I'm telling you this in a letter, but I know I suck at
saying it out loud because I have been trying to tell Aden for
weeks. Basically, I found out my dad has been having an affair,
which has been going on for years. When I confronted him, he
told me it would ruin everyone's lives if my mum found out,
which is true, and no one else in my family has any idea. And
I've just been struggling with it all. I haven't really been able to
concentrate on work or anything and I knew I needed to get out
of London and I knew I needed to see you.
I know it's extremely selfish of me to turn up like this.
Genuinely, please tell me to fuck off if you need to. I just didn't
know what else to do.
I'm not really sure how to end this. I've never been any good at
ending things with you, hey?
Your J

And my mind is blank.

I wait for something to switch on, but there's nothing there. Nothing. And then, like a reflex, I step towards him. I pull him close to me. His posture slackens. I don't smell his hair or clutch his shirt the way I'd imagined one hundred times I would if I ever held him again. I just hold him close to me. At first, I don't even notice that he's started to cry. He feels small, delicate. These are thoughts. I'm having thoughts again. I try to speak. I want to tell him that he shouldn't have to go through this. My voice is quiet, 'Of course you can stay.' He clears his throat, nods. I picture his mother, Ruth, and her generous smile and hearty laugh and delicious green curry and rosey perfume. Ruth, who made me a kilo of chicken soup (no less) and bought me flowers when I got pneumonia, who texted me after Josh and I broke up to tell me she loved me and wished me every happiness.

We're still outside the restaurant. There's a faint echo of cathedral bells in the air and an out-of-sight busker playing the oboe with a static piano backing track.

'This is completely—' I can't find the words.

'Fucked up? Yeah.'

'So your brother doesn't know? You're the only one?'

He shakes his head as a group ask us if we're waiting for a table. We're hurried inside. Fuck, it's warm in here.

'I realise there are a lot worse things that could have happened, but it's just—'

'Suffering is absolute, not relative,' I tell him, one of our old refrains.

'Suffering is absolute,' he repeats. Closed-lipped smile. We join a queue to order by the counter.

—

Miznon is loud, chefs bellowing the names of customers to collect their food. *Friedrich! Friedrich! FRIEDRICH!*

The décor is mostly edible – lemons piled high by the windowsills, onions and garlics on strings swinging from the ceiling, great silver bowls brimming with tomatoes. A man with a bun greets us in English, so we order in English from a laminated sheet of A4 – cauliflower and ratatouille pita wraps and a baked sweet potato to share. Man-bun hands us a silver tray with saucers of chilli, oil, and tahini. When he asks whose name the order is under, Josh says my name. We find a table in the corner, as far away from the shouting and chaos as we can manage. A brown straw basket filled with brown onions decorates the ledge next to my chair.

The only conversation topic on my mind is the one Josh doesn't want to discuss – his parents, his parents, his parents.

'So, is something going on with you and Lucia?' he asks. Ah, yes, the thing I'd least like to talk about. Sure, why not? It was naïve of me to think he might not have noticed.

'Oh. Umm. Kind of. It's casual.'

'Right.'

'What about you? Are you seeing anyone?'

Josh pauses. My stomach twists. Then he shakes his head. Right. Relief floods through me. I can't help it.

'Tell me something else that's changed about you since the last time we saw each other,' he says. He's changing the subject, fine, but actually there is something I've wanted to tell him for approximately ten months.

'MAYA!'

'Hold that thought!' Josh jumps. A freckled woman in a sunhat stumbles into the restaurant, knocking into a hanging chain of garlic. She unabashedly checks Josh out as he collects our food, though he doesn't seem to notice.

He sits down and slides my wrap towards me. 'Okay, go on, go on, what's changed?'

'I lost my diary. You know the black one I used to write in? It was so stupid, I left it on the Tube and I tried everything to get it back, but—' he looks distressed '—yeah, I never found it.'

I take a messy bite of my cauliflower wrap, smearing a line of tahini from cheek to cheek like a painted smile. I watch a bead of sweat roll down the side of Josh's neck.

'That's—'

'I know.'

I'm pleased he understands the severity of this loss. The diary I wrote in every day, the book which documented most of our relationship in my ineloquent, grammarless prose, gone. Josh looks away, does something with his jaw, looks back at me.

'So, like, our whole relationship you wrote about in that book?'

'Yeah, it's gone, all of it.'

'That's fucked, Maya.'

I watch the muscles in his jaw climb the side of his face as he chews, his cheekbones pressing firmly against his skin.

'All I have left is this recording of a masterclass I played in just after we broke up. It was quite the scene,' I flick my hand away, as if this was no big deal, and knock the chilli saucer to the floor. I reach to pick it up.

'Performers playing post-breakup would be an excellent concept album,' Josh jokes, covering the corner of the table with his hand. I cannot believe we are joking about this. 'Can I watch it?' he asks casually, like he's talking about a Netflix short. Why did I mention the recording? Of course he wants to see it

'I deleted it,' I answer.

'Right,' Josh interlaces his fingers and stretches his arms. I used to hypersexualise small movements like this, like the way he chopped vegetables or brushed his teeth or took off his mismatched socks. I'd search for the bouncing muscles in his forearms or the way his veins pressed against the skin of his hands.

'Why did you delete it?'

'Because I played terribly.'

'And you say you're not a perfectionist,' he laughs at me, mouth full of ratatouille.

'It's not just that. I think I kind of wanted that music to exist outside of time,' I say.

'*SARA!*' screams a waiter.

'But the world is ending whether you're scared of time passing or not,' he has sweet potato at the corner of his mouth, 'and since the world is ending, why not let your ex-boyfriend watch your recordings?'

I've never heard Josh refer to me as his 'ex' out loud before. I've always found 'ex' a jarring word, but it's especially bad in his mouth. Something about the crunching sound of the consonants; our whole story reduced to a single, brittle syllable. Josh is smiling, clearly pleased with his throwback joke.

I laugh a fake laugh, 'Since the world is ending, why not delete your recordings?' I say.

'Touché,' he wipes the sweet potato away.

'*DAVORIN!*' screams the same waiter.

I freeze. How many Davorins can there be in Vienna? The odds of him seeing us are quite low. I am sitting with my back to the counter and we really are tucked away in the corner.

'Maya?' Josh says. I turn around slowly to see the back of Davorin's head leaving the restaurant with a takeaway bag. I flick my head back to Josh.

'Sorry! I thought I saw someone from work. What did you say?'

I should probably warn Elsa he took her number from my phone.

'What if I let you read an entry from my diary? Since I randomly rocked up in Vienna and you lost yours, it's probably the least I can do.'

What? 'Wait, are you serious?'

'It would be rude to refuse, wouldn't it?'

I've never read Josh's diary. Even though he used to leave it out and about, all over the flat we shared. On our bed, next to our sink, tucked into the crevice of our couch, dangerously close to our stove.

'So which entry do you want to read?' he asks, leaning forward, cupping his chin in his hands.

'God, I don't know, um—' *Fuck is he serious?* '—How much did you write? How often?'

'Did you really never read it?'

I'm offended, 'No, of course not.'

'Well, you know me, it's mostly drawings and bullet points and the occasional stream of consciousness.'

I do know you.

'What about an entry from just after we'd met?' he suggests.

—

Josh ducks as he climbs down to my apartment. His shirt

pulls so that I'm face to face with a sliver of his back. I look away.

'Can I ask you a question?'

I respond automatically, 'You just did.' Another silly old routine of ours. Josh touches a finger to his temple and shakes his head, mocking embarrassment. Then he looks away from me.

'Is it really okay that I'm here?'

'Yes,' I answer quickly. Silence. 'It's good to see you.' I sound more pained than I intended. His eyes are glassy. I can just make out the outline of his contacts in this light and the familiarity of it, of him, is disarming. He suggests we put on some music while I read his diary.

One of our early dates was a Christine and the Queens concert on a rooftop in south London. So much of that night is hazy, smudged by alcohol and time. But the warm brown of his eyes is still clear in my memory. And the way our bodies pressed into each other as we danced in the sweaty mosh pit and Christine's synthesised swells and the way she breathed on the offbeat. And the sex we had afterwards.

God.

The way those rhythms stayed inside us, guided our bodies.

God.

I wonder if I'm playing her music now to remind him.

Meeting Maya　　　　　　　　　　　　　　　　　　　*7 Feb*
Writing on the Bakerloo – hence shitty handwriting
I was there for Rothko. Aden was there for Grindr . . .
Met Maya – facts & impressions:

- *Violinist*
- *I'd guess early to mid twenties*
- *Green eyes, short hair, great smile*
- *Extremely expressive face*
- *She basically sat on my lap*
- *Bold – I think she just says what she thinks and does what she wants – not thoughtlessly – but not overthinking things, like most people*

I like her

<u>*Coffee in members' section*</u>

- *She ordered decaf coffee but doesn't really like it??*
- *Swapped "On Repeat" Spotify playlists. I didn't know these were a thing*
- *Mine was maybe a bit too Top 40, but think I made up for it with Christine & the Queens – think she was impressed that I'd heard of them*
- *I joked we should also swap phone Internet histories – she said okay??? Mine was all studying-related, thank God*
- *She'd looked up: '100 best films to watch', 'Violin auditions' and some essay about charisma by Jennifer Schaffer-Goddard (will look up later)*
- *She has several apps meant to limit screen time on your phone??*
- *We learnt about each over by swapping iPhones but actually she's trying hard not to be on her phone – funny – didn't point this out*

- *Showed her some of my drawings – think this was overkill*

Waiting for lift
She invited me to get a drink at Gordon's on Thursday night – we exchanged emails, not numbers, which is kinda weird?

I'm jealous Josh has access to these details, though I wish he'd written more. I want to add to his notes. I was at the Tate that day at the suggestion of Professor Forrest. I was in a 'Bach phase' and she thought that I might be inspired by the structures and colours of the art. Josh was sitting on a bench facing a large red and black Rothko painting – I hadn't noticed him or said bench – and I was backing away from the painting to get a better view. Then I basically fell onto his lap. I found the whole thing more amusing than embarrassing. He apologised to me, more than once, and told me he was sitting because 'walking around a gallery is tiring in the way that walking along the street isn't', which got my attention because I'd never considered this, so I introduced myself, offering him my hand like I'd just remembered this was a job interview. An awkward exchange followed, something like:

'So why did you choose this room to sit in?'
'I used to want to be an architect. I like stripes and lines.'
'Fair enough! I like lines too.'
'If you were a fruit you would be a fine-apple.'

Silence.

'You said you liked lines.'

Silence.

'I mean, wow, I'm sorry. I honestly don't even know who said that.'

He looked completely shocked at himself, which I found endearing, so I asked him to get coffee with me. And I remember the busker who played on the South Bank as we said goodbye. He was playing country music on a guitar with an over-the-top American southern drawl. He'd interrupted his set to exclaim, 'What a fabulous audience!' in a thick Bristolian accent. I'd laughed out loud. I was fizzing. Jolly. Flying. And there was the old man in the purple corduroys feeding pigeons bread out of a plastic bag. And the Millennium Bridge, the bionic rib cage. Fuck, it's so close now – this memory, London.

When Josh typed his email address into my phone, the .com autocorrected into .completely and I almost left it like that. josh.greenberg@gmail.completely
    And then his eyes crinkled and the melody of his laugh got stuck in my head and I thought *God help me*.

———

Four years later, Josh leans back on my couch, eyes closed. I flick to the most recent entry he's written and tear my gaze away from him to read the single line on the page:

Since the world is ending, why not go to Vienna?

There's a small thud as I snap the book shut, though Josh doesn't open his eyes.

'I'm sorry I'm here like this, I'm sorry I'm such a mess.' He has his head in his hands, eyes still closed. He groans. 'I feel like a child.'

He sounds as if he is talking to himself, so I don't know whether or not to answer. Christine sings along in the background, undisturbed. She tells us she's been sad. I tell him something my therapist told me about the 'golden era' in someone's life, a period when everything is fine and just carrying on as it should be.

'Supposedly, the golden era ends the first time something traumatic happens.'

He looks at my ceiling, 'Yeah but I don't think that's what this family shit is.' He says, 'For me, to be 100% honest, that ended when we broke up.'

'Right,' I say.

'Right,' he repeats.

—

Josh switches off the music. I unfold my couch into a bed and we fit the sheet together.

'I haven't done this with someone for a long time,' he says softly. I give him one of my pillows and tell him to help himself to anything he needs. He thanks me. We don't touch. I switch off the lights and shut the door to my bedroom.

—

Lisa told me that when our dad died, I used to punch pillows before bed. I have a vague memory of this, but it might well be false. In my mind, I would lay the pillow on the bed, almost affectionately, and then I'd punch until I could barely breathe. These days, to calm down, I shower in the dark. Josh actually recommended I try this, back in the day. I'd expected to fumble for my shampoo, slip on the wet tiles, knock my head against the nozzle. Instead, I am transported to a steamy, clean new world. The absence of light heightens my other senses, so I can melt into the gentle massage of hot water on my shoulders, so the nerves in my skin can follow individual drops down my thighs and calves, so I can tune into the crashing sound of the water on the tiles and savour the lavender trail of soap along my arms.

And everything is fine. I almost say this aloud to myself. Yes, Josh is staying because he needs me, but he's in the other room. And I can support him without my life unravelling. And things seem unchanged with Lucia. And I'm mostly prepared for the audition on Sunday. And I'm making 300 euros I didn't expect to make. And I have therapy tomorrow morning, just in case I wake up having forgotten just how okay I am.

Still dripping, I tiptoe towards my towel. I switch on the lights and change into my pajamas. In the mirror, I study the three light lines on my forehead with a kind of gentle fascination. I'm even okay with these pre-wrinkles. I wonder if Josh noticed them.

—

But

But

But

I'm agitated, too hot, uncomfortable. I'm lying on my front, heart pounding against my sheets, falling in and out of memories.

> *Memory: I Choose You*
> *Before we slept, I used to choose a limb to*
> *hold onto and say 'I choose you'.*

I flip my pillow and throw the blanket far away. That's better. Now, I just have to—

> *Memory: Sweet Dreams*
> *The first few nights Josh was gone, I fell asleep by*
> *pretending he was still lying next to me. Sometimes I spoke*
> *aloud, wishing the air 'sweet dreams' or 'sleep tight'.*

No! I wrestle with the sheets and roll over, so that my ankle is dangling off the bed. I breathe through my nose and count to—

> *Memory: Red Fiat*
> *The sex we had in the back of a rental car, parked just*
> *metres from our Airbnb in the Lake District. The*
> *way my leg jutted out the window, and Josh—*

Enough.

Maybe I need a glass of water. I wonder whether my fight with the bedding is audible from the other room. I wonder whether Josh is already sleeping. I need my head to stop spinning. I can't afford a sleepless night. I open WhatsApp to message Lucia, but what should I say? I put my phone away. I need to sleep. 40% of me is tempted to read Josh and my old messages, but I cannot afford to get lost in the archeology of our break-up – the digital bones of dead love. Dramatic. But in all seriousness, text trails are bizarre. Cruel, even. Transience frozen in its purest form. They aren't memories you can edit. They're this thing in your hand, written by someone who once loved you who is no longer yours. I plug my phone back in. My body feels heavier. Good.

I'm going to play the Schubert Op. 100 in my mind and fall asleep.

Thoughts and pictures visit between bars.

He's keeping his dad's affair from the rest of his family.

I'm going to wear my black jumpsuit to the soirée.

Does Josh read our messages?

Tomorrow I'm going to start my practice session with Études. After scales.

But I'm drifting

Digital bones

Broken romances

The dreamy,   thoughtful,

expansive, lyrical, perfect

dance, relationship, chemistry, conversation

between violin and piano in the

first movement of Brahms' second violin sonata.

The lines on Professor Forrest's forehead

Am I finally in a country with

someone who loves me?

And Lucia?

Is he

she

sleep

ing

SATURDAY

I remember instantly that he is here and I am awake. I barely wait for the fog in my mind to clear before I check my phone. Nothing from Lucia. I don't know what I was expecting. My mum has messaged me unprompted. Unusual. Oh, I'm due a smear test in London. Lovely. I haven't quite figured out how to straddle two healthcare systems. It's probably been too long since I called her, but I can't deal with this now. When I stand, my stiff body creaks and clicks. I don't know when it started doing this. I should probably exercise more than I do, but I'd rather be in a practice room. There are only so many hours. I wrap my gown around myself like armour and creep out of my bedroom. My voice cracks under the weight of morning.

'Josh?'

He sits up on the couch.

'Morning Maya.'

His hair is flat but for a familiar unicorn-horn-like tuft. He looks boyish, untroubled.

'What time is it?' he asks, sounding foggy, rubbing his eyes.

'I'm going to take a call outside, but you should sleep as late as you'd like.'

'I'm already up, I'm already up.' He stretches his neck, left, right, up, down, and smiles, sleepy, eyes not quite focused. I offer to make him a cup of tea, but he waves me off.

'You go take your call. I'll sort myself out.'

—

The first time my bow shook during a performance, I was playing Shostakovich's *8th Quartet*. Yes, exactly, the one with its own gravity. Five movements of melancholic minor. At first, it didn't even feel like my arm. I was deep in my memory drawer when the floor shook beneath me. I lost my balance and a frightened voice interrupted me: *Yes, this is real. Yes, this is happening. You need to stay on the string. Don't panic. You need to play as softly as you can.* I waved my bow arm, adjusted my grip, moved a little around the stage, relaxed my breathing, tried to reroute the adrenaline. *Are your muscles fatigued? Have you eaten too much sugar today? Was that coffee really decaf? Are you falling apart? What the fuck is happening? Is this who you are now? What the fuck are we going to do?*

I finished the gig, walked out of the hall, and vomited into a bin. That night, I cancelled an upcoming concert of *The Lark Ascending* and, as punishment, forced myself to fall asleep listening to perfect violin recordings – Itzhak Perlman, Hilary Hahn, Jascha Heifetz. I let the music play all night. The violinists appeared in my dreams as ghosts, caressing my face with their bows and flaunting their immortal perfection.

This was exactly a month after Josh and I broke up and the first time I admitted to myself (and my sister) that I wasn't coping. I had to say something. I'd failed my violin. Publicly. I needed help. Lisa started coming back to London every other weekend, and insisted I attend online therapy sessions with Julie, a psychiatrist with a specialty in 'anxiety'. I've never seen her legs. I don't think my mum ever knew I was in therapy. Lisa paid. I know what you're thinking, and, yes, you're right: mental health only took priority when it affected my music because, really, music takes priority. Josh could tell you that.

—

This is the first time I've been in a Viennese café before 9
a.m. and it is busier than I expected – mostly students with
laptops – one hand galloping around a keyboard, the other
cradling an espresso. They look anachronistic beside the
polished stone columns and musician-less grand piano. I'm
not in the mood for high ceilings and refined interiors, so
choose a seat outside under a sleek black umbrella and open
my laptop. Beside me, two dogs at separate tables are whim-
pering, pulling at their leashes, desperate to be together.

I gesture to a passing waiter that I would like to order. He
delivers a coffee in a tall glass topped with a swirl of whipped
cream before coming over to my table.

'That looks delicious,' I say in English.

'It is the *Maria Theresa*. With orange liquor. A very old
recipe.' His voice is startlingly coarse.

'Oh. A bit early for me, I think.' I switch to German. I don't
know why.

'*Ich hätte gerne eine Soda Zitrone bitte.*' The Austrian Classic.
The waiter nods an approving nod and disappears. I'm
yet to find a café in Vienna without the venerated lemon
juice-soda water mocktail on the menu. Stefan, an Austrian
violist in our orchestra, swears it improves his health and
mood. '*Soda Zitrone für einen gesunden Geist*'. '*Gesunden Geist*'
meaning 'healthy mind', not 'healthy ghost', as I'd initially
misunderstood.

8.59 a.m. WLAN connected, earphones in. I brace for the

hollow ostinato ringtone, but my laptop is quiet. Strange. I check the time again – 9.01. Julie is never late. I'll send her a quick text.

Me:
Hi Julie
Ready when you are!
See you soon
M

Julie always looks immaculate, with a carefully coordinated outfit, perfect, blow-dried fringe, and painted nails (usually a *calm* ocean blue). Her face is lightly wrinkled around the eyes and lips and she wears a thin gold wedding band. I've hunted for her on social media with no luck. In our last session, Julie asked me to 'assign music to my relationships with Lucia and Josh'. I like that she unapologetically asked me to communicate in 'my language'. I told her Lucia would be a Strauss sonata for violin and piano. I was surprised at the depth of the choice – that piece makes me *ache*. There isn't a part of me it doesn't touch, burn, massage, or pleasure. Julie asked me what the music *meant* to me and I said it was like an X-ray, which was far more poetic than I'd intended, but I didn't know how else to describe it. 'It sees through you?' she'd said. Brutal. For Josh, I chose a Wagner Prelude. I explained that his preludes are 'almost alive, they don't resolve, it feels like Wagner won't complete things, like, there are so many moments when the music just feels unfinished.' I'm about to tell her Josh is in Vienna. Maybe we'll laugh about it. I cannot believe I'm going to do a therapy session in a café.

9.06 a.m.

She still hasn't seen the message, so I play through the *Piano Trio* in my head. My left hand follows on an imaginary fingerboard. People underestimate the value of silent practice, how it creates space to problem-solve and consider musicality away from the instrument. I imagine how I'll articulate each of Schubert's phrases to bring out the melody's introspection. This melody is a silken thread, and it needs to be a thread that the listener can hold onto. The trick is to know when to pull them towards you and when to let them guide themselves. Schubert wrote this piece only months before he died. It's contemplative music, gentle, exactly what I need. I can hear the instruments converging in my mind, notes suspended and fragile and iridescent.

Ah, finally, she's online. Thank fuck. I was starting to worry.

Typing . . .

> **Julie (Therapist):**
> **Hi Maya**
> **I am so sorry for the**
> **misunderstanding.**
> **I should have been**
> **clearer. I have availability**

next Saturday morning
for a session but am not
available right now.
Could next Saturday
work for you?
Julie

Right. I feel my jaw clench, throat constrict. Actually, I feel suddenly, completely, overwhelmingly exhausted. I focus on relaxing my jaw while I type.

Me:
Hi Julie
Ah, okay, I misunderstood.
Will message on Monday about our next session.
Have a good weekend!
M

Julie (Therapist):
You too, Maya. Take care.

The waiter arrives with my *Soda Zitrone*. Laughter bursts from me, a frightening sound, almost a cackle. The man at the table in front of me jerks around, clearly annoyed, and I offer what I hope is an apologetic smile. His white shirt is almost transparent. He has a large tattoo covering most of his back but I can't quite make out what it is. Actually, I don't know why I'm apologising to this man. I quickly retract the smile, but he's already looked away. Fuck's sake. I breathe out. I've told Josh I'm taking a call and I have a soda to drink, so I'm going to use this time to sort my head out myself.

Okay, what would Julie have said? She'd ask me what *exactly* I was worried about, and I'd answer that I was worried about losing my shit again. I can't afford to unravel the way I did last year. Not just after what happened with Josh, but with what happened before. I'd tell her I feel out of my depth dealing with Josh, that there's no social script for your ex rocking up at your door in a new city after finding out his dad is having a long-term affair. I'd tell her I was anxious that Lucia didn't know explicitly that Josh was my ex. She'd say there was an easy fix for that . . .

The man at the table next to me is quite obviously watching me mutter to myself, but I don't care. I stare at him and his extravagant moustache until he looks away. Wait, should I not be using this time to practise? No, this is productive. I'm screwing my head back on so I'll be able to cope with this weekend. Okay. Then what?

Julie would probably ask me what I could do to make myself less anxious. I'd tell her I just needed to make time to play the violin and not get emotionally re-attached to Josh. Easy. Who needs therapy when you can do it all in your head?

The man with the indistinguishable tattoo in front of me adjusts his chair, scratching the legs against the floor. The sound is horrendous and, while he scratches, I can think of nothing except the shrieking pitch. My heart is racing. Last year, when it was all unbearable, I burst into tears on the Central Line because of a similar feral screeching. But I will not re-enter that darkness. I will not.

Okay, action points! Make time to practise. I realistically don't need more than an hour or two each day, which is very doable. No alcohol. No caffeine. Come clean to Lucia. Be a friend to Josh. I'm sure Julie would mention something about boundaries.

The man in front drags his chair against the ground again and I am about to tell him to stop when he leans forward, shirt pulled taut against his skin, and I realise what the tattoo is. Though I must be wrong. I look to see if Extravagant Moustache on my right has noticed, too, but he is bopping along to his headphones, caffeinated and carefree. He stands, throws a few coins onto his table, and marches away from the cafe. I realise I've hardly drunk my Soda Zitrone and gulp it down. I check the time. It's almost half past nine.

I lean back in my seat, staring at the empty chair, and play through the rest of the Schubert in my head. But I'm distracted. I wonder how many neo-Nazis there are in Vienna. I can't see the waiter and don't want to hang around, so I leave five euros on the table and stand. Then I check the price of my Soda in the menu, because I am still the same old broke musician who can't afford to pay for her own therapy, and leave four euros next to my empty glass.

Five texts.

> Lucia:
> We should talk today, I think
> Baci

Right.

> Georgia:
> Baaaaabe how are you
> feeling this morning!?!
> X

Fuck knows.

> Elsa to Philharmonia Frauen [group]:
> Girls, do you know how Davorin got my number?
> He has called already three times this morning.
> I did not add my phone number to the orchestra list
> because I didn't want him to have access to it!
> But someone must have given it to him!

Fuck.

> Lucia to Philharmonia Frauen [group]:
> No!
> Can you report this?

Yes!

Elsa to Philharmonia Frauen [group]:
What would I say?
Help! Help!
Davorin called me three
times?
They would laugh at me.

Right.

I should tell Elsa that Davorin got her number from my phone, but I'll call Lucia first.

'*Buongiorrrrno*,' she answers just as I turn the corner into my street. I pause alongside a rainbow crossing. The floor is covered with a sheet of shiny metal, freckled with small holes. It must once have been a water fountain.

'Hey, I'm glad you messaged.'

'I am glad you called.'

Silence. Then we both speak at the same time:

'Listen, about yesterday, I feel a bit odd that I didn't tell you about— Wait, sorry?'

'I think there will be an encore at the gig today and I wanted to check— Oh, what did you—'

'You go,' I say, pacing along the dormant fountain floor.

'I just spoke with the conductor about this soirée, and he thinks he and I should play the Rachmaninoff Cello Sonata as an encore. I wanted to check that this was okay with you?'

Right. Work chat. Obviously. Heat spreads across my face like a rash.

'Yes, of course that's alright with me! I'm sure you'll play it beautif—'

Water. Water everywhere – in my sandals, dripping down my calves. My lower back is soaked.

'Fuck me!' I scream into the empty street, hopping gracelessly away from the erupting fountain. I can hear Lucia's laughter, even though my phone is far from my ears.

'Sì, per favore!'

'Shit, I'm sorry,' I yell at the speaker. I shake my hands free of water and wipe my phone on the small dry patch at the front of my shirt.

'Sorry, I was standing on a water fountain, which I thought wasn't working, but it just—'

Lucia is giggling, 'Oh, I want to see! Please! Put me on video.'

She's calling from her bedroom near her window, soft light brushing her face, painting her eyes a light, almost golden brown. I look like I've narrowly avoided drowning in the Danube.

'Oh no,' she says, giggling in my phone screen. I pan the camera down my body to reveal the extent of the damage while she laughs. Now that the initial shock of the fountain attack is behind me, the cool film of water on my skin feels refreshing.

'Okay cara, I should practise.' Her eyes flick sideways. I imagine her cello leaning against her art-covered wall.

'Wait, before you go!'

'Yes?'

Pause.

'I need to tell you about Josh.'

Maybe this isn't necessary. It feels very dramatic all of a sudden. I don't know, I don't know, I don't know.

'What do you *need* to tell me?'

'I just felt a bit weird. I should have told you yesterday that Josh is my ex,' I say as casually as I can.

'Yes, Maya, I know.' She looks distracted.

'You do?'

'*Certo.* I wasn't sure at first, but then I saw how your friend with the red hair reacted when she saw us all together in your apartment. Do you feel okay with him there?'

'Yes, yes, 100%.'

'Then thank you for telling me, but it is all okay. I really do need to go, but I will see you at the soirée, yes? Unfortunately, Josh cannot come because it is a closed event.'

'Oh, of course, yes, we said yester—'

'*Ciao cara*, see you at two!'

—

Josh is wearing a navy T-shirt, a towel around his waist, and steamy glasses. New glasses. Round wire frames. A few wet curls fall across his forehead. A tiny dot of foam on his earlobe could be a soapy piercing.

'That was a long phone call. Wait, why are you covered in water?'

I always loved the way he pronounced 't's. Soft, more like a cymbal than a drum. Almost Irish. I know this is a weird thing to enjoy, but I'm a musician and sound matters.

'I picked a fight with a fountain,' I say from the bottom of my stairs, 'you should see the other guy.'

He chuckles.

'I bet you made a splash!' he says, then shakes his head. Josh is so often embarrassed at his dad jokes. I fucking love them.

'Actually, it wasn't just a phone call. It was meant to be an online therapy session.'

He looks at me like I made up the word, smile disappearing, 'Therapy?'

'Yeah.'

'That's new.'

'Well, I got the timing wrong, so tried to wash all my troubles away myself.' I shake my hair like a wet dog. Josh laughs again.

'Right. Did all that fountain fighting make you hungry?' he asks, gesturing to the stove.

I realise one half of my table is set for two and the other half is covered in breakfast supplies: eggs, blackberries, a fresh loaf of bread (a full bakery loaf. Not the half-loaves I usually buy), and a carton of orange juice without pulp. Josh prefers orange juice with pulp, but probably couldn't understand the label.

Josh prides himself on being 'good at breakfast'. When we lived together, he would make porridge, hop in the shower, and return just as it finished cooking. He'd top it with peanut butter or chocolate chips or frozen berries and eat half-naked in a towel and steamy glasses.

'The woman at the supermarket was terrifying. I've never seen someone scan groceries so quickly!'

I laugh. He's right. I'd also found Austrian grocery scanning rather alarming at the beginning. Now I hurry, bagging my items to match the grocer's scanning speed. It feels competitive.

'Okay, so you have two options: fried eggs or French toast.'

The idea of pushing into the yolk of a fried egg until it bursts seems overwhelmingly sensual and I opt for French toast.

I change into a black, soirée-appropriate jumpsuit in my bedroom while Josh finishes dressing in my living room/kitchen. I sit at my dining table while he cooks, his broad back bent over a bowl. The soft scrape and whoosh of his whisking is rhythmic, soothing. Familiar.

Josh slides two thick slices of steaming, cinnamon-y French toast onto my plate, topped with molten blackberries.

'This is really kind of you, thank you.'

'Not at all.'

'Did you sleep alright? Did I ask you that already?'

'I slept fine, thanks. So, therapy?' he says as he sits across from me.

'Yeah. It's been really good for my playing.'

He raises his eyebrows.

'And for me in general.'

'Uh huh.'

The French toast grabs me by the tongue and drags me back to the Acton Town flat we shared. We had dark wood floors and burnt orange walls. The ceilings felt high, by London's standards, but the kitchen and bathroom were tiny. Josh took care of the aesthetic choices. We had a gallery wall of artsy black and white prints: a half-empty wine glass, the reflection of our front door in a puddle, the silhouette of a drenched man in a trench coat holding an umbrella over a dog.

'Diyuverosideri?' I cover my mouth with my hand as if this makes my mumbling more polite.

'I'm sorry, I didn't catch a word of that,' Josh jokes, mirroring my hand-over-mouth movement.

I laugh, chewing faster. Swallowing feels like a gesture. I try again, exaggerating the consonants, 'Did you ever consider therapy?'

Josh has already finished his first piece of French toast. I'd forgotten how fast he eats in the mornings. In a few moments he'll be complaining that he ate too quickly. He licks a few runaway crystals off his lips and stares at our chaotic painting from the night before.

'Yeah I considered it. Just never found the time. But I really am glad you're doing well, Maya.'

Buzz.

Elsa to Philharmonia Frauen [group]:
He just called again

Ah, shit. I should message her. Josh raises a fist to his mouth and swallows uncomfortably.

'Sorry, I think I ate too quickly,' he says.

—

The heat is already oppressive. On the stuffy tram to the opera, Josh stares out the window, frowning. When I ask what's up, he says, 'It's all just too—'

He stretches his neck from side to side.

'—Are they just trying to pretend all the violence didn't happen?'

I don't know what to say. I don't tell him about the tattooed man at the coffeehouse. I close my eyes.

Outside the opera, the Mozarts circle us in the searing heat, dripping with sweat, red robes swishing, shouting in a chorus of unintelligible languages. I grab Josh by the wrist and drag him towards the stage door.

'And is this your boyfriend?' Julius, one of the friendlier porters, asks in German. His smile takes up most of his face. I hesitate and he says something to the effect of, 'We cannot admit visitors, but we make exceptions for boyfriends and girlfriends.'

'Oh,' I manage, my tone universally registering as 'surprise', and glance at Josh. He seems at ease in his lack of understanding.

I turn back to Julius, 'Okay, *ja.*' I tell him in German that Josh is my boyfriend. (The word for 'male friend' and 'boyfriend' is the same in German, so I'm not strictly lying.)

'*Wunderbar!*' Julius beams at me, like this false disclosure has brought us closer. '*Willkommen an der Wiener Staatsoper!*' he bellows at Josh.

'*Dankeschön,*' Josh says confidently.

'What was all that about?' he asks, once we're in the corridor with only the opera singer photographs for company.

'You're not technically allowed back here,' I say.

He nods, 'Trust you to have the whole system sorted,' and then, 'lucky me.'

I've promised Josh a tour before I practise but my knowledge of backstage is limited. I guide him through practice rooms, rehearsal spaces, and the orchestra pit. They are less than inspiring, I realise. Mostly hot, colourless empty rooms with glorious acoustics. We have just under an hour before I have to leave for the soirée. Josh asks whether we can see the main stage and, the truth is, I don't know. I think it's highly unlikely I'd be allowed on the stage, but I won't be fired for this if we're caught.

Still, adrenaline is surging as I say, 'Yeah, course, follow me.'

We take the stairs to the second floor, ignoring the flashing red *ACHTUNG* sign. I raise my finger to my lips and Josh mirrors me. We tiptoe across the storage area behind the curtain.

'It's huge!' Josh mouths.

Apart from a few men in *Technik* shirts, the vast backstage is empty. I've seen them store entire opera sets back here – castle balconies, dancefloors, giant medieval cauldrons filled with popcorn.

'Okay,' I whisper, 'I haven't done this before, but I think we can probably stick our heads out from the side of the stage. You game?'

'Oh, I'm game.'

We pass what I assume is a props table, and Josh pauses to admire a bucket of red felt masks, plastic daggers, small American flags. Beside these sit a neat line of fake rolled joints. Josh raises his eyebrows and I shrug. He picks up a 'joint' and sniffs theatrically. He places the prop back on the table and leans into me, whispering in my ear so that our cheeks touch and I feel his breath on my neck, 'Just tobacco. Shame.'

My eyes roll. My cheeks and neck rejoice.

We move stealthily towards the side of the stage, pausing by the lush, blue-black velvet drapes. I raise my hand and count down from three with my fingers like we're recording for television. When I reach 'one', we poke our heads out and take in the horse-shoe auditorium. Red, gold, ivory. The balconies are majestic, decorated with intricate carvings. They float above hundreds of plush red seats.

'Wow,' Josh whispers, and I follow his gaze up towards the enormous crystal chandelier. He creeps forward and I join him so we are standing side by side, exposed, on the empty stage of the *Wiener Staatsoper*. We definitely shouldn't be here.

'This is ridiculous,' Josh sighs. He's looking up at the golden ceiling, at the glittering ring-shaped chandelier, at the gilded ornamentation, and I am looking at him – at his dark curls, the crease between his eyes, the strong line of his jaw, his soft, slightly parted lips.

Josh walks a few steps across the stage with his hands in his pockets, while I trace the outline of his shoulders with my eyes.

'This is amazing.' He turns, beckons me to join him. When our eyes lock, something changes in his expression. He looks curious or confused. Or like he's asking something of me. *What are you—*

But there's a shuffling from the back of the stalls as two men enter the auditorium. One has long white hair and an impressive leather jacket. The other, dressed in suit and tie, is bald and stooped. His face is astonishingly turtle-like. They are absorbed in hushed conversation until the suited man turns towards the stage, where Josh and I are not supposed to be standing. He raises a hand in the air, silencing his colleague. His turtle features curl into a 'you-shouldn't-be-here' scowl and he stalks towards the stage. He's yelling, yelling, yelling and I freeze. Then I run, tugging Josh along with me.

I can't hear what the shouting man is saying – I doubt I'd be able to understand if I could – but I run with Josh at my heels towards a set of double doors. We make a right. Yelling, yelling. The shouts are amplified by the hallway acoustics. But they couldn't have followed us backstage? Another right. We sprint down a passage I don't recognise. I don't know where we are. *What the fuck was I thinking?* In a perpendicular corridor, an elevator dings and I drag Josh towards it, still running. Oh, this is the service elevator I'm not supposed to take. The sounds of the shouting men *decrescendo*, then disappear, as the doors close behind us. I press the ground floor button and we collapse against the mirror, panting. I can feel something – acid or blood – gurgle in my chest.

'Fuck me that was stressful!'

Josh's 'fuck me' is almost too much for my vibrating body to handle. I only realise our elevator is climbing when it opens on the fourth floor. A woman looks us up and down before smiling and mumbling, '*Grüß Gott*,' as she leads a small donkey in a colourful saddle inside. Josh lets out a small guffaw. We ride back to ground level with the donkey, who looks at himself in the mirror the whole way down. I worry the men will be there when the door opens, but the hall is empty. The donkey handler wishes us a good day and Josh replies again, '*Dankeschön*!' As the doors close, I collapse into him, my head falling against his shoulder, and our bodies shake together with adrenaline and laughter.

———

The opera canteen's design is almost school-like – sparse tables and chairs, boring white walls, a simple wooden serving counter. We study the lunch options on a blackboard menu with wonky chalk scrawls. The handwriting is too messy to read, but a group of men are eating nearby – an assortment of old-looking ham sandwiches and plates of greasy schnitzel and spinach. We opt for Coke and lemonade and sit opposite each other on a pair of hard red chairs. The wall beside us is a collage of small, colourfully framed production photos.

'Compared to the rest of this place, this canteen is so plain?' Josh sips his Coke.

'Mm,' I agree into my glass. A flurry of balletic swans glide past us in matching winged eyeliner.

'Do you know much about the architectural history of the building?' Josh asks, pre-empting my answer by reaching for his phone.

'Yes, of course,' I lie, gesturing around me. 'This canteen

was built in the 1800s by Franz Joseph himself. He was quite the craftsmen, would you believe? And you see these tables? They're carved from the finest trees of the Viennese woods!'

'Okay, okay,' Josh chuckles, brushing my fingers with his without looking up from his phone. He scans the *Wiener Staatsoper* website.

'This is cool – apparently the two fountains outside are meant to represent two different worlds. On the left: music, dance, joy, and levity. On the right: seduction, sorrow, love, and revenge.'

'Dramatic,' I say. 'Which world would you rather inhabit?'

'The left, obviously,' he raises his eyebrows, 'isn't that the only answer?'

I don't reply.

'Oh,' he says, 'neither of the architects survived to see the opening of the opera house. Classic. I think about this a lot, actually, all those architects who work so hard on projects they never see come to fruition.'

Schubert's Unfinished Symphony

Mahler's 10th

My mind swirls with incomplete masterpieces.

Puccini's Turandot

Berg's Lulu

Mozart's Requiem, of course, the unfinished one they played at countless big-deal memorials – the reburial of Napoleon, the funeral of Chopin. The piece commissioned by a count who wanted to pretend he'd written it himself. The commission was anonymous, and Mozart believed he was being paid to write a Requiem for his own funeral. I wonder how many times the Requiem's been played here in Vienna. I let the music bloom in my mind. If a dictionary of sound existed, the word 'glorious' would be defined by these first notes. The classical stairway to heaven, the first—

'Oh,' Josh knocks me out of my trance, 'one of the architects committed suicide.'

The music stops. He puts his phone away.

Davorin and his headband appear across the room, towering over the rest of the men. He waves at me. I scowl at him. *Fuck! I still haven't replied to Elsa!* I doubt he'll come over here. I'm wrong. Davorin squeezes through a group of singers queuing for the water dispenser, and drops into the chair beside Josh. Josh looks at me, eyebrows raised. I feel an intense discomfort spring at the base of my stomach, like a hot coil.

'Josh, this is Davorin, he plays in my orchestra here. Davorin, this is Josh.'

I don't want to introduce Josh to Davorin with any additional information.

'Hey, man!' Davorin says, slapping Josh on the back.

'Why are you here? We don't have rehearsals?' I sound hostile. Good.

'I like this *Kantine*! Though it is sad we can't smoke here anymore.' Davorin juts his chin in the direction of the 'smoking section', now an awkward, aimless space separated by unnecessary automatic glass doors. A few nostalgic men sit slumped on the benches sharing the stale air. Wistful. They're probably reminiscing about the glory days – Austria, the 'ashtray of Europe'.

'Cigarettes are kind of Austria's Marmite,' I tell Josh. 'The far-right Freedom party overturned a ban last year, but then the coalition fell, right in time for my arrival.'

'God, I miss smoking,' Josh says. 'I nearly—'

'Why are *you* here?' Davorin interrupts.

'I was giving Josh a tour of the Opera *Haus.*' I say *Haus* with a German accent. I don't know why. Josh is smiling at me.

'Oh, cool. Are you a musician, Josh?'

Josh shakes his head as the two men from the auditorium walk into the *Kantine.* They are facing the illegible chalkboard menu, backs towards us.

'Shit,' I say under my breath, and Josh follows my eyes towards the men.

'What's up?' Davorin asks.

I don't want to tell Davorin why I'm afraid of these men and I don't have time to lie as the leather jacket is scanning the *Kantine* for a place to sit. He catches my eye. His posture stiffens. His eyes narrow. Then he puffs his chest and stalks towards us, leaving Turtle Face by the counter. Long strides. He's standing over our table and looking from me, to Josh, to Davorin, back to Josh.

'Hello, can we help you?' Davorin asks in English.

'You were on the *Bühne.* This is *verboten.* Who are you?' the man addresses Josh.

Davorin, catching on, replies, this time in German. He says something like, 'We just arrived here together. What do you mean "on the stage?"'

The leather jacket huffs and speaks quickly. I don't

understand. Anxiety induced by a foreign language is anxiety in technicolour. The man's eyes dart between Davorin and Josh. Honestly, I don't think he'd notice if I stood and left.

'I have seen you on the *Bühne*,' he says to Josh, who shrugs and looks desperately at me. Following the man's lead, Davorin switches back to English, 'We never go on the stage, we are orchestral musicians in the Habsburg Philharmonic, and we just arrived here in the *Kantine*. I am sorry, but I believe you mistake us for other people.' The man flicks his long white hair and makes a grunting sound before he leaves. I can feel my pulse in my palms. I realise I am holding my breath.

'Why the fuck didn't he look at you?' Josh asks, like sexism is our most pressing concern. Davorin gives Josh a conspiratorial smile, 'What were you doing on the stage? Naughty boys and girls.'

'Doesn't matter,' Josh shakes his head.

But the leather jacket is back with his stooped, turtle-faced friend and they're saying something like, 'Aren't these the people from the stage?'

'*Ja, auf jeden Fall.*'

They address Davorin with speedy, complicated German. The words blur in my mind as I try to translate. Davorin's face is serious as he nods and hums. *What are you agreeing with?* Then the men leave. I watch them disappear into the smokeless smoking section.

'What happened? What were they saying?'

'They know it was you on the stage, I'm afraid. You have to go to a suspension meeting on Monday.'

The walls of the *Kantine* seem closer suddenly. It's too hot in here. Panic.

'A suspension meeting? Are you serious? For walking on the stage for ten seconds?' Josh looks at me with concern, dread, maybe apology, but he's also starting to blur. *What the fuck was I thinking? I knew something like this was going to happen.*

'No, no! I'm just joking!'

What? 'What?'

'They were just annoyed and told you to be more professional. They don't have the power to suspend you.'

The *Kantine* comes back into focus.

'What the fuck, Davorin?'

Buzz.

> **Georgia:**
> **Outside!**
> **PS – I'm expecting a tour**
> **of my own at some point!**
> **X x x**

'Look, we need to go, anyway,' I stand, face hot, shoulders tense. Josh follows.

'Oh no!' Davorin smacks the table with his enormous hands. 'I thought we were bonding! No stress, no stress. You are coming to the party tonight, or?'

'What party?' I say, though I know this answers his question – I was not invited.

'Jacobo's friend is hosting a party. He invited us all after rehearsal yesterday.'

'Oh, maybe, yeah,' I say without enthusiasm.

'Jacobo is one of the horn players in our orchestra,' Davorin informs Josh, before turning to me with a disturbing smile. 'Do you know if Elsa will be there?'

'Davorin, you need to stop calling her. It's creepy. You're colleagues.' My voice trembles. For fuck's sake. I fold my arms like a child.

'Oh, just like you and Lucia?'

My eyes fly to Josh, who looks stony. Unblinking.

'Davorin, I don't—'

'Did you tell Elsa you gave me her number?'

'I didn't give you her number!' I raise my voice. The swans at the neighbouring table turn their beaks towards us, sinister, threatening.

'So, you didn't tell her. Well, I think she should come to the party. And I think you should come, too. Lots of important industry people will be there, lots of conductors, you know, good party to go to.'

I falter, as he intended.

'Right.'

'So yes, I think I *will* see you later.' His pale eyes are glowing.

Josh follows me out of the *Kantine*. We take the furthest door from the smoking section.

'*That's* what your colleagues are like?' he says as we wave to smiley Julius.

'Not all of them.'

'Uh huh.'

Outside, Georgia is leaning on a pillar, looking impressively modern against the old bricks in her gold-rimmed sunglasses. She's wearing what she calls her 'self-cleaning shorts'. They're a light, faded blue, ripped by the pocket and just under the left butt cheek. She's holding a beige tote that says 'Emotional Baggage' in large black letters. Georgia looks like she's had a full night's sleep, been to the gym, and drunk both a green smoothie and an oat-milk *mélange*.

'Morning!' she sings, though she knows it's after one.

'Morning!'

'How do you look so fresh after all that prosecco last night?' Josh asks.

'Darling, this all takes a lot of work.' She twirls red finger-nails in a circle in front of her face. 'When I first wake up, not even my iPhone recognises me. Oh, I love the First District! If cities had clits, this would so obviously be Vienna's. How was the tour?'

I roll my eyes.

'Great,' Josh says. 'Though we nearly got caught sneak-ing around on the stage. And we met one of Maya's creepy colleagues.'

Georgia's laugh sounds rehearsed, too melodic.

'I'm sorry you can't join us, Maya,' Josh says. His tone is earnestness distilled.

'Alright you two, it's only a few hours,' Georgia winks at me.

'I'll text when I'm done with the soirée!'

'Bye Maya,' Georgia says and pulls at Josh's elbow. 'So, did the chandelier also remind you of a great, big jewel-encrusted cock ring?' she asks him as they walk away from me.

I watch them wait for a horse and carriage to pass before crossing the road. The air smells of manure.

—

Mozart, Beethoven, and Haydn have all, at some point, lived on Theobaldgasse. It also houses the headquarters of Austria's populist right-wing 'Freedom' party. And the location of my soirée concert. But I'm not quite there yet.

I'm on Friedrichstraße, pacing beside the Secession building. The white structure is enormous and dramatic, topped with a shimmering orb that resembles a giant golden falafel. Written above the entrance:

Der Zeit ihre Kunst. Der Kunst ihre Freiheit.

(To every age its art, to every art its freedom).

I've just texted Elsa to tell her Davorin stole her number from my phone. She's read the message and hasn't replied. Two blue ticks and an 'online' stare at me as I pace. I don't have time for this, and I haven't practised today, and all the rooms at the opera were occupied by the time Josh left. And the audition is tomorrow.

Typing ...

I find some shade next to the Secession building and check the temperature. It's 34 degrees. My God. Here I am, a cluster of atoms in a world-on-fire, sweating over love and work. I wish *perspective* would assuage the panic, but somehow *perspective* only makes me feel guilty.

When I return to WhatsApp, the *Typing* has disappeared, but Elsa is still online. I don't have time for this. I resume my walk to the soirée. One street. Two streets. Sweat. Swig of water. Ah. I need to call her, don't I?

It takes her nine rings to answer. I almost hang up.

'Hi Maya.'

'Hey Elsa, sorry, I'm just walking and thought it would be easier to call than to text.'

Silence.

'Are you okay?' I ask. I need to check Google Maps to figure out where to turn, so put her on speaker.

'I—' she starts. Okay, I'm taking the next right. Silence.

'I—' she says again. 'It's not your fault he has my number. I just wish you had told me sooner. I have been driving myself crazy trying to think about how he could have got it.'

Fuck.

'I'm really sorry, Elsa. You're right, I messed up,' I say, as another thread of my perfect Vienna life catches, pulls, frays. 'I should have told you earlier, you're right, I'm sorry.'

'Thank you. Well, I know now. I just need to decide what I'm going to do.'

'Are you going to this party tonight? I saw Davorin at the opera just now and he's definitely going to be there.'

'Of course I'm going,' she says. There's a tiny wobble in her voice.

'I'll be there, too,' I say as I turn onto Theobaldgasse. I wanted this to sound comforting, but my voice is hoarse from stress and dehydration. Across the road from me, Lucia is leaning against the mustard wall of Theobaldgasse 9, earphones in, faraway gaze.

'Okay, see you tonight, then,' Elsa says and hangs up without waiting for me to reply. Right. I put my phone away, clear my throat, and walk towards Lucia. She looks—

My God.

She looks hot. White linen dress, red heels. She catches me staring and smiles. It's a warm smile. It's almost a 'Hey-I-was-just-thinking-about-you' smile, but that could be in my head. Still, I smile back and wave with my violin-free hand. She's whistling Bach as her gaze slides down my body.

'Hello *cara*.'

'You look amazing,' I say and she nods.

'I *feel* amazing! I am excited to play with you!'

Fluttering heart, hot cheeks – my palpable attraction to Lucia is soothing, somehow. The breeze in the tree beside us makes a sighing sound. We don't kiss. I don't wonder what Josh and Georgia are up to in the First District, 'Vienna's clit'.

Inside Theobaldgasse 9, the elevator buttons are gold and the cabin is encircled by a baroque wrought-iron gate. It's the kind of elevator door you have to open yourself. Somehow, despite the extra effort, it feels chic. Or *schick*, as they say here. I watch Lucia paint her lips red while we ascend. My head feels crowded, indistinguishable lines of thought clashing into one another like badly written polyphony.

'How long is Josh staying with you?' Lucia asks. My frazzled brain tries to read her tone.

'Just for the weekend, I think.'

Lucia hums in reply, a low F#. The elevator dings on G and the dissonance makes me wince. More blurry thoughts. But hey, at least my musicality is intact.

In the corridor, the floor is ornate, decorated with a gold, symmetrical leaf-like pattern. I follow Lucia towards a door hanging ajar. Its polished hardwood surface gleams in the harsh sunlight and the brass handle is hot to the touch.

The soirée apartment is heaving with guests, who sweat through their pastel suits and colourful cocktail dresses. In the centre stands a glossy grand piano. Lid open, teeth bared. A woman in Klimt-y gold admires her reflection in its body. We pause by the entrance. The whir of the aircon is too high in pitch, like a relentless buzzing insect.

'Maybe I should have worn something classier,' I whisper to Lucia, pulling at my black jumpsuit.

She whispers back, 'You look *radiante*.'

We needn't be whispering – no one has noticed us enter. I check my phone, though I don't know who I'm expecting to hear from. Lucia sets her cello on the floor with a thud. A few heads turn, including a tall man in a debonair grey suit with a cloud of white hair. His face breaks into a broad smile as he beelines towards us.

'And here are our young musicians!'

American. He greets us as he walks, his rich, tenor voice booming around his apartment.

'Welcome! Lucia, how charming you look!' He bends down to kiss her on both cheeks. His skin is bronzed, almost youthful, but for a cluster of wrinkles around his mouth and eyes. 'And is this lovely lady part of your trio?'

'This is Maya, my violinist.'

Your violinist?

'How do you do, Maya.' He takes my hand.

'You have a beautiful home!' I say. The Conductor's enthusiasm is contagious! Though the white noise in my head plays on! And the aircon buzz is fucking annoying! And it's tragically ironic that air-conditioning is part of the problem! Isn't it!

'The pianist, Sergei, is on his way. *Come stai, Maestro?*' Lucia eyes a tray of champagne flutes walking by. I love it when she speaks in Italian! Even just the odd word. I think I've mentioned!

'I'm well, I'm well. Wait right here, let me fetch my wife. She is so excited to see you!'

Impossibly, the Conductor's smile is wider as he hurries away.

'He's a character,' I say into Lucia's ear. The familiar vanilla heat of her perfume throws me back into her bedroom, naked, my lips are on her neck. My God. I need to sort out my head before we play.

'He's the best,' she says.

Someone taps my shoulder. I jump, I'm blocking the entrance.

'*Entschuldigung*,' I excuse myself automatically. In front of me is a short man, with slicked-back blonde hair and round glasses. His lens thickness rivals the score in my hand. He's wearing a suit – no tie – and thin black gloves despite the heat.

'I am Sergei, the pianist,' he replies in English. He has a cool, creepy voice, with the qualities of both a whisper (air, rasp) and a shout (volume, lack of melody). His BO is so potent, it's almost spicy.

'I'm Maya.'

'Sergei! *Wie geht's dir?*' Italian accent, Russian name, German how-are-you, Lucia kisses Sergei on both cheeks as the Conductor returns with a tiny lady in a silk white gown and a navy shawl. Their height difference is almost comical. She has perfectly painted lips and feline grey-green eyes. Her hair is cropped and black, with red, feather-like highlights.

'My wife, the fabulous Soprano!' He beams as she ushers us inside.

'There's no point standing in the doorway.' Her voice is shimmery, resonant. I can't place her accent. 'Welcome to our home. Come in, relax a while, play for us, and then you can enjoy some champagne.'

'Would you mind turning your phones off and popping them over there? House rules, I'm afraid!' the Conductor points to a woven basket overflowing with iPhones. 'You can leave your instruments in the corner.'

A waiter walks past us with a pyramid of colourful macarons on a tray. That pyramid probably costs more than my fee today. We are not offered macarons.

'Lucia, there is someone I would like you to meet,' says the Soprano, taking Lucia's hand and leading her into the crowd.

'A woman on a mission, my wife,' grins the Conductor, 'we'll begin with the music in about fifteen minutes – first my wife and I and then, after a little pause, you three. Does that suit you both?'

I know I don't have a choice in the matter, obviously, but he makes the question sound sincere. Sergei and I nod together. The Conductor smiles again, clasps his hands, spins on his heel, and rejoins his guests, like a vibrantly choreographed dance. We turn off our phones and place them in the basket.

Sergei and I explore the oversized living room without speaking. He seems taken by the commandeering shelf of musical scores – chaotic and colourful – suites, symphonies, opera, songs. Hanging by the shelf is a collection of photographs of the Soprano at different ages in a host of wigs and costumes. I recognise a few famous faces alongside her, though I wouldn't know them by name. I wonder what the couple calls this room – the Music Room? The Library? The Memory Room? I quite like the idea of this musical power couple. I'm curious to hear them play together.

Ambling through the crowd, I hear snippets of conversation in English and German: a recent exhibition at the Mumok

Museum, the extraordinary queue outside the Café Central, the best English translation of *Gemütlichkeit* ('a friendly kind of cosiness?' 'A type of warm belonging?'). There must be at least a hundred people here. I eavesdrop on a pair discussing the latest gossip at the Opera – the first main-stage work composed by a woman in the house's 150-year history.

'Yes, Olga Neuwirth – do you know her?' says an elderly British lady in an odd, loose-fitting leopard-print caftan/dress. 'It's based on the Virginia Woolf novel, *Orlando*, but I went because I heard the costumes were designed by Comme des Garçons! Rei Kawakubo. Can you imagine? Truly fabulous.'

I saw the first act of the dress rehearsal with Elsa and Lucia before work last week and found the whole thing quite frenetic and exciting. Watching Kate Lindsey, the singer who played Orlando, was a masterclass in focus. Her outlandish costumes doubled her size – three-piece tartan suits with exaggerated shoulders, ruffled white shirts and neckties, pin-striped shorts, lavish embroideries, metallic leather netting. But then she sang, and her voice! Her voice flooded the auditorium, and we forgot all about the costumes. The next day, I saw her drinking coffee with her score in the plain *Kantine*. I spent a few moments watching her lips on the mug, entranced by their ordinariness.

'Oh, that whole opera was a shaaaaambles,' says the man next to the leopard-print caftan. 'I'll be frank with you, I was one of the people booing at the end. It's a pity that the composer made such a mess of it, really, because I doubt they'll put on another modern opera after all this nonsense.' He leans closer to the woman and I have to step towards them to continue eavesdropping.

'I do wonder,' he says, 'if it wasn't all a bit of a publicity stunt. What I mean to say is, would they have agreed to put on this opera had it been written by a man?'

I groan.

Inwardly, of course.

I am the entertainment. I cannot politely disagree with this man, nor can I throw his champagne in his pink face. *'Why am I here with these people?'* asks one of the voices in my head. *'Because you need the money,'* answers another. When did that become the answer?

Sergei is beside me – I don't know how long he's been here – pointing to a framed poster amid the pictures of the Soprano. *'TEATRO ALLA SCALA'* it reads in black CAPS. And then, underneath, *'La Voix Humaine, Francis Poulenc.'* Sergei explains that the Soprano was famous for this role – 'a forty-minute, one-woman opera'. Then he summarises the plot. Unsolicited.

Elle, the protagonist, answers a phone on stage. Her ex-lover is calling. The two discuss their past relationship. Elle blames herself for their romantic problems. After a few signal failures, she admits to taking twelve sleeping pills in a suicide attempt the night before. Elle hears jazz music on the other side of the call and suspects her ex-lover is out with another woman. She admits to having become obsessed with her telephone, sleeping with it at night in the hope that he would call. Their connection cuts out. Elle panics. When her ex-lover calls back, she tells him that she has the phone cord wrapped around her neck. She tells him that she loves him, over and over, *je t'aime, je t'aime, je t'aime,* before the music ends and Elle drops the receiver.

The party reforms around us.

'Bloody hell,' I say to Sergei. 'Surely performing that would completely destroy you.'

Ding.

A few heads turn.

Ding.

The Conductor commands our attention clinking together two glasses of champagne. The room falls silent. I can easily imagine this man leading an orchestra, long fingers wrapped around a baton, infectious energy, encouraging smile.

'Good evening guests and, once again, welcome to our home.'

A few people raise their glasses. I search the crowd for Lucia and find her standing next to the Soprano on the other side of the room. She isn't looking at me.

'As you know, this has been a musical house for many generations, and we are very happy to continue the tradition into the twenty-first century! This evening, we have a young trio playing some Schubert for us all: I'd like to introduce: Lucia Rizzo, Maya Evans, and Sergei Molchalin.'

The guests applaud and the three of us wave from where we're standing. Lucia's eyes find mine, and she winks at me. The Conductor continues, 'But first, because you all asked so graciously, my wife and I will perform a little excerpt from Poulenc's *La Voix Humaine.'*

A few people clap. Sergei looks at me knowingly over the rim of his glasses, like he himself wrote the opera.

'So, make sure you're comfortable and please top up those empty glasses! The music will begin shortly.'

Lucia appears beside me and grabs my hand, leading me towards our instruments in the corner of the room. Her fingers are warm. Her grip is firm. I kind of love the way she pulls me along, splitting the crowd as we walk, like I won't find my way without her. The anxiety simmers in my chest, then dissipates. Long may that last. Sergei follows behind us, gloved hands in his pockets.

The Conductor removes his blazer and takes a seat at the piano. Oh, there's no sheet music. He'll play by heart? The Soprano stands beside him, a new grace to her posture. They lock eyes. There is a fresh intensity between them. I almost feel as if I'm intruding on a private moment, but I can't look away. The Conductor begins with piano trills, relentless trills, trills, trills, trills. I feel my pulse quicken. Here we go. The guests have stopped breathing, they're making space for the music. Good. The Conductor lifts one hand from the piano; it floats just above the keys. With the other, he plays a simple melody – the ringing telephone. The Soprano takes her mobile from her pocket. I want to roll my eyes at the theatrics until I see her face. Pain, grief, panic, desperation have rendered her features almost unrecognisable. Her full lips are thin, worried. Her once-piercing eyes are vulnerable, doe-like. She looks so fragile. Her stomach pushes against the fabric of her dress as she breathes.

'*Allo? Allo?*'

The way she speak-sings, it's almost naturalistic. Between each phrase, the piano clangs sound obtrusive. Dizzying. This music is designed to make you shiver – it's almost scientific.

'*Je ne sais pas . . .*'

She touches her fingers to her temple. The phone rings again in the piano.

'*Mon chéri—*'

Her voice is honeyed with tenderness. I can feel Lucia breathing beside me. She touches her fingers to mine so lightly it might be my imagination.

'*Tu es gentil. Tu es gentil.*'

Then everything is hectic. There's something frightening about the way she repeats herself. Fear, nerves, fixation, suffering. Her posture tightens and her gaze fixes on a spot in the distance. Her breathing quickens. The phrases accelerate. Her voice spins around the room like a lasso, pulling us closer. I want to reach out and hold her. She needs to be held!

I only realise the audience is applauding because Lucia's fingers leave mine. The Soprano bows her head, touches her hand to her heart. She looks almost giddy; she's grinning at her guests, and I feel anger rumble in my chest. Anger at the man on the other end of the phone, sure, anger at lost love, yes, obviously, but most of all, I'm angry at the Soprano for leaving her character behind so swiftly. She seems completely unchanged by her performance. I don't understand, I don't understand, I don't understand. I'm angry that she's able to smile at us while I'm still shivering with the violence of her music. I feel cheated. Surely, she gave herself over to the score. I saw it! I felt it! Was she really so detached? Isn't that dishonest? The applause thickens as the Conductor stands and takes his wife's hand in his own. I wonder how many times they've clasped hands and bowed together.

Lucia squeezes my arm before disappearing with a group of especially well-dressed strangers. I find the bathroom. The walls are decorated with old-fashioned tiny white and blue tiles and framed anniversary dinner invitations. I don't think I've ever seen a frame in a bathroom. I wet my hands and trickle cold water down the back of my neck. I think my body is experiencing emotions that my jumbled thoughts are yet to catch up to. There is a dull ache in my chest and neck. My lungs are somewhere near my shoulders. There are butterflies in my stomach. They might catch fire in this heat. Someone taps on the door.

'The trio is about to play!'

'Right,' I say to the violinist in the mirror.

—

When the Conductor re-introduces us, he says, 'I remember when I realised I finally understood Schubert – that's when I knew I was completely mad.'

His guests laugh politely.

'This piece, from Schubert's *Opus 100*, was one of the last works composed before his untimely death at 31 years old. Funnily enough, it was first performed at a private party much like this one. There's something very special about listening to chamber music in intimate spaces such as these. Goethe once likened listening to a string quartet to hearing a conversation between four intelligent people, and, well, I think the same can be said of a trio. So, please welcome our three intelligent, brilliant young musicians: Lucia, Maya, and Sergei.'

Reunited with my violin, this decadent outside world seems dimmer. Sergei adjusts his blazer, then the piano seat. I don't understand how pianists play a different instrument every-where they go. I try to still my whirring mind as Lucia and Sergei begin together. I watch for the familiar line to appear between Lucia's brows and feel a jolt of pleasure when it does. It's different, the way she presents this music. She performs a concerto for her audience, but she plays this Schubert for herself. Even the colour is special – warmer, deeper, with more core to the sound. Sergei's piano sounds severe beneath her – metronomic and harsh. The volume is bruising. And the buzzing aircon is distracting and dissonant. I count, two, three, and join them, but something feels off. My hands aren't shaking, but I'm prickling with the nakedness of chamber music. It feels like Sergei and Lucia can read my mind each time I move my bow. I don't want to feel naked in front of Sergei. I don't want Lucia to read my mind, even though I don't know what she'll discover there in the mess. I wonder what Josh thought of St Stephen's Cathedral – the single soar-ing spire, the ancient columns, glistening chandeliers, the candles burning for the dead. *Focus, Maya.* Sergei's notes are flowing and flowing, encouraged by the *sostenuto* pedal, but they are ugly, dirtying the air, insulting the manuscript on the stand, wounding my ears and, still, flowing and flowing. I glance at him. He's chewing on nothing, like he's on ecstasy. His chewing is out of time with his playing. I don't understand. His sound is polluting mine. In music, everything is contagious. *Damn it, focus!*

What is the music asking me for? This music is asking me for tenderness. Schubert is imploring me from his nearby grave. But every bone in my body is aching with some variation on longing – lust, sadness, yearning. I can feel the cool metal handle of my memory draw in my hand, but I refuse to open it. I refuse! It's too much! And I can't let my bow shake. I'm distracted. And noticing my distraction is distracting. And chastising myself is distracting. The majority of people in this room won't realise, sure, but still, I'm ashamed. Embarrassed. I will myself to focus. I try furrowing my brow like Lucia, but my face feels unnatural. I feel a weight press against my temples, my neck, my jaw. I'm splitting in two, three, half-living in parallel worlds – I'm dancing with Josh in our Acton Town kitchen, and I'm pressed against Lucia in the gold elevator. Fuck. I catch Lucia's eye and she blinks once, slowly. It seems like a deliberate blink. In it, I read, 'You're okay. Breathe.' I'm not sure if she even blinked consciously, but we lock eyes like this for one phrase, then another. Finally, finally, finally, I fall into the music, carried by the melody like a gentle wave. Our bodies move together. Even our breathing has synchronised.

When the guests applaud, I burn with the displeasure of imperfection. No, 'displeasure' isn't right. Revulsion. I am revolted. I feel filthy. I cannot play like this for Maestro García tomorrow.

—

Lucia returns from an adjoining room with three glasses of champagne and a handful of falafels.

'Are you okay?' she says under her breath. I don't like that Lucia can hear the death in my music. Josh never could.

'Fine, sorry, just a bit distracted.' I pop a falafel in my mouth and decline her offer of champagne. Sergei downs his drink, then mine, then excuses himself to hunt for another. He's one of *those* musicians, I guess – gagging for sweet, sweet release even as he takes his bow.

'Don't be sorry, it was still beautiful,' she lies, reaching for my arm. I fight the urge to shake her off. I am angry at myself, not Lucia.

'There is a French saying that I like from Voltaire,' she says, '"*Le mieux est l'ennemi du bien.*" "The better is the enemy of the good."'

'I didn't know you spoke French as well?'

'That is not the point, *cara.*'

'I know.'

There's a moment of pause between Lucia's sip and her swallow, like she's enjoying the feeling of the fizz on her tongue. Lucia Rizzo, star cellist, casual lover, who used to think I played like the music in her head.

I catch a glimpse of the Soprano standing alone by the window, holding an empty champagne flute. You know what? I think I need to ask her how she does it, how she performs with such convincing emotion, and then leaves it all behind.

'I'm just going to speak to the Soprano.'

'*Certo cara*, see you later.'

I sidestep guests on my way to her, who tell me:

'*Vielen Dank, das war
wirklich so schön!*'

> 'Thank you so much for your
> playing!'

I pick up a glass of champagne from a nearby tray and present it to the Soprano like a gift I've bought myself.

'Yes, thank you, exactly,' she addresses the glass.

There's a mistiness in her eyes I hadn't noticed before. They look unfocused, distracted. I wonder if now is a bad time.

'Is now a bad time?'

'For what, dear?'

'I'd love to speak with you about your performance.'

'Oh, it's you.'

I watch her search for my name.

'Maya,' I offer.

'Maya,' she repeats, 'thank you for your Schubert. I hear you only found out about our little soirée yesterday? Extraordinary. I don't know how you instrumentalists manage to play at such short notice.'

'Well, yes, but I've played the piece before, and—'

'The second half was particularly beautiful,' she interrupts, 'I love the way you interacted with the cello. The pianist, sadly, we could have done without. Too mighty, in my opinion, especially for Schubert.'

'Well, thank you, actually the reason I wanted to—'

The Soprano seems distracted again. She touches her throat.

'I'm sorry, dear, but I don't like speaking in large crowds. Why don't we step outside into the little sitting room?'

She takes my hand and leads me through her living room. We pass her wall of photos and it feels like travelling through time. She takes me through a closed door, into a smaller, still immaculate, room and sits on a rouge armchair. She gestures to the couch beside her. I sit.

'What is it you would like to speak about, then?'

This feels very official. Perhaps she's used to *official*. I wonder just how famous she was in her day.

'The piece, *La Voix Humaine*, it's so moving,' I say.

'It is. There is really nothing like it.'

'And your performance was so—' I search for the word '—believable. And emotional. I felt completely transported.'

'Thank you. It is not my first rodeo.'

A borrowed phrase from her husband, I'm sure. She smiles a more intimate smile than she gave her guests after the performance.

'I hope you don't mind me asking, but do you *feel* the emotions of the music while you sing?'

I nearly answer for her: *You must do. I heard them. And so how do you survive them? And why do you abandon them? And how?*

'Oh, that is an interesting question. My short answer is

no. I do not really feel the emotions while I sing. If I did this, if I really engaged with the feelings, I would not be able to sing.'

Something collapses inside me.

'I don't believe you,' I reply, surprising myself. I sound insolent. The door opens and a tiny blonde dog struts towards us, coming to rest beside the Soprano's feet. She ignores it, looking at me intently.

'You say my performance was emotional and I thank you for saying this. But I think what you mean is that *you* felt emotional during my performance.'

I don't speak. She's right, I guess. She continues, 'And this is wonderful. It means I have done my job. As a musician, it is important to remember that the listener is also a composer and also a performer. She situates our music. She finishes off our performance. She is our interpreter.' The Soprano looks thoughtful. 'You know, you might find this interesting: an old friend of mine published an article, years ago now, about the way our brains experience music. That is, in exactly the same way. Music activates the same regions in all of our brains. Yours. Mine. Every guest in my living room.'

I imagine my brain in a machine, lighting up like all the other brains.

'But even so – and this is the beautiful part – our experiences of music differ so greatly, for so many reasons, and I think *that* is what matters, really.' She takes a sip of champagne before continuing, 'May I ask, as my listener, what my performance meant to you?'

I am not ready with an answer. The full force of my feelings about her singing, Lucia's fingers, lips, music touching mine, Josh's morning unicorn hair in my living room, my own horrific playing, is overwhelming and ineffable. I try to keep my response analytical.

'I think what I found so emotional about your performance was that it showed, in this claustrophobic, completely one-sided way, the effect of lost love. You were so alone.' My voice breaks. Damn it.

'Alone, yes, that she is.'

She. Again, I'm struck by the distance between the Soprano and her character.

'So you really felt nothing?' I sound like a child. I need to get a grip.

'There is an important distinction between the experience and performance of emotion, but I sense this is not what you want to hear, so I will elaborate, in the hope of easing some of your distress.'

I'm sure she can read the devastation on my face. I laugh. I want her to think that I, too, find my distress mildly amusing.

'In my opinion, in order to give an emotional performance, you need to have experienced the emotion you're expressing, and you need to have left it behind. Learning to leave behind emotion is a skill. For me, and perhaps it is different as a singer, I require distance from an emotion to be able to use it artistically.'

'What kind of experiences were you drawing on, then?'

She doesn't answer. Maybe this is too personal. Oh well, it's out there.

Then she says, 'I've been rejected before. I've had to give up a love I thought was the only love I would ever have.'

Her voice is very matter-of-fact, but her face is nostalgic, younger somehow. Her eyes are wide, even glassy.

'Let's take this character, Elle, for example.' Her tone shifts again and she sounds objective, didactic. She almost reminds me of my violin. 'Elle feels obsession; I've felt obsession. I imagine what the man on the other end of the phone could be saying. In my imagination, he has the voice of an old lover. But for me, the easiest way to slip into character is to think of those words, *je t'aime, je t'aime, je t'aime ...'*

I see a glimpse of her character resurfacing.

'Tell me, have you ever said "I love you" when nobody was there?'

I don't reply. She nods. The noise from the party trickles into our little room. Sensing the end of our conversation, I lean forward, ready to stand. Suddenly she asks me, 'What do you think of Vienna?'

'Oh, um, I love it.'

'That doesn't surprise me,' she says with a half-smile, 'do you know why?'

I shake my head.

'Vienna is a city that romanticises the past. They are proud to have maintained their *Lebenskunst.* Have you marveled at the horses pulling carriages along the streets? Have you sampled the cream on the coffees, made from the same recipe for hundreds of years? They play their old music in their old buildings, while they sip their old wine, and they love it here. My husband, he loves it. It's why we carry on the tradition of these soirées. But for me? In order to really, truly live and, perhaps just as importantly, in order to really, truly perform, the past needs to feel far away.'

—

'You two disappeared for a while!' Lucia tucks a stray strand of hair behind my ear. Her fingers linger by my neck. She's carrying an empty glass of champagne. 'And you have no drink! A disaster!' She grabs a glass from a passing waiter.

'Actually, I'm probably going to head soon to practise for tomorrow's audition.'

She frowns at me. Only for a second.

'What did you two speak about?' she asks.

'I wanted to ask her how she did—' I struggle for the word '—that.'

I gesture to the piano, as if she was still standing beside it, singing 'I love you' to no one.

'And? Did she give you any good tips?'

'Kind of, lots to think about,' I say, my tone frustratingly void of flirtation. Lucia Rizzo is smiling at me with her red, red lips and I'm thinking about the Soprano and Professor Forrest and the memory drawer I might need to blow up. And yes, you know what, I'm mourning the *desire-ful* hypnosis I felt in Lucia's apartment thirty or so hours ago.

'*Entschuldigung*,' a voice behind us interrupts, dusty with age. I turn around to find a man in a navy suit, with severely cut silver hair and salt-and-pepper stubble. He has a small, shiny white card in his hand, which makes his skin look yellow and fragile. '*Englisch? Deutsch?*'

'English is better,' Lucia says confidently, saving me the embarrassment.

'Hello. Thank you for your Schubert. It was so lovely. You are the cellist, or?'

'Yes, I'm Lucia. And this is the violinist, Maya.'

Closed-mouth smile.

'Hallo, Maya,' he mumbles, turning back to Lucia. His snubbing of me piques my interest.

'I host a recital series in an art gallery, the Galerie der Kunstraum by the Ringstrassen-Galerien.' He offers her his card, 'Do you also play solo, Miss Lucia?'

'Yes, I do,' Lucia says without looking at me. She takes the card, *'Dankeschön, das freut mich sehr. Ich werde Sie dann anrufen.'*

He replies too quickly for me to understand, chuckling as he speaks.

'Super! Sie können auch Deutsch! Dann hoffe ich, bald von Ihnen zu hören!'

He smiles at me and turns away.

'Wow, get you!' I say.

A quick study of my feelings: I'm not jealous. From that performance, I'd also have scouted Lucia, not me. Still, I feel sick, my subpar playing reinforced. I need to practise. And I need to flirt with Lucia. And maybe I need to apologise to Elsa again. And I need to talk to Josh about his parents. Don't I? Josh, who is right now with Georgia in a dark, candle-filled cathedral.

'Yes. He must be looking for a cellist,' Lucia says, gently. 'Anyway!' Her tone brightens, 'Are you coming to this party tonight?'

'I'm not sure whether or not to go. I know important people will be there, but I have Josh with me, and I need to get an early—'

'I think you should come! Bring Josh! Show him how we party in Vienna.' She rolls her shoulders and I force a laugh.

A small splash of champagne.

'Okay, whoops,' she says, licking a golden drip from the side of the glass. It looks like a tear. 'You go practise, but I will see you at the party tonight?'

'Yes, probably, yes.'

I lean in to kiss her on both cheeks and she places her hands on my shoulders and slows me down. Instead of touching her cheek to my cheek and kissing the air, she places her lips on my left cheek, then my right. My stomach twists with desire. Thank God.

As I'm digging for my phone in the basket by the door, the Conductor once again demands the attention of the room with a champagne-glass *ding*. Oh, yes, Lucia is going to play the Rachmaninoff. Rachmaninoff, who was married all his life, happily in love, and still able to write his haunting second piano concerto. I don't get it. Should I stay? No, I really do need to go. Wait, she's going to play after drinking? I suppose it's an encore. Still. What? How?

I close the apartment door behind me. It's quiet in the corridor. Finally. I drink the silence like it's ice water and I'm dehydrated.

JOSH:

Hey!

I hope the gig went well!

Do you know what time

you'll be done? Georgia

and I are just having a late

lunch in the centre

Me:

Sorry for late reply!

They made us switch

our phones off!! Why don't

we meet back outside the

opera in an hour or so?

Does that work?

JOSH:

That works.

I thought we could go for a drink?

Maybe just the two of us?

Me:

Yes!

Umm in that case let's

meet at the 25Hours Hotel?

I think you'll like it!

Actually maybe 90 mins from now??

JOSH:

Perfect.

See you there.

Let me know if you want

me to bring you some food?

I'm by the elevator when I hear a distant piano play the opening notes of the Rachmaninoff. *Movement 3.* I've already pushed the button. The little arrow is glowing red. The lift arrives just as Lucia's cello enters with the melody. And I freeze. My heartbeat, which I can feel in my fingertips, almost stinging, slows. Even my thoughts still. Her melody is hot, liquid gold, even from far away, and I feel it coating me, heavy and solid against my skin. I've never heard her play Russian music before and it's like she suddenly has the Midas touch. And I'm walking back towards the soirée apartment. And I'm on the floor, leaning against the closed door, letting the music cover me. Her tender, agonising first few notes brush my arms. Her sighing melody coats my chest. Her lush lower register paints my thighs, across my knees, down to my ankles. But the gold pauses just under my chin. It can't reach my mouth, my cheeks, my eyes, because my face is covered with tears.

—

I've pulled myself together! All is well! I've just emailed Maestro García, asking for details about tomorrow's audition and I'm alone with my violin. At last.

This little practice room is windowless but cool, lit by old, fading yellow bulbs. Despite the size, it's very easy to breathe in here. I close my eyes and relish the muted hum of nearby practising musicians. I take my violin from her case and prepare the *Carmen Fantasy* score on the music stand. My stance is combative as we tune – legs wide, eyes fierce. We feel mighty, unshakable. Time slows with her in my hands.

'First, we practise for intonation, then we practise for colour.' My violin instructs, 'It's intonation that will hypnotise our audience.'

Mrs P decorated the neck of my first tiny violin with white tape, so I knew where to press. Professor Forrest told me to imagine eyes on my fingertips. We always started with scales – C Major, F# minor, it didn't matter. Single notes, double stops, thirds, harmonics, arpeggios. One note per bow, two, three, eight. When I protested – when can we move onto actual pieces?! – Professor Forrest told me scales were humbling.

'Scales aren't mechanics. They aren't warmups. You have to ask yourself – what does it mean to climb and descend? What does it feel like? How can we make the journey sound sugary or bitter? The sheer spectrum of colours and tastes that violins are able to produce ... It's *extraordinary*.'

And so we begin. Slowly, slooooooooowly, guided by the metronome app on my phone. We gradually increase our speed. So much of music's magic is in the tempo, right? And repeat. And repeat. Now we'll focus on vibrato. Some musicians think of vibrato as decoration with the left hand, but they're wrong.

'How much hubris must you have to think your left hand is governing vibration!' my violin interrupts. She sounds exasperated. She's right. Every room already has its own vibrato. Acoustics vibrate. Your instrument vibrates. Your bow vibrates. Your body. Your *soul* vibrates! It's the job of your left hand to respond to the sensations all around you.

Dynamics. We start *pianissimo*, at the lightest part of our bow. We appear from nowhere and then we *crescendo*.

God, it feels good to *work*.

And finally, melody. We practise out of rhythm, dotting notes so the first is longer than the second. Then reverse: short-long, short-long, short-long. It's like a dance. Healing, somehow, riffing on the tune. Freeing. Professor Forrest called dotted rhythms 'musical paracetamol'.

Études come next. Kreutzer's second Étude through to Paganini's caprices.
And
Finally
We are warm and ready for acrobatics! Bring on the *Carmen Fantasy*.

—

We have fifteen minutes or so before we have to leave, so I ask my violin what we should play, just for fun.

'Let's play something we love to play,' she says and I nod. 'Let's play something powerful, but unsteady. Asymmetrical.'

I nod again. We're undecided. But maybe we should *decide* to leave words at the door.

'Yes, Kant was dismissive of music's intellectualism,' my violin continues, her tone both didactic and passionate. 'He considered music in terms of sensation. So, right now, when you think of sensation, which piece comes to mind?'

She knows that I'm thinking of Brahms and she knows we won't play Brahms. I wonder if she misses him, too.

'Right now, I guess I'm thinking of Beethoven's *Kreutzer Sonata*,' I lie. Though we do love the *Kreutzer Sonata*, my violin and I. I think it might have even had its premiere nearby.

'Wonderful. So, let's think about the Tolstoy novel of the same name. Professor Forrest taught us that this piece was a conduit for adultery in the novel – music that can make even the most faithful cheat. So I want the music to sound dangerous, okay?'

I nod. Seems fitting. I can't believe that Josh's dad— No. I close my eyes, breathe through my nose. Back to Beethoven. I remember when music like this was a holy object I could only touch with gloves in a dark room. Now it feels like a friend.

Despite what my violin says, I don't think about how I want this music to sound. I don't want to *listen* to this music. I want it to taste like red wine, to smell of roses. No, fire. Smoky embers. I want it to feel like someone is pulling you towards them, running their fingers through your hair, down the sides of your neck. I walk past my memory drawer and into an empty room.

Adagio. The double stops are exposed, raw, vicious. I feel **alive**. Wait, we said no words.

Sweat covers my face in a slippery sheen. I lie on the floor, holding my violin like it's a bouquet, like I'm dead, like we're together in the coffin. But I am the opposite of dead – my every cell is pulsing with adrenaline. My body is an instrument. Percussive, vibrating, primal, hot, wild, thoughtless. Feeling is the opposite of thinking.

But this isn't the career, is it? I'm not going to play like this tomorrow because sometimes, when I play like this, it breaks me. Tomorrow I'm going to play the *Carmen Fantasy* and I'm going to show off my technique, phrasing, articulation, intonation, precision, because I want the work and because I need the work and because

ultimately

this

is

work.

—

We meet beneath a peach-coloured sky. It's finally cool enough to walk without sweating through my jumpsuit. Plus, the wind is feral.

'That's where we're heading,' I point the rooftop bar out to Josh as we wait to cross the road. Otherwise, we don't say much:

'Stephansdom was beautiful.'

'The soirée was fine.'

The bottom half of the 25Hours Hotel could be posh student accommodation – compact and dark grey, with dozens of uniform rectangular windows. The top half is a glass prism. From where we stand, I can just make out the bar, with its bland transparent railing and a few incongruous trees.

'Oh, wow, that is not what I expected.'

'What did you expect?'

'Something older.'

That makes sense. The lights change, by which I mean two women with a love heart between them flash green. This is one of Vienna's photogenic gay traffic lights. Apparently, these appeared after Austria won Eurovision in 2014. Georgia once told me that pedestrians are less likely to jaywalk when the lights feature couples rather than the usual lone red man. Romance = safety. Hah.

'I love the anthracite,' Josh says, eyes still on the building.

I don't know what anthracite is.

The door to the hotel is stacked with a hundred different analogue cameras, like some modern-art Jenga. Fluorescent red and orange letters spell *WE ARE ALL MAD HERE*. In the elevator, we stand side by side, facing the doors. We used to face each other in elevators. Neither of us have mentioned Georgia, or Lucia, or Josh's heavy backpack in my living room, or his letter on my bedside table. Nope. We crossed when the lesbians flashed green and Josh told me he liked anthracite.

On the eighth floor, the elevator doors open to dozens of hanging lightbulbs. A group of five tumble out of an old photobooth, narrowly avoiding us. A deconstructed drumkit hangs from the ceiling by the bar. Inconsistency is the aesthetic – there are stools, couches, and armchairs of different sizes, colours, and fabrics. The lights – lamps, fitted bulbs, cheap chandeliers – vary in shade and lustre. The music is loud and blurry. It's the kind of trance music you feel thudding in your chest. I don't love it.

I scan the room for a place to sit. Two older women – seventies plus – share a green velvet futon, sipping white wine. A group of maybe-underage teenagers in fashionable sneakers film each other doing shots at the bar. Men in suits (no ties) crowd around a messy stack of papers, half-finished beers obscuring their table. The drinks match the drinkers, it's true. It looks like we'll have to head outside.

'Do you think Gen Z's expressions have been influenced by emojis?' Josh points to the cartoonish faces of the maybe-underage teenagers at the bar. He's right. One boy is sticking out his tongue and crossing his eyes while another's wide stare matches his round, open mouth. I can't tell you the exact moment when I started separating myself from the generation below, nor when I started making 'oh I'm so flattered' jokes when asked for ID. But here we are. Tongue-out-eyes-crossed does a shot without using his hands. His friends applaud.

'Maybe,' I say, as we're pushed together by the rowdy crowd at the bar. My shoulder, his bicep. His hip, my waist. I want to lean into him and I want to pull away. Aden, Josh's best friend in London, once leant me his copy of Annie Ernaux's *Simple Passion*. In it, he'd underlined something about experiencing pleasure like a future pain. Right now, I think I'm feeling both simultaneously, existing now and tomorrow. Josh orders a Bloody Mary. Of course. The familiarity of him is comforting and melancholic. Like Bach, sometimes. Josh wouldn't understand this analogy. Lucia would. I'll order a lime and soda because it's cheap and non-alcoholic.

A sign by the bar reads:

could I have this dance for the rest of my life

No question mark.

do Gen Z deem punctuation unfashionable

No, actually, fuck it, I'm at least getting a mocktail. Treat yourself. Virgin Mary. Lucky me. We take our drinks outside, squeezing past the emoji-faces, their shots, the suits, their beers.

Outside is quieter, a little smoky. We lean against the balcony railing, gazing at Vienna, magnificent Vienna, brushed with sunset hues. A waiter lights a candle on the table floating between us. I suppose it was once that classic candle-in-gin-bottle design, but after countless replacements, any possible glimpse of the bottle is covered with hard wax. It looks like a monster.

'Cheers,' Josh clinks our glasses together.

I sip my drink, letting the smooth stream of overpriced, spicy tomato juice burn my tongue.

'Hey, are you alright?'

'Yes,' I answer too quickly. He waits. I bite my celery stick, a cool relief from the salty drink. Josh doesn't like celery, and I watch him decide whether to put his stick in my glass like he used to.

'Would you like my celery?' he asks.

I'm a little sad he had to ask. I nod and sigh, and our candle-monster shudders.

'I played terribly in the soirée.'

'Okay, I got the vibe you maybe didn't want to talk about it. But Maya, I'm sure it wasn't—'

'It's not just that.'

He waits. Our celery stalks lean against each other in my glass.

'I'm not really sure what to say. I feel weird.'

'You feel weird?'

'Yes.'

But I don't really want to think about why I feel weird. I don't know why I brought it up. Do I sound weird to you? Do you remember the Maya from Lucia's bed yesterday morning? I wouldn't blame you if you flipped back to that opening scene, read it over and over. I would if I could, I think.

'I'm fine, really,' I say. 'But I think maybe we should talk about what's going on for you in London.'

Josh looks at me, considers me, continues, 'Yeah, I don't know. It's weird. Sometimes I think the right thing would be to tell my mum everything – give her the information and let her decide what to do with it. Sometimes I think that would be cruel, like I'm just trying to get this all off my chest.'

'It's an impossible position to be in. I think it's completely normal not to know what to do.' I sound like therapist Julie.

'I dunno.'

'How did you find out about the affair?'

'Oh, I went to his office to drop off a late birthday present and heard him talking on the phone to her.'

'Bloody hell, I'm sorry.'

'When your sister's ex cheated, did she think – did any of her friends—?' Josh shakes his head and pinches the bridge of his nose, 'Like, would she have wanted to know if a friend heard what was going on?'

'Yes, she would have.'

'Right.'

'But I think it's different with your mum. You're her son, not her friend, and that distinction matters, doesn't it? In terms of your responsibility, I mean.'

He looks unconvinced. I can't tell if I believe what I'm saying, or if I'm saying what he needs to hear. Maybe it doesn't matter.

'Plus, Lisa was only with her ex for a few years so, yes, her life fell apart with the knowledge of an affair, but it wasn't her whole life, you know? I think, when you're married, with a family ... I don't know. I just think it might be different for your mum.'

Josh sips his drink once, twice. He looks away from me, and I want to take him into my arms and fly away from here.

'My mum loved you, you know. She was devastated when we broke up.'

'Yeah, well, so was I,' I laugh, but it's a strange, forced laugh.

Josh buries his hands in his pockets. The woman to my left blows her smoke into the view, and the wind carries it closer to us. I turn my head away, but Josh closes his eyes and breathes deeply. His body buckles.

Josh had just quit when we met. His body used to buckle just like this whenever he encountered second-hand smoke. Memories collide and engulf me, an immersive slideshow of our early romancing: a group of teenagers breakdancing in my local park, scratchy sand in my shoes on a day trip to Whitstable beach, hazy back alleys in the West End. I watched him then, and I'm watching him now because I love watching his body crave things.

'You know, when we broke up, my mum called me and yelled at me,' Josh says. 'She told me to follow you wherever you needed to go.'

I feel like someone has slapped me across the face and punched me in the gut and poured my drink on my head. The idea of sipping my Virgin Mary or taking in the view feels ridiculous in this very real world where Josh's mum told him to follow me. And he told her no.

'Sorry,' he mutters, shaking his head, 'that wasn't a very sensitive thing to say.'

'No, it's okay. There's no real script for this kind of hanging out, is there?'

'I guess not.'

'When did you decide to come to Vienna?'

He sighs. 'It wasn't actually as spontaneous as you might think. I wasn't sleeping and I was so tired all the time. I felt on the verge of losing it, but still kind of had control over my behaviour. It was weird – I would just stand up and leave tables, drop out of shabbat dinner last minute without giving an excuse, that sort of thing. It made me think a lot about

Hamlet, actually. Like, acting crazy before actually going crazy. Anyway, then my sleeping kind of improved and I kind of calmed down and things began to feel more normal again. But – I know this sounds strange – I didn't really *want* to feel better. Because if things resembled normality, that meant I had to exist in this new normal where my dad was this—' His eyes fill with tears and he wipes them angrily. '— Sorry,' he grunts. My throat tightens as his throat tightens. 'It's insane how much I've cried about this.'

'Obviously there's nothing to apologise for,' I say, and take another bite of his celery.

'I just felt like if I let myself sleep or try to forget about it or be happy, it felt like I was betraying my mum,' he runs his fingers through his curls. 'I want to be angry and I *am* angry, but I'm mostly just so fucking sad. Jesus, I'm sorry, I know what I sound like.'

'You sound human, Josh.'

'Mm,' he hums, and sips his drink. 'And then, on Thursday night, my dad called to ask if I could cover for him with mum while he was with this other fucking woman. And I hung up on him and booked a ticket here. And I didn't really think about how that would affect you, or how selfish it was of me to just show up. To be 100% honest, all I could think about was getting out of London. I really am sorry for just rocking up like this, Maya.'

My face does something out of my control – grimaces or scowls or winces. It used to make me smile when Josh said 'to be 100% honest', like he was acknowledging the degrees of honesty.

'It does sound like maybe you should talk to someone professional about this,' I say with my strange new face.

'I dunno. I can just imagine a therapist telling me I've done the wrong thing by not telling anyone.'

'I don't think it would be like that, Josh.'

'No, maybe not.'

I don't know when it happened, but we're no longer facing one another. I steal a sideways glance at Josh but he is focused on the skyline. It's turned from a pale purple into a deep blue, closer to the colour of his shirt.

'Did you stop connecting music to your life because your therapist told you to?' he asks.

'Hmmm,' I hum.

'And how does that make you feel?' Josh's eyes find mine.

'Hmmm,' I hum again.

The world around us, all of it – the sweaty bodies and fuzzy sounds – dims when he looks at me like that. His eyes flick to my lips. Just once. Just for a second. Maybe even half a second. Maybe I imagined it. I take a step back.

'Right!' he says loudly enough to catch the smoking woman's attention. 'So, important question, are you ready to party?'

He takes a step back, too.

'Josh, maybe we shouldn't go.'

'No, I think let's leave the family breakdown and therapy talk at the 25Hours Hotel. We should definitely go to the party. It sounds like it will be a good networking thing for you. We don't have to stay long, but we should definitely go.'

'I hate networking.'

'Everyone hates networking.'

I wonder if this is true.

'Hey, sorry to be "that guy", but will people be speaking English?'

It's comforting to hear my own worries echoed back at me, even if he's just trying to change the emotional channel of the evening.

'Some people will, yeah, I'm sure.'

'Oh, also, I invited Georgia. I hope that's fine?'

'Of course,' I smile. I feel dizzy, almost jet-lagged, I haven't caught up to this abrupt tonal change. 'Yeah, fine, I'll text her the address.' This comes out harsher than I intended.

—

We pass a fountain on Museumstraße near the entrance to the 25Hours Hotel. It's ugly by Vienna's usual standards – statue-less and colourless. Next to the fountain sits a busker and her guitar. She's wearing a white vest, brown corduroys, and a quasi-mullet (neat, stylish, and with a fringe). Despite this, the nose ring, and the dramatic eye-liner wings, the most noticeable thing about her is her Sloaney drawl. I don't think Josh will appreciate the rarity of this – a Brit singing on the streets of Vienna. A cardboard sign with her stage name – APHRODÏTE – balances on her open guitar case. We pause beside her as she sings 'you were the perfect stranger' to no one. I feel in my bag for loose cash and rub two coins together while she plays the folky outro. I can feel Josh fidgeting beside me, but I want to hear a little more. I like her voice. It's cool and smooth. Aphrodïte – I might look her up later. I drop both euro into the guitar case, and she grins at me from beneath her fringe. In my peripheral vision, I can see Josh admiring the fancy, pastel-coloured apartment blocks across the road.

Aphrodïte is singing about a 'Tinder babe'. Her eyelids are heavy, like the too-thick eyeliner is weighing them down. The chords are fun – two half-diminished minor chords followed by the dominant seven. Aphrodïte's thoughts seem miles away from the Seventh District. I wonder what she's doing in Vienna. I almost ask Josh whether he's been on Tinder, but then I remember I really, truly, deeply don't want to know.

'Hi,' Aphrodïte is grinning at us.

Josh answers first, 'Hello! That was great! Thank you.'

Aphrodïte looks at me with a face I recognise – *compliment me, audience.*

'It's such a pleasure to hear an English accent in Vienna,' I try. This isn't a compliment. 'Your voice is so cool and smooth,' I try again. Josh chuckles.

'What a review!' Aphrodïte laughs, too. Her laugh is warmer than her singing voice, somehow more resonant. 'Do you two live in Vienna?'

'I do, yes. But Josh is just visiting. And you?' I nearly put my hand on Josh's shoulder as I say his name, but catch myself. Aphrodïte's eyes dart to my awkward floating hand.

'I'm here for now, but Vienna isn't my final destination. What's your relationship, then, if you live here and he's just visiting?'

'Excuse me?' I say. I'm sure I've misunderstood.

'That's quite a personal question,' Josh laughs again, but this time he sounds uneasy.

'I'm sorry, I didn't mean to pry. Well, I did mean to pry.

But if you'd rather not say, that's cool. I've just been trying to figure it out since you started watching my set. It helps me play when I make up stories about the people around me. Busking can be boring as shit.'

'Okay, if you had to guess our relationship status, what would you say?' I'm surprised by my own engagement/ deflection. Maybe I'm desperate for an outside perspective – someone to observe our situation and tell me what the fuck is going on. Maybe I should invite Lucia here to the ugly fountain, so Aphrodïte has more of the picture. Maybe Georgia, too. Aphrodïte looks coy, suddenly, averting her gaze and strumming an E major chord.

'I don't want to stir any pots,' she lies. The fifth is flat, her second string. Neither of us respond. 'I think you're friends. But—' Broad smile. Very large teeth. '—You're in love!'

She strums another chord. A diminished something, but I'm paying less attention.

'Oh, are we now?' I say, trying to lighten this needlessly intense interaction. I don't look at Josh. I wonder if she'll write a song about us.

You're just friends, but don't you see?
Vienna's not your final destination, but she might be.

'But you don't want to be in love,' she continues. Another slightly out-of-tune chord. 'Shit. I hope I haven't struck a nerve?'

'No, no. You're quite the detective, though.' Josh's smile doesn't reach his eyes, 'Anyway, we're just heading to a party. But lovely to meet you.'

'Lovely to meet you, too!'

Aphrodïte adjusts the capo on her guitar. As we're walking away, she yells, 'Hey! I'm playing a concert at the Mayer am Nussberg Heuriger tomorrow afternoon if you're around. It's a beautiful spot! For friends and lovers alike!'

Neither of us turn around. Did she say *Maya*?

We pass posters of old Austrian royalty taped to street poles like ads for rock bands. In most of the posters, Empress Sisi has a sharpie moustache and/or devil horns. Our destination is a tall, thin building, decorated with a series of graffitied cartoon mouths – open, then closed, then pouting, then kissing, then biting – with increasingly red lips. I glance at Josh, who is smiling at the mouths. Then he smiles at me.

———

Fourth floor, breathless. As the door opens, music floats into the hallway – Julie London's 'I'm in the Mood for Love'. I know the 1950s album from Spotify, the one with the nostalgic vinyl static. It's quite an *aesthetic* musical choice for a party. Erudite, yet somehow cosy. Maybe this will be fun.

'*Willkommen*! Welcome!' In the doorway, an Australian woman with startlingly blue eyes and hair tied in a messy bun introduces herself as Cali. She hands us each a shot glass of clear liquid, a piece of paper, and a yellow Bic pen.

'I'm Maya.'

'Josh.'

I once notated the rhythm of our names together in the diary I lost: Maya, Josh.

'Shot those bad boys, then write a poem, then I'll let you in.'

'You're joking,' I say.

'I am not! It's something I picked up living in Oslo and I've found it a rather magical exercise.'

This doesn't strike me as a particularly Norwegian tradition. I catch Josh's eye and gesture with my chin to the stairs – *We can leave if this is too much. Maybe we should leave. Should we leave?*

'No, it's okay, I'm into it,' he answers, shotting both our vodkas, then pressing his paper against the wall. The beige surface is bumpy and rough. He'll end up poking a hole. Maybe someone will think it poetic. Cali waits, staring into the distance with a fixed, almost heated gaze. She doesn't seem to mind me not drinking. Maybe she's often surrounded by boring musicians.

Josh scribbles enthusiastically against the wall. No discernible holes. But writing poetry is not his thing. *Was* not his thing. *How much can a person change in a year?* I envy Josh his lack of inhibition. Words are not my medium. I suppose it doesn't matter. He turns to me, catches me staring. Oh, he's finished already? It can be that short? Fine. Easy.

'You can use my back if you don't want to use this bumpy wall?' Josh smiles at me. He knows my hesitation is not related to deciding which surface to write on. When I press against his back, I try to ignore its contours, the muscles that firm to greet me. Josh covers his poem with his hand. 'Absolutely not, you are not reading mine.'

'Fine, fine,' I laugh into the back of his head. His hair looks silky in this hallway half-light. It's lighter, too, closer to the colour of honey than almonds. Fuck me, this is ridiculous, pressing onto Josh's back instead of the wall, meditating on the colour of his hair.

A Poem, I title my paper, but nothing comes to mind. Obviously. I cop out and write:

This is not a poem.

'Don't worry, no one will know who wrote what,' Cali explains as we fold our papers. We're still standing in her doorway. She bends down and picks up a scrap off the floor.

'Well, well, well, I must have dropped this earlier.' She sounds excited. 'Should we read it together?'

This seems staged, and I am about to roll my eyes when I notice that Josh is *captivated*. Cali's Australian accent is more pronounced as she reads – broad vowels, juicy dipthongs, Ls falling to the back of her throat:

I'm mourning the language that died
On the night when I lied and you cried on the floor.
I'm mourning the words that were ours
And I'm cursing the verse I don't write any more.
How before we'd begun, with your hands on my tongue,
You wrote like a plane in the sky:
'Baby answer my call?', now these words mean fuck all,
But they'll stay in my mouth till I die.

'I don't love rhymes,' she says, flatly. I find it strange that someone who doesn't love rhymes asks her guests to write a poem on entry to her apartment.

'Who wrote that?' Josh asks.

'Wouldn't *you* like to know?' Her coy smile flowers into a smirk as she pockets our poems. Finally, she opens the door and invites us inside.

'So is this your place?' Josh asks Cali as we take off our shoes.

'Yeah,' she sounds distracted.

'What brought you to Vienna?' We're still in her doorway.

'Poetry,' she replies, again without making eye contact.

Josh raises his eyebrows at me. *She didn't really answer my question, did she?* The thoughts in my head are the thoughts in his head.

Is Lucia here already? We both wonder. *When's Georgia arriving?*

Cali beelines for a man with long, knotty blonde hair and a bottle of tequila, leaving Josh and I to puzzle at the strange living room. The living room is strange because it doesn't look lived-in at all. We could be standing in the show room of an upmarket Ikea. Glossy white candles are arranged in a line along a glass table. The table's rose gold perimeter matches the rose gold of the punch bowl at its centre. Interspersed between the candles are smaller bronze bowls of hummus and guacamole, and matte-black, asymmetrical plates of thinly sliced meats (folded into tiny parcels), pitas, and cheeses. The sofa, whose navy-blue velvet matches the armchair and ottoman, is cushion-less. All this contrived elegance is juxtaposed with a gaggle of shoeless guests – shiny foreheads and windswept hair. A small group of men are huddled together by the bedroom door, sucking on vapes like lollipops. Conductors? Industry people? Unlikely.

I spot Elsa by the punch bowl and join her as Josh leaves to find the bathroom. Beside the bowl are a stack of wooden coasters that say: *'DON'T FUCK UP THE TABLE.'* This aesthetic is confusing. Elsa's face is paler than usual, with dark half-moons under each eye.

'Maya! *Willkommen!*' She squeezes my shoulder with tipsy affection. 'Would you like some punch?'

Looking at the off-pink liquid brimming with swollen orange wedges and floating brown banana makes me woozy, and I shake my head.

'No,' she agrees, 'it looks horrible. Why don't I pour us some gin and tonic?' Elsa takes two gold paper cups from a stack.

'Actually, I'm not drinking at the moment, but can you pour one for my friend from London?'

'Oh yes! The ex-boyfriend?'

'Well, yes.' I sound surprised.

'Lucia told me he was here.'

Elsa's gin:tonic ratio is almost 1:1. I can smell the pine-y botanicals from here.

Are you alright? Are we? I don't ask. This isn't the time. Or I don't want to bring it up. I don't know. Instead, I say, 'Hey, what's with this apartment?'

'What do you mean?' She swigs her drink, and winces as she swallows. I wonder whether she always pours such strong G&Ts. Or maybe she is already too tipsy to mix sensible drinks.

'Don't you think it looks like a showroom in here?' I ask.

'What is a "show room"?' She hands me Josh's G&T.

'Like, a room you'd see in Ikea advertising furniture.'

There don't seem to be alcohol-free options on the table. I love gin, but you know I won't drink it. Because of the audition, yes, but even without the audition, it's important I keep my head screwed on tonight. It feels like a choice between zero G&Ts and too many.

'Cali gave all the shared things to her ex in the break-up and decided to start again with new furniture,' Elsa whispers theatrically.

'Love is a natural disaster,' I say, wondering whether this translates.

'Skål! Let's cheers to natural disasters!' Elsa smashes her cup into mine without meeting my eye. The fifty:fifty gin-tonic blend sloshes over the rim, marring the new rug.

'Are you alright, Elsa? With Davorin and everything?' I ask. I've changed my mind. I should have asked earlier.

'I don't want to talk about it. We have a party to enjoy!' Elsa gestures around us with her cup, again, redecorating the rug. 'You should say hello to Zofia!'

She points to a woman with short blonde hair lounging alone on the cushion-less sofa. She looks comfortable in her solitude – unfocused gaze, bare bronzed legs resting on the ottoman.

'Zofia is a Polish conductor. Very talented. And a good person to know.'

'Right,' I say, as Josh joins us. I hand him his drink and grab a few almond-stuffed olives from one of the fancy plates.

'Hey, I'm Josh.'

Elsa smears guacamole on her chin as she bites into a mini pita, 'Hello Josh, I am Elsa. Maya is my colleague and friend.'

'Colleague *and* friend! Nice to meet you,' he chuckles. 'What are we all talking about?'

Elsa repeats her sentence identically. I wonder whether this is a second (third? fourth?) language thing: 'You should say hello to Zofia. She is a Polish conductor. Very talented. And a good person to know.'

'Great! Let's go say hi,' Josh says as I shovel pita into my mouth. I haven't eaten enough today. I really need to eat. If I don't eat, I won't sleep. If I don't sleep, I'll play like shit at this audition.

'I will leave you,' Elsa says, eyeing the shaggy blonde by the balcony door. Or the bottle of tequila in his hand. I wipe the guacamole from her chin with my thumb, though she doesn't seem to notice. Her ringlets bounce as she walks away.

'She's a character!' Josh takes a sip of his G&T and coughs, 'Fuck me, this drink is strong!'

The Polish conductor moves her legs from the futon as we approach her.

'Can we join you?' Josh smiles his charming smile and sits beside her. He was always a good career wingman.

'*Bitte!*' she says in a lush Slavic accent.

'I'm Josh.'

'Maya.'

'I'm Zofia,' she continues and points at me. 'You are a musician.' She points at Josh. 'You are not.'

Josh's mouth falls open. 'How did you know?' he asks, as if Zofia had just shown him the card he picked at the beginning of the trick.

'Conductor's intuition.'

'Really?'

'Instrumentalists don't tend to introduce themselves so confidently to conductors. I assume you know I'm a conductor?'

We nod. I wonder how many times she's going to say the word 'conductor'.

'What do you play, Maya?' Zofia looks me up and down in a way that is not judgmental but attentive. 'Wait, let me guess.' She studies my fingers, mouth, bare shoulders. I notice her notice the faint outline of my violin hickey. 'Aha! Viola?'

'Close! Violin,' I say, massaging my neck. I feel Josh's eyes on me. 'In the Habsburg Philharmonic. Here in Vienna.'

'Maya plays first violin!' Josh adds, voice shimmering with pride. Once upon a time, he didn't know what that meant.

'I see. I guessed viola because I find the violin more combative, and you do not seem combative to me.'

'Oh, I disagree!' I say, and smile so she sees this is kind of a joke.

'Ah but I love the viola. I love how close it is to the human voice. I'm here in Vienna to conduct a double bill of Wagner and Mozart's *Sinfonia Concertante*, which is an incredibly special piece for violas, as you know. It's grand, but also so playful, I find. Maybe I should hear you play while I'm here.' She smiles back at me.

'That would be great,' I say, and Josh nods enthusiastically. I can hear the Mozart playing faintly in my head, that point near the end of the first movement when everything suddenly slows and the viola and violin sing their tender duet, melodies coiling around one another like bare legs wrapped together after sex.

Zofia leans towards Josh, 'And you? What brings you to Austria?' I've wondered before whether conductors deliberately lead conversations like they lead orchestras.

'I'm here visiting Maya,' he lies. The music in my head stops.

'And what do you think of *Wien*?' Zofia gestures around the room, as if the city were squeezed inside.

'I like Vienna, what I've seen of it, anyway. There's definitely an air of history about the place, which is cool, but also – how do I put this? – it's only the history they've chosen to share.'

'Have you ever been to Warsaw?' Zofia's eyes flick to mine. She could be cueing my entry in the *Sinfonia Concertante*.

'No,' we say together. Zofia responds, overlapping with our 'no' chorus as if she is the soloist and we are the *tutti*. I don't know where this conversation is going. 'I find it an interesting comparison. Vienna is living in the present and their *chosen* past, perhaps. But Warsaw, at least in my opinion of Warsaw's old town, wants to recreate the very old past. The old town was bombed completely during the war and they rebuilt it to resemble exactly how it looked in the fourteenth century.' Zofia mimes hammering into a nail, 'It is almost like a Disney set.' She puts down her imaginary hammer.

'Are you from Warsaw?' I ask.

'No, I'm from Krakow, but I often go to Warsaw to see friends and visit Chopin's heart.'

I know at least five musicians who have made the Warsaw pilgrimage specifically for this reason. I notice Josh's open mouth and explain, 'Chopin spent the first half of his life living in Warsaw, but he died and was buried in Paris. The Poles dug up his body years later and removed his heart so that Warsaw would be its final resting place.'

'Bloody hell.'

'What do *you* think of Vienna?' I ask. I know I am just recycling Zofia's conversation starter, but I want to move the topic away from hearts removed from bodies. *Also is Lucia still not here, or did she arrive without coming to find me?*

'I like Vienna, too, but I think it lacks violence. It is too clean and beautiful here.'

'Yeah, exactly,' Josh replies, nodding seriously.

'You're Jewish as well, yes?' asks Zofia and Josh continues nodding. Elsa appears on my left, perching on the edge of the couch.

'Halloooo!' she sings, oblivious to our conversation about post-mortem heart surgery and Vienna's violent history.

'*Hallo,*' I answer. Josh waves a sweet wave.

'*Hallo* Elsa,' says Zofia, 'and how is the punch?'

'*Gefährlich,*' Elsa warns, stretching the middle syllable. *Gefäääääääääährlich.*

'Dangerous,' I translate for Josh under my breath.

'Oh! *Du sprichst Deutsch* Maya?' Zofia asks.

'A little,' I say, glancing at Josh as I steer the conversation back to English. Elsa is carrying four shots of tequila in one shaky hand.

'Oh, don't worry, I prefer to speak in English,' reassures Zofia. 'Improvisation is easier in English. I feel like I have to prepare whole sentences in my brain when I speak German—'

'Zofia,' Elsa interrupts, swaying, 'I want to ask you something. I will ask you in English.'

'So ask me,' Zofia replies. It sounds like a dare. Actually, it sounds almost flirty. 'But only after we do these shots together.' I worry Elsa is going to make a fool of herself in front of a conductor, but it seems they know each other well. Josh nudges me. Elsa hands us our shots.

'*Skål! Prost!*' Elsa toasts loudly while the others drink. I rest my shot on the table beside us. We wait for Elsa's question while she bites into a wedge of cheese like it's a sandwich. She returns the teeth-marked wedge to the serving plate. 'Zofia, you are here to conduct Wagner, right? Does that feel weird for you as a Jew?' Elsa's gaze is hazy, unfocused.

'Aaaah,' Zofia sighs. 'Obviously I cannot speak for all Jews. But, personally, I have mixed feelings. Even if Wagner wasn't a Nazi, he was publicly antisemitic and would have been a Nazi had he been born later. Though that can be said for a lot of people. And, actually, a lot of Wagner's operas are critiques of power and don't align with the ideology of the Third Reich. What do you think, Maya?'

Hm? Oh. Me. Um. I avoid answering directly while I sort out my thoughts.

'Well, when I was a teenager I used to kind of ignore Wagner because everyone I met that liked Wagner was a bit of a dick, so I assumed his music was for dickheads. But the professor who kind of built my musicality from scratch helped me understand that so much of his music is surprisingly … gentle.'

'So you think we should just forget about who he was?' Zofia asks, eyebrows raised.

'To be honest, to be 100% honest, I don't— Ah, well, no. I guess not.'

'It's hard to gauge the appropriate distance between life and art,' she says.

You're fucking telling me, I don't say.

Pleased with the conversation she started and then did not contribute to, Elsa refills Josh and Lucia's glasses, which they shot with cheese chasers as my phone buzzes. Lucia, finally! No, it's an email.

Dear Maya,
Great to hear from you and my apologies for taking a while to reply.
I'm sorry to say I've been called out of Vienna to jump in to conduct the Berlin Phil, which means I will not be available to audition you this weekend. Unfortunately, I have to submit my choice of soloists to the Salzburg Festival by Monday, so have organised a separate set of auditions with violinists here in Berlin tonight.
I'm sure our paths will cross again one day in the future and wish you lots of luck in what I'm sure will be a wonderful career.
Warm greetings,
Lorenzo García

Stomach somewhere near my knees, tongue down my throat, heart in my face, like some fucked-up Picasso. My head is buzzing as I tune back into the conversation. Elsa is explaining, 'Yeah, I nearly quit myself a few years ago. It's a pretty shit life. My brother was a cellist and had a nervous breakdown and now he's a lawyer who goes on fancy holidays twice a year with his kids. Obviously, I'd never be able to quit, but sometimes I daydream about something terrible happening to my hand that would make the decision for me.'

Dark. Drunk. But, I mean, she's right. You kill yourself in this industry for no money, year-long probationary periods, and non-reportable harassment, and the industry just fucks you over. And you let it fuck you over because the music is worth it. We love the music. We worship the music. The music is love and sex and food and air. I reach for my still-full shot glass. I don't even grimace when the tequila burns.

'Oh, yes Maya!' Elsa is already refilling my glass. 'Welcome to the party! Have another one, you need to catch up!'

'Oh, I thought you didn't want to—'

Josh looks at Elsa, then at me, then back at Elsa, completely dazed, then stunned, then outraged, as if Elsa has just suggested we light the apartment on fire or drown a puppy.

Shot two as the doorbell rings.

'Audition was cancelled,' I say, fire riding my breath, voice husky with alcohol.

'Riiiiight?' Josh's voice slides into a question mark. His vowel sounds slippery.

'One more, let's go!' I say, and Elsa whoops as she obliges.

You know what? It feels good, surrendering. Since the world is ending, what even is consequence?

Speaking of which, Lucia has just appeared in the doorway.

She's changed back into yesterday's linen trousers, though it's too dim to see the shadow of her legs beneath the fabric. The dark skin of her décolletage is framed with a silky white cami, dipped low at the back. A revelation of skin that makes me blush. I watch her chat to Cali in the entrance hall. How well do they know each other? She has an empty shot glass in one hand and a folded poem in the other. Josh is watching her, too. Maybe Georgia won't bother coming tonight. I can't believe my audition was cancelled. It's almost laughable, right? Are you laughing? You know what? Fuck the Maestro. Fuck the Salzburg Festival. Fuck the *Carmen Fantasia*.

Lucia walks alone to the drinks table and pours herself some of the off-pink punch. Elsa offers me her cup of 1:1 gin:tonic and asks, 'Hey, I heard about the soirée, how did it go?'
    'It was fine. Lucia played beautifully, but it wasn't my best.'
    'Why do you think?'
    I swallow my irritation along with the bitter gin mix. My God, that's disgusting. 'I don't think I was in the right head-space for Schubert.'
    Lucia catches the end of my sentence as she sits beside me, leaning over to kiss my cheeks. I feel Josh stiffen on my other side.
    'Oh Maya, you played beautifully,' she says. 'And *guten*

Abend to both of you,' she kisses Elsa, too. To my right, Zofia asks Josh something about British politics, but I can't hear his reply. Conversation and pop music fill the room like water.

My focus feels a little h a z y.

'You know,' Lucia says, 'one time I played the Brahms trio when I was in a really bad mood, and I just could not find a way into the music. Then before the concert I drank too much vodka – I used to like playing drunk when I was young – and that scary octave slide was so, so smooth.'

'So you still played well?' I ask her. *Do you just always play well?*

'No, no, it was *terribile*.' She laughs.

Oh, someone changed the playlist from jazz to EDM. *When did that happen?* In the centre of the room, Cali dances alone in an exaggerated display of sensuality. She rubs her hands along her body while she rolls her shoulders and bends her knees, slowly, in time to—

'Okay, okay, do you want to know why I'm so drunk?' Elsa's voice in my ear. 'It's because I tried to speak to the orchestra management team about Davorin and—' she sips our gin, 'they laughed at me, of course.'

'Oh, Elsa, I'm so—'

She doesn't wait for the rest of my apology before she shoots upwards and joins Cali in the centre of the room. Cali is dancing with her arms above her head, and Elsa grabs her hand and twirls her once, twice.

'Tequila?' asks the shaggy haired guy, offering us the bottle. I hadn't noticed him take Elsa's place on the side of the couch. I half register his Australian accent.

'Why not?' I hear myself say, as if from a distance.

He flicks his hair out of his face like his neck is spasming, 'Still not used to the long hair, sorry.'

I think he likes flicking his hair.

'Yeah, I guess I do.' He laughs.

What?

'Why did you grow it?' Lucia asks. She's sitting so that not a single part of her is touching me. Lovely.

'I've been thinking a lot about my *brand*,' the Australian says. Hair flick.

'What do you do?'

'I'm a guitarist. Classical guitar.' He lifts up his hands and wiggles his fingers, as if to say, this is where the magic happens, and I roll my eyes before I realise he's actually showing us his fingernails. The nails on his right hand look like talons, birdlike. I imagine him flying away.

'I *am* my music, you know? So picking the right haircut is important.'

'Why are you in Vienna?' beautiful Lucia asks.

'I like to travel and I basically organise gigs in whatever city I want to visit. I asked Cali if she could help arrange a concert and she did! Fucking champ!' He raises his bottle of tequila towards the dancing women.

It takes my vision
a few moments to return
to our couch.

Uh oh. I push my foot into the floor to brake.

'My greatest goal is to not end up back at my parents' place. Us artists, we're boomerang kids, aren't we?'

'Sure,' I simulate interest.

'FUCK I never gave you the tequila,' he says, managing to interrupt my one-word sentence. He laughs a honky-tonky laugh and shoves

the tequila

into

my hand.

'Thanks,' I say. I don't really taste it this time. I pass the bottle to Lucia.

'Anyway, I kind of fucked up the concert. I was playing these exciting pieces and, like, man, I really wasn't prepared enough. But that's kind of what I'm thinking about. With my brand. Like, do I want to be this polished clean-shaven guy who plays the right notes all the time? You know?'

'I don't know. Do you?' I ask, glancing at Josh, who is absorbed in conversation with Zofia. They're both frowning but I can't separate all the s o u n d s enough to hear what they're saying. The tequila bottle is in my hands again, but I don't take another sip. Or do I?

'Do you want a smoko?' the guitarist asks. Besides his offer of tequila, I'm pretty sure this is the only thing he's asked us.

'*Non grazie*,' Lucia says, watching Cali and Elsa entwined on the dancefloor.

'*Non grazie*,' I say and giggle.

'Maya, you are tipsy!'

'I think I am not sober, yes! You don't seem tipsy, Lucia!'

Do I use her name as often as she uses mine? Does it have the same effect on her as it does on me?

'I don't know,' she smirks, 'people use my name quite a lot.'

What? 'Did I say that out loud?'

'*Si.*'

The guitarist offers Zofia a 'smoko'. She nods and raises a hand, presumably expecting him to hand over a cigarette. Instead, he tugs her from the couch. They stand, unlit cigarettes pointing towards each other like tiny swords.

'I'm Andrew. I'm a guitarist.'

'Zofia, conductor.'

'A chick conductor! That's awesome! What's it like conducting as a woman in Vienna?'

'What's it like? Well, it's not like my breasts get in the way of my baton.'

Guitarist Andrew's body buckles as he laughs, hands on his knees. Then they walk outside together. So it's just Lucia, Josh, and me on the couch. Wonderful.

'What a weird man. Do you want to dance?' Lucia asks me, or Josh, or us both.

Josh shakes his head and I do the same. It almost feels like we're dancing.

'Okay, well if you change your mind.' She stands and joins the others in the middle of the room.

Elsa dances by stepping from side to side and looking beautiful. Cali dances mostly with her head, like she's being pushed back and forth by the beat. I like it. Lucia's body is sensual and alive. I wish her hips could paint the air. It would be nice if the air was filled with her hips' colourful swirls. Her bare back has more structure than my thoughts. I lean back so that my shoulder presses into Josh's shoulder. This is confusing. I am confused.

'Do you want me to grab you some water?' Josh asks, scanning the alcohol-only drinks table.

'No, but thank you for offering.'

'God, I forgot how polite you are when you're tipsy!' he laughs again, leaning closer to—

'You don't seem totally sober yourself.' My voice breaks on a hiccup and I roll my eyes while he laughs harder.

'Do you remember that party we threw when we moved into the Acton Town flat? That the police hit up?' I ask, my voice mingling tequila and nostalgia. It doesn't feel like a melancholic question.

'I don't think you call it "hitting up" when it's the police,' he's chuckling again, 'but yes, I do. You were so polite and steady that they thought you were sober.'

'It's a gift,' I sing. I didn't mean to sing. Maybe I should slow down. Maybe not. Josh says something I can't make out over the music. I lean in closer. Our mouths aren't far apart. I realise my shoulders have been tense because suddenly they loosen and relax. *Relaaaaaax.*

'I *am* relaxed,' he says and I don't kiss him. 'Oh, great, look who's here.'

Alone at the drinks table, Davorin does three shots in quick succession before joining Elsa, Cali, and Lucia in the middle of the room. His height is even more pronounced from our sofa view. Cali and Lucia dance between Davorin and Elsa, though the movements more closely resemble sports defence than dance. The song ends and Davorin skulks off towards the balcony. I guess Zofia and the guitarist are still outside.

'He's so creepy,' I say and Josh nods. His eyes are narrowed and his mouth is tense.

'I thought he said there would be important industry people here.'

'Yeah, I guess he exaggerated. Though that guy in the dorky shirt at the drinks table is a conductor.' I wonder how loudly I said *that guy in the dorky shirt.* 'Let's go talk to him!' I stand up and only

wo

bb

le slightly.

'Maya, are you sure? Maybe we should—'

I don't hear the rest of Josh's warning because I'm at the other side of the room with the dorky shirt. He has one white eyebrow. How eccentric! 'Hello! How are you doing?' '*Hallo, gut,* thank you. Not so much

English.'

'*Das ist* okay.
*Wir können
Deutsch
sprechen.*'

'Haha *ja wir
können*. You
good *auch*?'

'*Ja*, I'm good
auch.'

The doorbell.

'Fun night?
Spaßßßßß.'

'*Ja. Möchtest
du etwas zu
trinken*?'

'I am taking
a little break,
actually. Did
you try the
punch?' I
point at the
empty bowl.

'Oh! You fin-
ished it!'

'*Ja, es hat
geschmeckt!*'

He gives me
two thumbs

up. His
hands are
very beau-
tiful – long
fingers, short
nails, gently
protrud-
ing veins.
They look
made up.
'Your hands
look make-
believe,'
I tell him
and he nods
seriously.

Georgia doesn't see me as she walks straight to the balcony,
dodging the dancers on her way. Josh whispers – wait, how
long has he been standing with me? – 'I'll tell her we're inside'
and runs after her. Bye!

'Your friend?'
'*Ja*, exactly,
*genau. Sie
schreibt* a
novel. Her
Deutsch *ist
besser als
mein.*'
'*Nein! Dein*

*Deutsch ist
gut! Du spielst
Violin, oder?'*

German! German! German! is EASY when you mostly
know what someone is going to say!

'Ja! I play
violin. Good
memory! We
met before
at a different
party. You
conduct?'

I mime conducting.
Holy shit! All conducting is mime! I laugh.
Outside, Georgia's white dress billows in the wind like . . .
Pick a simile, I can't choose:

- Frothing milk
- A cloud?
- Marilyn!
- A GHOST

Lucia grabs my hand and excuses us. It's basically the first
time she's touched me all night. But who cares? We're **casual**.

'It looked like you needed rescuing.' *Did it?* She hands me
a drink. 'It's water,' she says quietly. Tenderly, I think. She
watches me finish the glass. She's so beautiful.

'This is nice, thank you,' I say. 'I didn't have dinner. Or lunch, really. I'm normally more responsible. Very disciplined, me.'

'I know you are. I'll go get some more water and some food, wait here.'

'Hello hello, someone is sleepy.' I think it's Davorin's voice.

I force myself upright. Only a little dizzy.

'No, no, I'm fine.'

I hope I sound soberer than I am. *Soberer. Is that a word?* Davorin laughs.

Then there is water in one hand and pita in the other and Lucia's voice, 'Here you go.'

'Hey guys, we're going to read the poetry all together soon,' Cali interrupts. I didn't see her join us. Her face is shiny with sweat and her cheeks are—

Why do people keep appearing? What are Josh and Georgia doing outside? Why isn't there music in my head?

'Lucia, hey! Look at that picture!' Davorin pointing. Generic, cartoonish painting on the wall behind us. Naked woman playing the cello.

'It's you, but white!'

'Sure.'

'But I think the painting is hotter, sorry.'

'That's fine.'

'Yeah, you know, more my taste.'

'Very nice, Davorin.'

'What the fuck is wrong with you?' I erupt. Undermined by slow, slurred speech. Someone's loud breath.

'Leave it,' Lucia's quiet voice. Severe. Hand squeeze.

'Freedom of speech, man! It's not racist, it's just my—' Davorin's horrible smile. His giant fist in the air.

'Just stop talking, you piece of—'

Glass no longer in my hand. Water in my eyes. Dripping down my face. Clothes cling. I'm cold.

'What the fuck, Davorin?' Lucia pulling me from the couch.

'Oh it was a joke! Relax! Relax!' Horrible laughter.

'Hey! *Könntenwirbittealleinsein?*' Lucia's voice. Opera entrance cards cutting lines of coke. Trembling men. So many men. Always so many men. Bathroom. Dizzy. Cold.

'*Eine Minute,*' frustrated man. Waiting.

Lucia's thumbs under my eyes. My makeup on her fingers.

Lucia Rizzo.

Star Lover.

Casual cellist.

'Davorin is bad.' I used to know other adjectives.

'I'd just rather not pick a fight with him.'

Annoyed? With me?

Cali in the doorway with Elsa. Black towel thrust forward.
'Is *this* okay?'
Squinting to clear my view.
Alone to dry.
Sit on toilet seat.
Close eyes.
R
O
        M
             O
       S
P
     N
              I

First 'tactical chunder' in years. Pray no one can hear me.
Glowing green Austrian mouthwash. Sip cool air like from
straw. Drink from sink like animal. Slip out. Find bedroom.
Lie down. Fuck this. Just fuck—

—

My eyes are closed, but I can see dark, corner-less shapes in the blackness. I stretch my neck and stand slowly, trying to ignore any residual dizziness. I need to get out of this room.

What the fuck should I say to Davorin?

Wait.

Why won't the door open? I try again, jiggling the knob, pushing and pushing, but it doesn't give. Someone must have locked me in. Davorin, I bet it was Davorin. Fucking Davorin! My silly hand trembles as I bang on the door, but it's futile over the music. I shake the handle, vicious, panicked, pushing, pushing, pushing then pulling. The door flies open.

Oh.

Maybe I should lie down a bit longer. I close the door and collapse on the stranger's bed. Ten more minutes. Ten more minutes, get some water, rejoin the party.

—

Hi again. I'm leaning against the door to the living room, where the shoeless party guests have formed a circle around four white candles. It's a little séance-like. Cali sits cross-legged in the centre beside a small pile of ash? At least I think it's ash. Two men I don't know are chuckling. Their laughs are very similar, heavy, deep, with the croak that comes from tobacco, or nicotine, or whatever it is in cigarettes that cracks our voices. Lucia isn't here. Josh and I make quiet, diagonal eye contact and I feel my eyes accusing. His brows are raised. Is he questioning my accusation or wondering where I've been? Georgia smiles and waves like she hasn't spent the last who knows how long outside with Josh. Davorin's long legs are spread, of course, and jutting into the middle of the circle near the candles. His face calls to mind Munch's *Scream*. I glare at him, but he isn't looking at me. Cali announces that, 'oh, this last poem is by William Blake. Cop out! Whoever wrote this down! Cop out!' She reads it out anyway:

He who binds himself to a joy
Does the winged life destroy;
But he who kisses the joy as it flies
Lives in eternity's sunrise

I am not sad I missed the rest of the poetry reading, though I need to know what Josh wrote. And what Lucia wrote. And Elsa, actually. And Georgia. And what the fuck would Davorin have written? A haiku, I bet he wrote a haiku. Cali holds the paper against the candle fire. The initial catch is beautiful, poetic, like the candle is sharing its light. But then the fire begins to spread, blackening the poem, ruthless. *Since the world is ending, why not burn the poetry?*

—

'She went home!' Elsa shout-slurs over the music. We're dancing in the center of the room with the cocaine men, stomping on the ashes of poetry I'll never read. Josh and Georgia are back on the balcony.

'I know you two are together!' Elsa shouts again and I step back.

'Who?!'

'You and Lucia! I know! It's obvious!'

'We're not together!'

'You and Lucia!'

'I heard you! I'm saying—'

'I think you are good together! Is your ex-boyfriend here to win you back!?' She gestures with her chin towards the balcony. A wave of something crashes through me.

'No!' I yell back and part of me registers sadness somewhere as I say it.

'Are you sure!?'

'It's a bit complicated!' I say, focusing on the consonants, though I'm slurring less than before. *Is it complicated?*

'Why did Lucia leave?'

'This party is a shitshow!' Elsa laughs into my ear, but there's a shadow in her tone. Something close to vulnerability. Or maybe fear. I look around for Davorin but he's not in the living room.

'Yeah!' I say, as someone turns the bad music up.

'Do you want to know something crazy?' she yells.

'Sure!'

'I think, out of the seven billion people in the world, I might be the most drunk right now!'

Cali joins us, interlacing her fingers with mine.

—

Josh and Georgia dance on either side of me. I can't even hear the melody anymore, just the rhythms, just the beat. Maybe that's the style. Georgia said something like, 'Maya! Babe! I can't believe we haven't even said hello yet!' when she joined us. I didn't reply. She's a good dancer. Comfortable in her body. And she anticipates the changes in tempo flawlessly. I find this infuriating. She leaves our group to dance with the conductor with the white eyebrow. Her arms are around his neck. Of course they are.

Josh smells of tobacco, tobacco, tobacco. We're shouting at each other, bodies pressed together under the pretense of dancing, though neither of us are really moving much.

'How's it going?!'

'Look, is something going on with you and Georgia?!'

He looks as though I've slapped him. 'Can we not do this here?!'

What?

'Right,' I say. Full stop. Fuck it, paragraph break.

Josh surprises me by erupting with laughter. Proper chest-shaking, thigh-slapping, roaring laughter. I feel my eyes widen.

'What? I don't get— Are you—?'

'Oh Maya, Maya, Maya, Maya,' he cries, eyes filling with tears. He starts to dance, shaking his head from side to side. I can see the beat reverberating through him, down his neck, through to his mismatched socks, covered in ash. 'Obviously there is nothing going on between me and your weird friend I met five minutes ago.' He pauses. 'In what universe—'

'Okay, okay, okay,' I say.

His body is vibrating with laughter. His chest collapses as he bursts into hysterics again. And it's infectious. I have to hold onto him to steady myself, fingers on his shoulder, bicep, elbow, forearm, wrist. I keep trying to speak, which only makes me laugh more. He pulls me over to the side of the room, buckles over, tears falling from his eyes.

'You're hilarious, Maya. Has anyone ever told you that?' His hand hovers over my jumpsuit strap.

'It's not the go-to adjective, no,' I say, finally catching my breath. There are maybe two centimetres between his fingers and my neck.

'Are you feeling okay? You were out of it earlier. I don't think I've seen you that drunk since that night near Baker Street. Do you know the night I mean? God, you just started running through that park?' he shakes his head, smiles, 'What were we even doing there so drunk?'

—

Have you ever felt your blood freeze? Ice clogging your veins? Protesting. Refusing to oxygenate the rest of you. It's heavy. Thick. An alien matter weighing down every part of you. You don't feel numb. You don't feel attacked, but invaded. Colonised from the inside. Stuck. Broken. Unmoving.

And then your furious, burning, capricious heart pounds against the ice. There's a crack, spread, shatter, crash, and you're free. And your blood is hot once more and pumping. And the shouts of the boy who loves you and the strangers in black fill your ears as you start to run. You left your shoes in the church, so the grass and sticks bite at your toes. But the stinging feels good, doesn't it? It means sensation has returned to you. The blood between your toes is warm. So you keep running, while the boy you love runs after you.

And the woman who taught you everything lies cold and still. Further and further away.

—

'Maya, fuck, I'm sorry. I genuinely didn't remember what we were doing in Baker Street until I'd already said it. Fuck, Maya, I'm sorry. Are you alright?'

—

When they asked you to play at her funeral, you answered without thinking. You didn't consider what it would be like to stand in the dark, freezing church, next to her body, holding your bow the way she taught you. You opened your memory drawer, but you fell inside. And you kept falling. And blackness covered you. And not even Brahms could pull you out. His rich melodies, the same lines that used to make your stomach rumble and your mouth water, were tasteless and dry. And then your blood turned cold. And you shook. Not just your bow, but your shoulders and your knees and your lungs. You shook so much, your vision blurred. Your lips and fingertips tingled.

And so, you haven't touched Brahms in two years.

And so, you nodded and said 'Yeah that makes sense' when your therapist told you it was dangerous to tie your music to your life the way you do.

And so, you locked the memory drawer you built and filled with her.

And now, Venezuelan conductors can sit in on a single rehearsal and tell you they hear a light dim when you play. What they can really hear is the death in your music.

They buried your musicality when they buried her. And so, they buried you.

—

'Maya. I'm so sorry. Do you want to get out of here? We can go outside or we could just leave?'

Absolutely not. I'm fine.

'No, no. I'm fine. Come on, Josh. Let's dance.'

—

Zofia and Elsa have moved towards the corner of the room. They're wrapped around each other. It's a beautiful, cinematic kiss. Their bodies are pressed together. Elsa has her arms around Zofia's neck. It's the kind of kiss a film would show from multiple angles. Close up, the way their mouths move together. From further away, tangled limbs, bodies blending into one.

Davorin appears and grabs Elsa by the shoulder.

'Davorin! Get off me!' She snaps to face him. Her voice is loud but controlled. She pushes his hand away. He grabs her by the wrist. I step towards them. I can barely hear the music. I can feel the adrenaline in my face.

'Mate!' Cali has her arms in the air, 'What the actual fuck?'

'Come on, Cali. She's clearly in the mood for fun!' Shark smile. 'I want some too!' He's drunker than before.

'You're disgusting,' Elsa says, less calmly. Absurdly, 'Dancing Queen' is playing.

I step towards them. 'Leave her alone, Davorin. She's not interested in you. Jesus, why do I even have to intervene?'

Davorin's grip tightens on Elsa's wrist. He pulls her towards him, bending over, pushing their bodies together, laughing.

'*Sluta! GAH!*' I catch a glimpse of Davorin's shocked expression as Elsa knees him hard in the groin. It all happens in slow motion – Davorin raises his giant hand, but

My fist

    My fist

        My fist

           Davorin's jaw.

His headband flies. His scream is wordless, just hateful sound. My knuckles immediately start to throb. I have never punched anyone. Never. I am a fucking violinist. Blood. I've made him bleed. Someone is yelling in German. Davorin's face drains of colour until he is almost translucent. I know the saying – 'drained of colour' – but I've never actually seen it happen before, not like this. Elsa's body crumples and she falls into Zofia. Her tears are dyed black with mascara. Georgia is here and she's saying, 'hey hey hey', raising her hands in a 'let's-all-calm-down' gesture. I try to stretch my fingers but feel only hot, hot pain. Fuck. Fuck. Fuck.

'You bitch!' Davorin's scream is thick with venom.

'What the fuck is going on?!' Josh's voice.

'I'm calling the police!' Cali shrieks.

Davorin is upright, fuming. 'You should be flattered!' He spits at Elsa, 'And you should stay out of this!' he yells at me or Josh or Georgia.

Georgia answers, 'I think we should—'

But Davorin lunges at me. Georgia steps in the way, her hands still raised, and he slams into her. They fall to the floor with a brutal thud. She scurries away from him. What the fuck is going on?

'Well, fuck you all,' Davorin growls, wiping the blood from his lip on his dirty sleeve.

The door slams. Georgia gets up quickly, her whole body shaking. She stands next to Josh. He puts an arm around her, and she closes her wet eyes and leans into him. Someone switches off the music and the lights are brighter than before.

'Show's over!' Cali's yells. 'Time to get the fuck out of my flat, I reckon.'

—

A doctor once told me to befriend my body as if it were separate from me. I'm thinking about this now, as I press frozen peas onto my throbbing knuckles. I can move my fingers. I think they're just bruised. But we'll have to wait until tomorrow to see the damage. And I cannot think about this right now.

'Let's get out of here.' Josh's voice is gentle, almost hoarse. I know that voice. It's the voice that asked me how I'd slept before he'd opened his eyes, the voice that good-morning-ed me with tea in bed. Georgia nods and links her arm through mine. We don't make eye contact with any of the gawking men as we leave. In the hallway, I flick a light switch and realise too late that it is the doorbell of Cali's neighbour. Another switch, another metallic *ding!* Why do light switches and doorbells look the same in these stupid old Viennese buildings!? We give up, fumble for our phones in the darkness, and use the torches to light our four-flight descent.

'I think I'm just going to take an Uber,' Georgia says when we reach the ground floor. Her voice is steady.

'Good idea,' Josh replies. I still haven't said anything. Georgia and I are basically neighbours, though neither of us suggest we all ride together.

'Are you alright?' I ask her.

'Yeah, yeah, you?'

I don't answer and Georgia doesn't ask again. Josh's fingers brush against mine. We wait in the wind for the Uber. Josh sighs loudly.

A black Toyota.

Georgia turns to us before she opens the door.

'Well, that's one for the novel!'

Though she isn't smiling. Then she kisses both our cheeks. I can still feel Josh's fingers against mine. He leans into me, slightly, and squeezes my hand twice.

We watch her Uber turn the corner before we begin our walk home. I study my bruised hand, which has begun to shake.

'Just the adrenaline,' I say.

'Do we need to go to the hospital?'

Wave of dread. I try to stretch my fingers.

'I think it's okay.'

'You sure?'

'Yes, I'm sure.'

'I cannot believe you punched someone.'

'Me neither.'

'He deserved it.'

'He did.'

'Okay, let's go home.'

—

I can feel my messy brain taking notes on this moment – that strange experience of memory as it occurs in real time. The faint echo of faraway trams, the light wind on my face.

'Did you know about Georgia's engagement?' Josh asks.

'What? No?'

'I had a feeling she might not have told you. It's what we were talking about outside. She was engaged to some asshole in her early twenties who had been cheating on her for years. And her parents divorced when her mum had an affair with a colleague.'

'Oh,' I say. I sound shocked. 'Oh,' I say again. 'Right. Was it helpful? To talk to her?'

'I think so.'

'What did she say?' I ask.

'Basically, she said we all walk around with a story about ourselves, which we're constantly editing. Sometimes, something huge and terrible happens that knocks out a big chunk of your story so that it doesn't hold together anymore. And then you have to ask, "Do I change my story or do I continue with

the old one, even though the facts don't fit together anymore?"
Anyway, that kind of summed it up for me.'

'That sounds very Georgia,' I say.

The street is silent but for the polyrhythm of our shoes on
the pavement. I notate the rhythm in the air while we walk.
The 5 tram whizzes past.

'If we ran for that, we'd be home in like six minutes,' I say
half-heartedly, watching it go. But then I grab Josh's elbow and
we run.

The tram is empty but for an old woman with a small suit-
case on her lap. We don't sit down. The windows are dark.
There's nothing to look at except each other. When I study Josh
in the tram's harsh light, I am taken off guard. He is dazzling.
He makes the word dazzle dazzle. It fizzes with onomatopoeia.
His jaw and his eyes in this half-light look— Look—

'I don't have a ticket.' He doesn't sound worried.

'It's probably fine this late.' I don't sound reassuring.

The soft hum of the tram. I wonder if we're going to talk
more about the evening. I feel almost nauseous with exhaustion. Overwhelmed. Dehydrated. I try to stretch my purple
fingers but it's pretty painful. Fuck.

'I forgot what it was like to be at a party with you, Maya.'

'What do you mean?'

'I just— I don't know how to describe it. My attention is so
split between what I'm doing and what you're doing, it feels
like there's two of me.'

I try and process this. Two Joshes. One who exists with me.
Is that what he said?

'I didn't think you were thinking about me.'

'You've always underestimated how much I think about you.'

Josh shifts so that our bodies are parallel. I imagine this, our parallel bodies continuing through time without ever crossing.

At Westbahnstraße, two men board our tram with a muzzled dog. The old woman with the suitcase yells at them, though I can't tell what she's saying. Why are old women always yelling on public transport here?

'It— it wasn't my intention to come here for you,' Josh says with a delicacy that is almost tender. The old woman is still yelling.

'I know,' I reply. Do I look like I need reminding?

He breathes in like he's going to say something else, and I hold my breath, too.

'Maya.' He's blinking more than usual. His fingers are fidgeting. His fidgeting is beautiful. Humans aren't meant to be still.

'Maya,' he says again. The tram jerks and I lose my footing. He grabs my shoulder and pulls me towards him, and I step into his body like he's a time machine. He presses my palm to his lips and something like relief or surrender floods through me as if he's flicked a switch. Wait.

'This is our stop.'

Josh looks at me with a serious expression, like he's about to say more. But I step off the tram as the doors open. Whatever conversation he wants to have, I'm not ready. Right now, we're in the in-between and a conversation will take us somewhere.

And I think I just want to stand here and stare at the crossroads a while.

—

We pass a queue of people outside the twenty-four-hour sushi van. Mostly twenty-somethings standing in a long, quiet line.

'Hungry?'

I snort, but my stomach betrays me with a low growl.

'Actually, yes, I'm starving.'

Josh suggests he wait for the sushi, and I head home to ice my fingers.

—

When was the last time I was alone in my flat? I gulp down water by the sink, eyes fixed on the square of peeling paint on my wall. I wonder if it's a sign of damp. I'm holding a bag of frozen spinach to my fingers when I see Josh's diary on the couch. Well, fuck. I tell myself I'm not going to read it as I pick it up. I tell myself I'm disciplined, so disciplined, and so honest, as I turn it over in my bruised fingers. The leather is worn and scratched, rough against my palm. Josh will be back any minute, I think, as I don't return the book to the couch.

25 May

I wonder if she tries to read my mind like I try to read hers. Sometimes, when my housemates are out, I sit alone in the living room and try to imagine what she's doing. What she's eating, who she's with, what kind of building she's in, what she's thinking about. Does she think about me? How often? Does she ever think about coming home? Does she miss me? Etc. Yes, I know it's lame, but she has a picture of me hanging on her wall, so one-all??

And now I'm smoking on a bench outside her flat in Vienna of all places, with a bag of breakfast groceries, wondering who she's on the phone to for so long. Maybe it's the Italian cellist.

I've missed smoking. It feels good to smoke in Vienna because Hitler hated smoking. I read somewhere that Nazi scientists did a lot of research into the harmful effects of tobacco. Smoking is basically anti-fascist.

When Maya was practising last night and Georgia asked me if I was here to get her back, I told her no and she said she didn't believe me. She told me to go for it. But I'm not going to go for it, obviously. I just want her to be happy. But I still don't understand:

- *Why she couldn't be happy with me?*
- *Why she couldn't be satisfied playing music in London, or even just using London as a base?*
- *Why she couldn't commit to even considering building a family with me?*

Maybe I was completely delusional the entire time. Fuck knows. I don't even know how it all spiralled. I thought if I could just support her and give her time to grieve her professor that we'd be okay? But then she was just gone? And now she's here?

Did I use the family drama as an excuse to come to Vienna? No. Sure, ever since I found out about her move, I've daydreamed about coming here unannounced. I've imagined what it would be like to see her again and, like, what her face would look like when I stood in front of her and said Hey Maya. I swear to God I've even said it out loud. But I never actually thought I'd do it. It was all a daydream. But then I was really breaking down, and this really did feel like the only option.

It's funny, when my friends mention her, I try to put on this smile that's like – ah, yeah, I loved her, I lost her, but it's all good, I've re-covered. As if I wouldn't fucking fall to my knees if she came back to London and told me she wanted me.

Tb100%h I've worried there's something wrong with me – aren't most people over a relationship once a year's gone by?? What if I'm broken somehow?? I used to think if I could just understand why Maya left, I'd be able to move on. I thought it was the 'unsolved' that stopped me from letting go, moving on, etc. But maybe it's like quitting smoking – you have to want to move on. And here I am in Vienna with a bloody cigarette in my hand.

I can hear him outside. I throw the book onto the couch and dart back towards the kitchen counter. The pain in my fingers has dulled, thank God, and I return the mostly-still-frozen spinach to the freezer as Josh descends my crooked little stair-case with a plastic bag.

'I went for vegetarian sushi because fish from a van felt wrong.' He smiles and joins me by the sink, filling a pint glass with water. His lips are glossy and his hair has been styled by the wind. I feel like I should reintroduce myself: Hi, I'm Maya Evans, 27-year-old British violinist who punches people at parties and reads her ex-boyfriend's diary while he buys her dinner.

We finish the sushi in about four minutes. Neither of us sit down. The fortune cookies are dry and mostly tasteless, but Josh makes an appreciative noise while he chews. As we wipe rogue soy sauce from the table with our thumbs, I remember the chocolate orange he brought from London.

'Oh, I've got a great idea,' I say, opening the fridge and lifting the deformed ball into the air like something holy.

'Oh my god. I wanna say you should save it, but I would give a kidney for a bite of that right now,' Josh grins. 'Fuck, I'm actually salivating. What is *in* those things!?'

We use a knife to cut a few chunks from the ball of chocolate. I try to savour each piece, let it melt on my tongue, but I can't control myself. I chew. Swallow. Reach for another. Another. It's fucking perfect.

'God, this is good,' I say.

'So good.'

'Like, this is really fucking good,' I say again and Josh smiles at me.

'Let's put on some music?' he suggests when I tell him I'll probably be sick again if I keep eating chocolate. I will 100% get into trouble or be fined if we play music this late. But fuck it.

'Sure, what about Joni Mitchell? *Blue*?'

'*Blue* it is,' he says, returning the mangled ball of chocolate to my fridge.

—

We're lying on the floor side by side, not touching. We used to lie just like this on our rug, listening to albums from beginning to end. It was a colourful, scratchy-looking rug, but surprisingly cosy. I think Josh sold it when we broke up.

Sometimes we talked while the music played. The rules were simple. It was like being in a jazz club – we could thread conversation in and out of the melodies, but we had to listen to the whole album. And here we are again. But we're not talking. He's staring at the ceiling. And I'm staring at him – at his cheeks stained pink by the cold, his slightly askew shirt. And I kind of get what they mean when they say time isn't linear, because I'm studying past and present Josh simultaneously, like two photos superimposed onto one another. I run my eyes from his shoulder towards his upside-down watch, along the faded pale lines of his jeans. In German, 'lust' doesn't just mean sexual longing. It means appetite, delight, desire, gusto, joy.

Track 1 – All I Want

I give my thoughts permission to run. Sprint. I'm too tired to chase after them. Is this the opposite of meditation?

If albums were bodies, *Blue* would be skinless. All organs and nerves.

The guitar strumming, *travelling, travelling, travelling, travelling,* I can almost taste the metal strings in my mouth. I think I love it most when Joni repeats things. Or when she rhymes 'dance' and 'romance'. The Germans like to rhyme *'Herz'* (heart) and *'Schmerz'* (pain). Language is built to house heartbreak. Joni sings that she loves only when she can forget herself. Unravelling love taped to unravelling melodies. Fuck. A devotion so vast it can only collapse.

No, but I don't agree with this line. Do I? I love you when I forget myself? No. But I *want* you when I forget about me, us, consequence, needs. Or when I remember that none of this matters anyway

because the world is—
and since the world is—
why not—

I'm exhausted and my fingers ache. This album, this album, this album is a soul looking at itself in the mirror. A mirror that shows you what you want but can never have.

But then Joni sings that she wants to shampoo you. And my heart stops. Simple, perfect intimacy ... What else could she have said? She wants to feed you? Too basic. She wants to comb your hair? Too obvious. No, she wants to shampoo you and it is perfect and I can feel the warm silkiness of shampoo and Josh's curls between my fingers. Josh who splits himself in half at a party so that part of him is always with me. Is that what he said? I open my eyes and he's still there, lying beside me on my rugless floor.

Track 2 – My Old Man

Surprise. Surprise at the piano, at the register switches, at the chromatics, at this folk dressed in jazzy clothes, as we swing between major and minor, these silly third-less chords, oh Joni, maybe you can fix me. Josh shifts his posture like he wants to sink deeper into the floor. There are about thirty centimetres between us. Just thirty steadfast centimetres with a thousand reasons to stand their ground.

Track 3 – Little Green

Josh is breathing in time with Joni. I wonder if he knows. Joni wrote this song about giving her daughter up for adoption. Before her success. But this isn't music you write. This is music you birth. I'm sure it hurt. I bet it was excruciating. But she did it anyway. Singer-songwriters seem to have permission to write explicitly from life; no questions asked. Poets, too, I guess. But not novelists. Not really playwrights. Composers? People say Mahler's symphonies are autobiographical. I've read papers that describe his music as 'full of memories'.

But isn't instrumental music *abstract?* they all ask.

No. Words are an approximation, but music is the opposite of abstract. Music is concrete. Music isn't a metaphor for something real. Music *is* the something real.

Mahler's symphonies are
confessional,
eccentric,
grotesque,

gentle,

aggressive,

caustic,

idealistic.

You can hear the tragic beats of his life in the Sixth – his forced resignation at the Staatsoper, the death of his young daughter, his heart disease diagnosis. I once played in his Ninth in London – anguished, horrified, bitter. I cried when I first heard the final movement, his heartbroken acceptance, as the musical texture disintegrated in our fingers.

But I'm here now with Joni. Joni, who writes harmonies like she's colouring in the melody. It's weird that we find universality in such hyper-specific lyrics. Loss is inevitable. All change is loss. Joni and her daughter eventually found each other. What do you call that relationship? Is Josh thinking about his parents? His breathing is very even now, almost as if he's asleep, but his eyes have opened.

Track 4 – Carey

Shimmer. This one shimmers. Fuck the thirty centimetres. I press my shoulder into Josh's shoulder and he doesn't move away.

When a song addresses a person, does the listener turn into that person? Is Joni going to buy me a bottle of wine? I love the way she says 'bottle of wine', like 'boddle of wine', like she's drunk or excited or dancing. How many people were in love with her? How many people did she love?

Once, at a party years ago, I overheard Josh talking to one of his friends, Samantha, about me. Samantha asked him, 'When was the moment you fell in love with Maya?'

And Josh replied, 'I dunno. I don't think there was really a *moment*. But I do remember looking at her one morning and thinking, "God, I wonder how long I've loved you" Sorry, that was way too honest, wasn't it?'

And I cried as I eavesdropped. And I want to cry now. Because no one will ever love me like that again, will they? One day, I'll hold a telephone to my ears and sing I love you to no one with my own pathetic *voix humaine. Je t'aime. Je t'aime. Je t'aime.*

Track 5 – Blue

I take it back. Albums aren't bodies, they're mountain ranges, and the opening of Blue, this first word she sings, is the tallest peak. Fuck, and the

V   I   E   W

The colour of her voice makes the vowels sound make-believe. Vibrato teases out the notes. No, it doesn't tease. It torments. I don't know. She just sounds so vulnerable. She sings that songs are like tattoos. Maybe people are, too.

We went back to the Tate for our first anniversary and Josh spent a long time staring at a Rothko that looked like a child had tried to paint a sunset. I asked him what he was thinking about and he started listing red things: raspberries, blood, lava, wine, autumn leaves.

In one of Sarah Waters' books, she talks about wanting to kiss someone without skin, so it's just the nerves kissing. I felt that, then, with Josh at the Tate, as he listed the red things.

Track 6 – California

Maybe Joni's just telling us a story. Or putting us inside one. Like a snow globe. But hot. Sparkling. I like the relationships she creates between words just because of their sounds – vogue, rolling stone. I know all songwriters do this, but I like it best when she does. Will I ever be able to listen to this album again without thinking of Josh? I used to be very careful about where I listened to music. Fear of association. Music is sticky. You can ruin music this way. I would know. I would fucking know.

You're right. I can no longer ignore my throbbing fingers. I don't want to leave him, but I am a violinist with crumpled fingers and I need ice. Josh doesn't seem to notice when I stand. He's still staring at the ceiling. Maybe he's in a memory drawer of his own. Give me the key, Josh. Or maybe he doesn't want to look at me. Outside, a motorbike revs, then disappears. But outside doesn't exist.

Track 7 – This Flight Tonight

These chords sound more like a drive than a flight. I don't know much about the guitar, but something is tuned down,

I think, and something's bending. Joni's like a siren, maybe, pulling us into a story, rather than into the sea.

I open the freezer and grab the bag of refrozen spinach cubes. Josh always kept Magnums in the freezer. Those mini ones I assumed were made for children. He liked the ones covered in nuts. I don't think I've eaten one since we broke up. Do I even like Magnums?

God, the spinach feels good.

Track 8 – River

Oh, it's Christmas. Just like that. This moody, bruised jingle bells. She's magical. She stretches time. She can fill a bar with as many words as she wants. How long until Josh leaves? There's another dimension to this song, maybe all the songs, maybe all songs, but I feel it so strongly here. When she sings about flying, she flies.

Fly   yyy   yyy
                    yyy
                                        yyy
                                                      yyy
I'm back lying beside him.

What does it mean to love someone naughty? Imagine if Joni Mitchell and Mahler collaborated. What if songs were house items? I think I would want this one as my pillow. What does that say about me?

He looks at me.

Finally.

Track 9 – A Case of You

I think this one is my favourite. But I'm not thinking in words anymore. I'm thinking in sensations. She can do the words for me. She does them better than me.

Track 10 – The Last Time I Saw Richard

Piano, piano, piano. Neither of us is breathing. I almost want to tell him.

'You're not breathing.'

'No, I guess not.'

He presses his knee against mine, so that our bodies on the floor make a messy love heart. It's only with Josh that I think in bird's-eye view. When I finally exhale, it isn't a breath, but a hum. The softest possible hum. It wouldn't have stretched across thirty centimetres.

Josh's fingers on my cheek.

I melt into them.

'Is this okay?'

I nod. We pause. I count to three. Warm, familiar lips, hot, gentle, a current tears through me, my whole body responds to his tongue, my neck throbs, my chest rises, there is a blissful aching in my stomach. He pulls away, then pushes back. I mirror him. My hands are in his hair. Away, back, away, pausing between kisses like each is a new idea. He kisses down my body while Joni sings. He kisses my bare ankles and looks up at me. There are days I forget I have ankles and now they are the most important part of my body. I pull him to me and we kiss again. I want to keep kissing him until my lips collapse. We're tangled. We can share pleasure this way. The tips of his fingers push at my hip. Then he's grabbing onto my jumpsuit and I'm scratching down his back. I don't know whether what we're doing is right or good. But I know how it feels.

'Josh,' I say, winded.

'Yes?' He sounds like lust. Lust, all of it: appetite, delight, desire, gusto, joy.

'I'm—' I don't believe I'm saying this '—Is this a good idea?'

'Oh,' he leans away. 'Do you want to stop?'

When I don't speak, he leans further from me, and I have to clench my fists to stop myself from pulling him back. Discipline, surrender, discipline, surrender – at this point, it feels like flipping a coin. Which side are you hoping for? I don't know what I'm going to say until I say it.

'No,' I tell him. 'I don't want to stop.'

He leans closer to me.

'I don't want to stop either,' he says, and we dissolve into each other.

He slides the straps from my shoulders and kisses down my neck. I wrestle with his shirt and ignore the dull ache in my bowing hand. His breath catches when I stroke his bare chest.

'Are my hands too cold?' I ask.

He speaks into my mouth, 'No. Fuck no.'

He kisses my breasts, while his hands scratch down my sides. It's painful, how much I want him to touch me.

He knows.

He climbs down my body and his lips are on me, and heat races through me. He knows exactly what I want him to do. His tongue circles me faster and I want to hold my breath but

Not yet.

'Wait,' I say, 'let me get a condom.'

He follows me into my bedroom and lies down on my bed.

When I join him, he takes me in his arms. His eyes are dark, almost liquid. He stops breathing. So do I. I lower myself onto him.

Fuck.

Josh.

My body shudders as he moves inside me.

Josh.

His hands are on my hips. My hands are on his chest. I can feel his heartbeat against my palms and fit our rhythm to his pulse. I touch myself as we move together.

'Fuck,' he says softly.

The smiley boy I met in the gallery when I was 22.

The breathless naked man between my legs. Inside me.

The same, ridiculous infinity tattoo on his calf. He grabs my thighs. There are scratch marks on his chest from my good hand.

'Fuck,' I say back.

—

We're lying on top of my blankets, sweating, panting. It's late, so late, but I have no audition tomorrow. No rehearsal. No reason to get up and practise. I can just lie here with a listless, languid, blissful post-sex brain like a normal person.

'I have an idea,' Josh whispers.

'Oh yeah?' I whisper back.

'How does one more piece of chocolate orange sound right now?'

I laugh at the ceiling.

'Fucking perfect.'

Josh fetches the cold, deformed ball of chocolate from the fridge and we lie side by side on my bed, taking turns biting into it like an apple.

—

Josh is in my arms. I'm in Josh's arms. I feel gravity pushing me into the mattress and I succumb to it. I prepare for an onslaught of over-thinking, but sleep is instant, like fainting.

—

It's 4 a.m. when his phone rings. All these fucking ringing phones. I feel broken, diluted by exhaustion and oxytocin. Then—

'Fuck, Maya—' It takes my brain a few seconds to read his voice. He sounds panicked.

'What is—'

'It's my dad.'

I reach for his shoulder, but he's already out of bed, hunting for his clothes in the dark.

'I think they're in the other room,' I say as he disappears.

—

My door skids against the gravel road. Josh is pale, ghost-like, staggering down my stairs. His shirt is back to front.

'He told her. She left him.' His voice is barely audible, stained with grief or shock, and something somewhere inside me fractures. I shouldn't be naked. I pull the blanket to my chin.

'I'm so sorry.' I don't know what else to say. My brain is foggy with sleep or fuzzy with panic.

'Why did he have to call me? I'm their kid. This is not my responsibility. This is not on me!' His voice is louder. Livid. He fills and downs a glass of water.

'I'm so sorry, Josh—'

'What's going to happen now? Do I ring her? Just to see if she's okay? What if she asks me if I knew?' His voice cracks. His face reddens. For a moment it looks as though he might throw the glass against the wall. I almost tell him to. Just so he can act out his pain. Instead, he sits on the floor beside my bed, legs stretched. He looks up at me, 'Should I call her?'

'I don't know, but I don't think so Josh. It's half four. Call her in the morning. I think she probably just needs to be alone right now. Maybe you can text her? To say you love her?'

I don't know who ventriloquised this mature response, but

I am grateful. Seeing him like this feels like someone is sitting on my chest.

'Good idea,' Josh says, and types something into his phone that I can't see. 'Okay. I sent her a text.' Silence. I don't move. 'You know when you're sad, how you start thinking about all the times you've ever been sad? Like your brain has this catalogue of past sadness you feel the need to browse through? Why doesn't that happen with happiness? Imagine if every time you felt happy, you also felt happy about every fucking thing that's ever made you happy? You know? Did any of that make sense? Fuck, I'm sorry, I'm so tired.' Harsh laugh. His eyes flash with anger.

'It did make sense,' I say as he climbs back into my bed. 'And you're right, sadness comes in multitudes. When I cry, I think about all the things in the world that could make me cry. It's sick, really.'

Josh's knee is shaking. My body is aching for sleep.

'Are you okay, Josh?'

'Yeah. We should sleep.' He climbs under the covers and rolls away from me.

SUNDAY

Water. I need water. When I swallow, the walls of my throat stick together and, for a moment, I can't breathe. It's not just my head that throbs. It's my face and my eyes and the base of my neck. My knuckles are black, as if dusted with charcoal. And I'm naked. I check the time. Ten o'clock. My memory hasn't quite re-introduced full sentences:

The Polish conductor was sitting—
Cali in the hallway with—
Elsa kissed—
Lucia and the painting—
Josh and Georgia smoking—
Davorin bleeding.

Faster.

Josh in the tram saying my name. Josh on the floor with Joni Mitchell. Josh's mouth on mine.

The sentences transform into a slideshow of images, like a sexy exhibition or a broken film. The way he looked up at me from my ankles. His hungry eyes. His bare back beside me. Lying in bed, I felt his presence like a weight, like I was clay, or a pillow, the pressure of him changing my shape.

Josh's dad on the phone.

Okay.

I need to confess to you something I've been trying to ignore. Josh is no longer beside me. I don't know when he left. I don't know where he's gone. All I can tell you is that he's not here. But I will worry about this after I drink some water and shower. Disciplined Maya, welcome back!

Josh's showers are always scalding hot. He once said that he was suspicious of couples who shower at the same temperature: 'No one that similar should be living together.' Josh was the last to shower here and he has returned the handle to my preferred temperature. The thoughtfulness behind this gesture, coupled with my hangover, physically hurts.

The hot (but not scalding) water washes away about 15% of said hangover. I slip on a dress, swallow two painkillers, and down two glasses of water to soothe my pulsing temples. I spend a few more minutes stretching and studying my fingers. They're fine. The pills should help the dull-ish ache, and I'll be able to play today. I don't know what the fuck I was thinking. I'm lucky. I'm stupid.

Then I'm in a stare-off with two bottles of perfume: the one I wear every day and the one I used to wear every day.
    The doorbell.
    He's back! And I hadn't even worried! Not really. I decide on no perfume.
    'It's open!'
    The doorbell.

A quick once-over in the mirror – the whites of my eyes are a scary shade of red. And my lips are so dry they look like cracked cement.

I race up my crooked little staircase and fling open my door to a body like a barrel, a ginger moustache, and piercing yellow eyes. My neighbour is speaking without smiling, frantically waving his hands about, gesturing to the street, then to my flat, back to the street. He's furious. At first, I expect him to complain about the music we were playing too late last night. But I think he's saying something about moving my car? I try to cut into his monologue to explain to him that I don't own a car, as if I could afford a car – 'Kein Auto! Kein Auto!' – but he won't hear me. He continues ranting, gestures again to me, to the pavement, to the road, then slams my door in my face. I almost fall down the stairs with the force of it.

Right. Okay. *Where is Josh? Where is Josh? Where is Josh?* I'm stuck in a loop. His backpack is gone. But his toothbrush is still here. *Where is Josh? Where is Josh? Where is Josh?* He wouldn't just leave.

Pick up! It's ringing, ringing, ringing. *Pick up! Where are you?*
     Wait, isn't this the 'already-on-a-call' dial tone?
     For.
     Fuck's.
     Sake.
     I type with my left hand.

Me:
Where are you?
Are you okay?
Bit alarming to wake up
to an empty bed

Send. I hate this anxious version of myself. I crouch on my stairs and continue typing.

Me:
Hey Georgia
Wow
Last night got weird.
I hope you're alright?
Have you heard from
Josh this morning?
xx

I don't even care what this looks like.

Me:
Hey Elsa
I hope you're okay?
Here if you need to talk?
Again, I'm so sorry for
not telling you that Davorin
took your number from my phone.
If you decide to file another
complaint against him after

last night, I'm happy to corroborate!
See you at work tomorrow.
M x

I change 'corroborate' to 'help', delete the 'x' (Swedes don't use 'x' like we do), and press send. One tick. The throbbing is back: temples, neck, hand. I let my eyes fill with tears before I decide it's okay to cry. I put my head in my bruised fingers and sob, surrounded by every sad thought my dehydrated brain can muster, just like Josh said. They don't feel like tear-drops, they feel like a tear stream down my face, along my cheeks, chest, the floor.

The fact that Lucia hasn't messaged me leaves an acidic panic in my stomach, which makes me feel like a monster.

—

I'm still sitting on my staircase, face stiff with dried tears, star-ing at our Friday-night painting. What am I meant to do with this messy canvas? I think I need to talk to someone and con-sider texting Julie, but messaging my therapist seems ludicrous and excessive. The person I really want to speak to wouldn't charge me. She's definitely awake. And she's not at work.

Buzz. Two new messages. My shaky hands nearly drop the phone.

Georgia:
Hey darling,

No, I haven't heard from him.
Are you alright?
x x x

Elsa:
What an awful night.
I stayed here with Cali –
didn't feel safe leaving.
Fuck! Humans!
Thank you for helping last night.
It meant a lot to me.
But how is your hand?
I'm not going to say anything
to management – they will just
ignore me or laugh at me again.
Not worth the drama.
See you tomorrow.
Kisses

Fuck it, I'm going to call her.

'Maya? Hi?' Lisa sounds confused, maybe even annoyed. I
never call out of the blue. But despite her tone, the sound of
her voice is soothing in a way that must be biological.

'My?'

As a teenager, I hated that nickname – 'My'. I thought it
sounded possessive and controlling. But right now, it feels
so good to belong, even a little, to my sister. Why do I live so
far away?

'Hey, do you have a minute?'

'Of course I have a minute, it's Sunday morning.'

'Shit, yes, obviously.'

I tell her everything – about Lucia and the missed calls and Josh's arrival, about how I played in the soirée, the cancelled audition, the party, punching Davorin, sex with Josh, his parents, his disappearance. She's quiet. I have to check in a few times to make sure she's still on the line. I tell her that Josh brought up Professor Forrest's funeral, accidentally, and that I think I spiralled further. And I tell her how much I hate the way I *feel* things. When things hurt, they hurt too much. Cuts slice too deep. Bruises hit bone. I want to be one of those people who can raise their guard when necessary. Who can build walls from material other than paper or cellophane. Like the Soprano from the soirée. What did she say? 'The past needs to feel far away.' That's when Lisa interrupts me.

'So all of this happened over the last two days?'

'Right?' I half-laugh.

'Do you need me to visit?'

I didn't expect her to say this. 'No. Of course not.'

'Do you want to come stay here for a few days?'

'No, I can't. I've got to work.'

'Okay. Do you think you should get back together with Josh?'

Well, there you go. There it is, out in the open. A siren whooshes down my street.

'I don't know,' I answer honestly, 'I don't even know where he is.'

'That doesn't matter. He obviously hasn't just left Vienna without telling you,' she says. I can hear her husband Adam clanging pots in the background. She sighs. 'Look, My, your biggest strength is how deeply you feel things. I know that, you know that, even Mum would agree after enough wine. The way you care and love and emote and all that is who you are. I'm jealous of it, actually, because I think our childhood probably pushed me in the other direction, or whatever.'

'Lisa, you literally have a perfect life.'

'It works for me, but my perfect life is your living hell.'

She's right. Routine, stasis, loving your normal job the normal amount. I glance at my violin case and a wave of adrenaline crashes through my chest and stomach.

'Lise, I'm panicking. And I cannot go back to how I was last year. I'll lose my job.' *I'll lose my mind*, I don't say. Professor Forrest's death broke me. I knew I had to leave London, and I knew Josh and I wanted different things, so I broke him. And then my body broke. Betrayed me. And I couldn't do the only thing I knew how to do.

'What's making you panic?' Lisa asks.

'I'm panicking that I need to make a big, life-changing decision, and I have no idea what to do, and I also just feel ridiculous because what do my decisions matter in the grand scheme of—'

'Don't be absurd, of course your decisions matter,' she says. In the background, Adam asks what she wants for breakfast, but she ignores him.

'I don't—'

'Look, My, you called me because you want tough love and

I'm going to give it to you. It sounds like you've had one hell
of a weekend, but you're going to be fine. You do not need to
make any big decisions this weekend. You need to make sure
your hand is okay, and it sounds like you need a bit of space
from all of this, to be frank. What about this Lucia? It sounds
like you like her?'

'It's casual.'

'Lying to me is fine, but lying to yourself is boring. Don't
be that person, My, it doesn't suit you.'

I think of the of the art on Lucia's walls, the way her
eyes blaze in concert, the sleepy scratch in her voice when
she whispers *buongiorno*. I think of our first shy kiss, of her
smooth naked body twisted in sheets, decorated by fractured
morning sunlight.

'Fine. I like Lucia. A lot. Fine. She's completely amazing.
But I don't think she feels the same. And Josh—'

'Josh is going to leave, My, and you need to make sure he
leaves you with your Vienna life intact.'

I flex my purple fingers.

'Maybe you're right,' I say.

There's a knock at the door.

'Fuck, he's back.'

'You're fine. Call me again later, please.'

'Thanks, Lise—'

But she's already hung up.

'It's unlocked!' I yell, and the door swings open to reveal a
woman's silhouette. From the top of my stairs, she tells me, 'I
have your 300 euros from the soirée. Can I come in?'

'Of course you can,' I tell the silhouette.

Our fingers don't touch when she hands me the envelope at the base of my stairs.

'Thank you.'

'*Prego.*'

Lucia looks from my eyes to my lips, and I feel both desired and judged. I am hyperaware that my face is puffy from tears and distorted with exhaustion. I want to hide. I don't want her to see me like this. Her gaze moves to my floor, where my clothes are strewn from the night before – jumpsuit, bra, and underwear tossed into a haphazard triangle. Lucia's face is unchanged.

'You left the party early,' I say because one of us should say something.

'It was a terrible party.' She holds her breath. 'Can I have a glass of water? It's too hot again outside.'

She wipes her neck with her hand, fingers brushing her collarbone. It's absurd how far away she feels given the number of times I've traced that skin with my lips.

'Of course,' I say, and force my eyes away from her neck.

Neither of us speaks while I fill the glass. I pass it to her and am about to sit when she notices the bruising on my hand and reaches for me. As our fingers touch, a jolt of electricity shoots up my arm. Something shifts in her face.

'Maya! *Cara*! Your fingers!'

'I know,' I say and stretch them once to show that they look worse than they feel.

'What happened?' She lets go of me. I fight the reflex to grab her back. She's so far away.

'I punched Davorin.'

Lucia's eyes widen. 'You did what?'

'He took it too far with Elsa,' I shrug. 'It was a whole thing.'

'Are you okay?'

'I'm fine.'

'Will you tell me what happened?'

I expect her to sit down, but she doesn't move from the foot of my stairs, so I recount the whole affair while she stands and nods and sips water.

'I can't believe this. Are you worried he will report you?'

This hadn't even occurred to me.

'I think Davorin's too much of a misogynist to report being punched by a woman,' I say.

'Yes, I think you're right.' Lucia chuckles and smiles at me. 'Work is going to be interesting tomorrow.'

A flicker of frisson. She sighs. I sigh back. Then she takes her empty glass to the sink and looks again at my clothes on the floor. I feel like I should say something, but she speaks first.

'Where's Josh?'

She's not looking at me. A wave of panic.

'Out,' I half-lie.

'Okay. Well, I'm glad you're alright. I should probably go, but I'll see you at rehearsal.' She smiles at me, tight-lipped, then leaves.

———

But she hasn't left. She's standing on my steps. I don't think I've ever seen Lucia hesitate before. I've always assumed there's no space between what she wants to do and what she does. But here she is, floating.

'I heard the end of your conversation on the phone before I knocked,' she says, turning back to me. 'I didn't mean to. But I did.'

Fuck. I try to recall what I said to Lisa but 'recollection isn't remembering something in its entirety. It's re-collecting.' Scattered moments, right? I.e., I have no idea what the fuck I said. But I'm sure it was *intense*. Well, there goes our casual fun. *Tschü-üss!* I don't know what I was expecting. She wasn't even fazed that my ex was in town and staying with me.

'I don't know how you could think I don't like you.'

Wait. 'What?'

She repeats herself.

'I— But—'

I don't know what to say. She walks back down my stairs and stands in front of me so that our faces are very close together.

'Come on,' she looks me deep in the eyes.

'What do you mean? You've never said anything. And you didn't seem to mind Josh being here. And I didn't think we—'

'Maya,' she steps towards me. Her lips are still glossy from the water. 'We have never played a private concert together before. Do you really think a violinist happened to cancel the weekend your ex came to Vienna? I've never walked into a practice room you were in until yesterday. I knew it was occupied. I obviously knew it was you playing. Did you think it was a coincidence that I interrupted and fucked you against the door?'

My stomach twists when she says, 'fucked you against the door'. But my mind is still. Adrenaline has banished all thoughts. Even the ache in my fingers is gone.

'I can be much more vulnerable with music than with words, but I am here in your apartment delivering an envelope I could have given you at work tomorrow, trying to tell you that I want you. But I'm also telling you there is no rush with me. You need to look after yourself, and your music. And your hand.' She smiles. 'But when you are ready, will you come over?'

I nod. So it's going to be just like before? That's what I want. Maybe that's what I want?

'I'm going to make you *gnocchi* or *cacio e pepe*. We're probably going to talk about language and music and art.' She steps closer. 'To be *very* clear, this will be a date, because I also think you're "completely amazing". *Capisci?*'

I nod.

Lucia doesn't kiss me when she leaves.

But she does look back, just once, just for a moment, before closing my door behind her.

I stare after her. Then, slowly, in a shocked and hungover haze, I collect last night's clothes from the floor. I'm hanging the jumpsuit up in my cupboard when my phone buzzes on the kitchen table. I run to it, almost tripping over the corner of my bed.

JOSH:
I'm so sorry for disappearing!!

My mum called early this morning and
I didn't want to wake you,
so I grabbed my bag and
just started walking.
I've ended up near the Museum area.
She's doing okay, all things considered.
She's in shock, I think.
She had no idea.
It's fucked.
Everything is fucked.
Do you want to join me here?
Or I could come back to the flat?
Sorry again if I scared you!
X

———

The heat feels closer today, heavy, almost needy, pressing against me. Lisa texts as I board the tram:

Lisa:
Don't forget to call me later x

I wonder what she thinks of my mess. I wonder if she hung up the phone, turned to Adam, and rolled her eyes, 'nothing serious, just Maya throwing another grenade at her life'. Adam, who is so wholesome and so perfectly besotted with my sister, he burst into tears when I played the Massenet *Méditation* at their wedding. I was surprised when Lise asked for that piece. Surprised that she knew it at all, sure, but mostly surprised at her choice – it's a little erotic, a little religious, a little saccharine, even a little maudlin?

In the poker game of genetics, why did she get dealt stability and contentment, while I got what? Chaos? Though she'd call it 'excitement'. She did, once. The night before she got married. We were sitting in Mum's apartment, just the two of us, drinking room-temperature champagne we found in a cupboard, when Lisa told me she was jealous of my 'taste for adventure', of my 'exciting life'. Though she'd never do anything to change hers. We've not spoken about it since. Obviously.

Meanwhile, on a scorching Sunday in Vienna, passengers sweat and speak in hushed German, children are chastised for being too loud, and muzzled dogs blink lovingly at their owners, as I ride the 49 tram to Josh.

—

A group of men in *V for Vendetta* masks stand in a circle by the entrance to the Museumsquartier. In the centre of their circle is a screen playing a series of violent images. Dark Vienna, menacing Vienna. Josh is sitting with his backpack in one of the Museumsquartier's strange plastic armchairs. This spring, the blocky seats are an impressive violet.

'I've heard the chair colours change based on an online vote,' I say as I approach him.

'They kind of remind me of giant Tetris pieces.' He smiles up at me, eyes glowing in the mid-morning sun.

'Are you comfortable?'

'Absolutely not.'

'Hi.'

'Hi.'

The wind has whipped his cheeks a bright pink and wrestled with his curls.

'I'm so sorry I disappeared. I should have at least left a note. She called and I just— I didn't— I bought us breakfast.' He holds up a lush red box branded with gold letters:

Sacher Hotel.

'This isn't breakfast, it's cake.'

'When in Vienna ...'

I join Josh on the uncomfortable violet chair and pop the chocolate 'Hotel Sacher' seal into my mouth. I once kissed Josh in bed with a slice of Terry's Chocolate Orange in my mouth, sliding him the chocolate with my tongue. Have I told you that already?

'They take their cake very seriously here,' Josh says.

'They do.'

We smile. I carve a piece of the dense chocolate sponge. It is far too early for anything so decadent, yet my tastebuds are dancing, linking arms and celebrating the tangy apricot jam. I can't tell you the last time I was this hungover.

'He said they sell hundreds of thousands of these cakes every year! Do you think I should take some back for my mum?'

So he's leaving. Of course he's leaving. His mouth is covered in chocolate.

'Do you want to talk about your phone call?' I ask.

'Let's finish our breakfast cake first.'

How can he just *postpone* conversations like this? And they call *me* disciplined! He hands me back the fork.

'Okay, but will you tell me exactly when you're leaving?' I can hear pleading in my voice. Why don't we know what we're going to sound like before we speak and it's too late? It's the opposite of playing my violin.

'My flight's at three.'

His flight's at three. I can't read his tone. The cake suddenly feels heavy in my mouth.

Buzz.

Lucia? No.

> **Georgia:**
> **Did you find Josh?**
> **Can I join you guys later?**
> **x x x**

'I told Georgia you were missing this morning, and she's asking after you. Do you want to see her again before you leave?' I ask tentatively.

'I'd probably rather just hang out with you?' Josh has managed to get icing on the side of his forehead.

Me:
Yessss! Sorry for not messaging sooner.
He's off this afternoon.
I'll call you tomorrow? Xx

Georgia:
Yes!
Glad you're both okay!
Let me know if you need me x x

Josh is licking his fingers. Dimpled half-smile. My silly heart flies a quick loop around my body. My mouth is coated with chocolate and apricot, and my head is buzzing with morning sugar.

'I like this area,' Josh says. I follow his gaze towards the sad-looking Museum of Contemporary Art. Its exterior is prison-like – a dark grey box with a curved roof. Beside it is the Leopold Museum, a plain white box-building with a straight, flat roof.

'The architecture here really *is* amazing.'

'Is it?' I ask, re-assessing the monochrome boxes.

'Yes! The mixture of baroque and contemporary … This is exactly how I pictured Vienna. You're lucky to live here.'

This harmless comment cuts. *I* am lucky to live here. *Josh* does not live here. His flight back to London leaves at three o'clock. And then what? He takes a photo of the white box.

'For Aden. The white limestone. He'd love it.'

'You've changed your tune!' I say.

'Vienna's grown on me!'

'Okay, so what do you want to do with your last few hours here?'

'I googled that wine tavern the busker suggested last night.'

'Of course you did.'

'It looks kind of amazing.'

'I'm way too hungover to drink today,' I tell him. He's already digging in his backpack for his phone. 'Though it would be kind of nice to go somewhere new.'

'Let's get a soft drink or something? I think you'll love it.'

I throw the empty cake box away, while Josh sorts out our ride.

—

I'm staring out the window of our Uber at the too-early pale moon. We haven't touched since he left my bed this morning. I haven't told him about Lucia's visit. Actually, I have no idea what I think or how I feel about it all. He seems completely different this morning. Doesn't he? Do I?

'*Mayer am Nussberg Heuriger,*' the driver says in a low, accented growl. The aircon is so loud, I can barely make out his consonants.

'*Dankeschön,*' we chorus, stepping out of the car.

'Holy fuck,' Josh says, jaw dropping. The sun shines fierce and golden along an expanse of vineyards, freckled with mint-green umbrellas. Hundreds of people crowd long tables, eating meats and cheeses from wooden boards and drinking wine from tiny glass steins. This feels like *Sound of Music* Austria, hills alive with chatter, laughter, the clink of glasses, distant guitar strumming. We could be hours from the city.

We queue for drinks at a tiny wooden hut – *Soda Zitrone* for me and a *Radler* (lemonade + beer) for Josh – and find a bench near the bottom of the *Heuriger*. We sit side by side overlooking endless rows of grapevines. A little way up the hill, Aphrodïte is crooning into a microphone about her Tinder Babe. I stifle a yawn and close my puffy eyes, while the sunshine massages my stiff neck and shoulders. Aphrodïte sounds faraway. I take my first icy sip of *Soda Zitrone*, holding it in my mouth a little longer than necessary, letting the tart bubbles pop on my tongue.

'So,' Josh's voice comes out of sun-speckled darkness.

'So,' I say, opening my eyes, facing him. Near Josh's cheek, a mosquito bounces in the air like a jerky ball. I flick it away, leaning in towards him. We lock eyes. I freeze and straighten.

'How's your hand feeling?' he asks.

'It'll be fine, I think.'

'Yeah?'

'Yeah.'

'Okay, well thank fuck.'

'Are you ready to talk about it?'

I'll let him decide what *it* I'm referring to. But we're going to talk about *all of it*, eventually.

'I'm sorry. I know I'm being weird today. I don't want you to think it has anything to do with you,' he says. Profile to the light, half of Josh's face is golden and sun-kissed; half is dark and exhausted.

'What's making you feel weird?'

'I just— Speaking to my mum kind of made my selfishness hit home. You know? My selfishness at coming here and bursting into your life unannounced and also, like, leaving my family when they needed me.'

'I think that's a bit reductive, Josh.'

'Look, am I glad I came? Yes. I'd be lying if I said I wasn't fucking elated to see you. I'm just— I'm sorry. I want to do what's right for everyone without completely breaking down.'

'You're doing your best, Josh. I think we both are.'

'Mm,' he hums into his drink. Each time he swigs from the bottle I watch the foam charge to the surface, then recede. It's almost meditative.

'I mean it,' I say and he finds my gaze, holds it.

'You're pretty fucking amazing, Maya.' He raises his hand as if I'm about to protest. 'Just take it.'

I raise my hand to mirror Josh and he reaches out and holds it. Our first touch in hours – I expected some sort of shock, I think, something revelatory, anything! – but it feels like a normal hand. He lets me go and we sip our drinks in silence for a moment. Then another. The sun casts long, umbrella-shaped shadows on the grass all the way down the hill. Is this silence just the absence of sound or are we both trying to figure out what to say? I rehearse the sentence twice in my head before I say it out loud, like I'm about to speak German: *Even though you're leaving, I think we should probably talk about what happened last night*. But Josh speaks first. 'Can I ask you a risky question?'

'You just did,' I joke without a smile.

His mouth is tense. His face colours. 'Were you planning on never speaking to me again? If I hadn't just turned up here?'

I breathe through my nose and rub the condensation on my glass.

'No. I don't think I ever thought we'd never speak again.'

'That's a lot of negatives . . .'

I laugh. 'Fine, fine, I'll try again. Yes, I did think we'd speak again.' I try to appear blasé but somehow sound impassioned. Classic.

Josh nods meaningfully, though I don't know what he's thinking. The wind catches on the *Radler* bottle neck and the glass begins to whistle.

'I've read all these books where characters meet someone in their early twenties and break up for some reason that feels very important at the time. They think they'll connect with other people, or whatever. But then they all get older and realise connections like that are rare, and—' He trails off, but continues before I can speak, 'Maya, what if we made a mistake?' he says, looking away from me. His voice is shaky, frantic, 'I think we made a mistake,' he says again with more conviction.

'Josh.' I swallow and face the hills. I don't know what to say. Maybe I've misunderstood. He wouldn't ask that of me. Surely he's not asking this of me.

'Maya.' His breathing is uneven as he follows my gaze. 'Don't you think we made a mistake by breaking up?'

My body is stressed, frazzled, jittery – mouth, throat, chest. I feel like a sum of my parts, each of which has a different opinion on the situation. I turn back to him.

'Josh,' I almost whisper, 'I don't think I do.'

His face is blank for a moment, then vulnerable, wide open.

'You don't?' His panic rushes over me, like ice water.

'I think you're in shock, Josh, you're going through a lot.'

That's not what I meant to say. I feel the air between us

changing the things I'm trying to project. I put my glass down and press my hands against our bench to steady myself. I'm angry again and I don't know if it's fair. Josh pulls away from me. No, come back! He looks at my shoulders like he might grab me, shake me. Maybe I want him to. I don't know. I don't know!

His look is one of uncomplicated, unquestioning love and yes, yes, yes I really do want to lose myself in it. But—

'We don't want the same lives, Josh. That hasn't changed!'

'But even after all of this time apart,' he says, 'I obviously still— How could I not—'

I ignore my somersaulting stomach, 'You're not being fair, Josh. I'm trying. I've tried so hard this weekend and now you're making me into the person that has to say no.' I wipe at my wet cheeks. 'I don't want to be that person, I fucking love you too Josh, obviously, but we both know this can't work! And it's not fair of you to ask me!'

'We broke up while you were grieving, Maya. Everything was falling apart for you, and I didn't know how to— What if we tried to figure things out? We have to be able to— to—'

'To what?' I feel more anger charge through me. 'What exactly are you asking me for?' I say. I think I might have started to cry.

'I'm not asking you to come back to London! I wouldn't do that. I can see how much Vienna suits you and—'

'But it's not about Vienna, Josh, it's about the kind of life that I want, and the music—'

'But I don't understand how could you choose that over us? I don't understand why it needs to be a choice.'

'Because it's the only thing that's ever made sense to me. It's what makes me feel alive, Josh! It makes me feel so fucking alive!'

'But don't *I*?' The whites of his eyes are red. The hazel flecks catch fire.

'Of course you do! You know you do! It's just—'

'Not enough?' His voice is fragility distilled. He hands me the knife I used to cut him open, points at the scar, tells me to do it again.

'Not who I am,' I sob.

'No, Maya! This is who you're *choosing* to be!'

'That's not fair, Josh,' I can feel snot sliding from my nose, 'What's the difference between who I am and who I choose to be?'

'It's just a job!' His eyes are wide and disbelieving; his face is streaked with tears.

'But it's not to me, Josh!' I still can't look away from him, even though the sight of his face is physically painful to me, 'How can you say that? Surely after all this time you know it's not just a job to me!'

We've had this conversation before. Why is he doing this? He breaks contact, turning towards the hills, where the clouds have thickened and darkened. The air feels waxy, denser than before. I feel the layers of who we are and who we used to be floating between us like smoke. I just want to reach through and hold him. Josh, who is the sound of pages turning, the smell of coffee, scalding showers. Josh, who is Christine and the Queens and my old perfume. Josh, who is Joni Mitchell and Rothko. Josh, who hangs on my wall, looking away from me. Josh, who is here with me right now, looking away from me. Josh, who is turning back to me and asking, 'What if I moved here?' His eyes are frantic, searching my face for – for what? Some sign of hope? 'If this were a film, people would be rooting for us!'

I've stopped crying. There's a sickening, sinking feeling in my chest and knees. And yes I'm angry! And maybe that's fine!

'But this isn't a film, Josh. This is your life. You want a home and a nine-to-five job you enjoy and the promise of a family.'

His eyes still. 'I do want those things.'

'I know,' I whisper, and we break contact again.

'And you still don't want those things,' he says, shaking his head.

'And I still don't want those things,' I say. I shake my head too.

'Fuck, I'm sorry. I'm sorry,' he says, 'I shouldn't have said anything. You're right. You're obviously right. I just – ah, fuck. I don't know what's wrong with me.'

'I take it now's a bad time?' Aphrodïte is standing behind us in a cowboy hat, nose ring glistening. I have no idea how long she's been there. Josh bends over and covers his face with his hands.

'There have been better times,' I croak. Suddenly, I can feel the heat of a thousand foreign gazes around us. Fuck me. Is public love always humiliating?

'I spotted you two and just wanted to thank you for coming! And give you this. On the house.'

She hands us a CD in a thin paper case. *APHRODÏTE*, it says beneath a doodle of a closed eye with winged liner.

'Thank you,' I say, taking the CD. Josh's face is still in his hands.

'Right, I'll leave you two to it. Good luck with whatever it is you're dealing with.' Aphrodïte tips her cowboy hat at us and walks away.

Josh's back is shaking and for a moment I think he's crying.

'Oh my God.' He looks up at me from between his fingers. 'I couldn't look at her. I'm so sorry, I just thought if I kept my eyes closed she'd go away.'

I hand him the CD, 'I think you should have this. I'll find her on Spotify. We can compare notes.'

'Uh huh,' he says. 'I'll call you, then?'

'I mean it, Josh. We'll figure it out.'

'Fuck, I'm so sorry. I literally just apologised for being selfish and then went straight back to— God, we are far too British to have had that conversation in public. I think I might die.'

'Oh, yeah, I'm 100% already dead,' I say.

He wipes his red eyes.

'I interrupted your life with no warning, I didn't immediately tell you why I was here, I made a mess of everything – everything! – then I suggested we get a drink outside the city, and begged you to take me back.'

'I mean, yes, that's all true.' *The anger is starting to make sense.* 'But it's also okay. It's all very—' I trail off.

'Very what?'

'Very human, Josh.'

He scoffs. 'Very human. My biggest fault. God, I'm sorry. And you hurt your hand.'

'Oh, I don't regret punching Davorin.'

'It was amazing. Amazing,' he says.

Neither of us speak for a while.

'Wait, is it raining?' Josh asks. Moments later, I feel a drop of water splash my forehead. Then another.

'Shit. When do you need to leave for the airport?'

He looks at his upside-down watch. 'About ten minutes ago.'

'Right.'

'How long has my watch been upside-down?' he asks.

I shrug.

'Right,' I say again, standing, shielding my face from the rain. 'Do you want me to come with you?'

'Ah, I think I'll be alright.'

Something already broken in my chest shatters anew.

Josh hoists his backpack up off the floor. He looks calm and completely disheveled, as if he's strolled through a hurricane. He draws me to him and I breathe him in – boozy lemonade, sunshine, rain, and tears. All around us, people are laughing, huddling under umbrellas, or running for the road.

We join them soon enough, tugging one of the mint-green umbrellas from the floor and sprinting for cover, clothes stuck to our bodies like skins.

'Are you okay to get home?' he asks, once we've made it to the road. All around us, groups are pouring into taxis.

'Yeah, I'll find a tram or catch a lift with someone heading in the same direction.'

'I'll wait with you until you—'

'Don't be mad, Josh, you'll miss your flight.'

He holds my gaze, then retreats into his phone. Rain keeps falling – on our heads, on the bench, on the thirsty grass beside us. In the distance, the trees shimmer against the darkening sky.

'Oh shit, it's going to be here in a minute.'

'That's great!' I lie, 'You shouldn't have any problem making it to the airport on time.'

'Thank you for this weekend, Maya. I—'

'You really don't have to say anything,' I interrupt, because I am one more word away from sobs that would put this storm to shame. My chest is tight, and the world's least genuine smile is stretched across my face.

'Are you sure I can't even drop you somewhere on the way?'

I shake my head. Josh nods because he knows I can't speak, and hugs me again. I hold him to me. Maybe a second too long. Maybe three. A hideous yellow car pulls up in front of us. Josh sighs and pulls away from me, wiping tears or rain from his face – I can't tell. I wave. He waves back, then bolts from our umbrella. I stand alone and watch the yellow car join the other cars, then disappear.

'You look like you could use a ride.'

Aphroditë's eye liner has run in artistic jagged lines across her cheeks.

'Or a hug?' she offers. The sad-clown state of her face does not seem to have affected her confidence.

'You know what?' I tell her, rain pounding the stolen

umbrella. 'I would love a ride. Are you heading anywhere near the Westbahnhof?'

'Sure,' she says, joining me under cover. Her guitar case is wedged between us. 'My Uber's coming in, like, three minutes. Where's the guy you were with? You'll probably have to squeeze in the back with my guitar.'

'He's gone.'

'Oh,' she says, but doesn't sound surprised. 'Are you alright?'

'Just ready to head home.'

'Totally.'

And that's how I find myself drenched and exhausted in the backseat of a silver Mercedes with Aphrodïte, the nosy guitarist.

'So he's an ex-boyfriend?'

'Yep.'

'Here to win you back?'

I catch the attention of the Uber driver in the rear-view mirror before his eyes dart back to the road. I could lie to this woman. I could tell her Josh is married. Fuck it, I could tell her that, yes, we dated until we found out he was a distant cousin. *It was a whole debacle.*

'No, no,' I say instead, 'just visiting.'

'Sure, sure,' she replies with an infuriatingly *knowing* look. I really just want to be alone. The driver takes my silence as a cue and turns on the radio. It's a song I don't recognise and I'm grateful for association-free music. Four chords on repeat with a bad bass line and too much percussion. Exquisitely generic. Perfect. I'm shivering in the aircon, which is absurd given how hot it's been outside. The hairs on my forearms point to the sky, like they're trying to tell me, *Look, that's where Josh is heading. That's where you've sent him.* Beside me, Aphrodïte takes a notebook out of her bag and scribbles. She doesn't stop until we reach my street.

'What do I owe you?' I say as the car slows.

'Oh don't worry about it. Just promise you'll come to another one of my shows sometime.'

'Sure,' I say, 'thanks.'

—

I don't know what I expected to find in my flat – an exhibition of our weekend? My melting reality preserved like one of Salvador Dalí's clocks? Instead, the only evidence of Josh's visit is our painting leaning against my wall, next to the photo of his back. I approach the frame in my wet clothes, hair dripping all over. It's lighter than I remember, so easy to lift from its hook and place on the floor next to the canvas. I don't know what to do with either of them.

I sit crossed-legged on my couch with my phone. I've already started crying when Lisa picks up.

'Hey,' she says. 'Hey, hey, My, you're okay.'

'I know I'm okay!' I sob. I am gasping for breath, 'So okay!' I say again. 'Practically thriving!'

'You've done amazingly,' my sister says, and I almost check to see whether I've dialled the right person.

'I have this photo of the back of his head,' I'm still

wheezing, 'and this painting we did on Friday night. What the fuck am I meant to do with them?'

'Why don't you leave them a while? See how you feel in a week or two? You don't have to do anything with them right now?'

'Why are you so sensible?'

'One of us has to be.'

I smile despite myself, tears still gushing. Why hasn't someone thought to utilise tears as some kind of hydro-powered renewable energy? They're fucking infinite.

'Fuck's sake. What a mess.'

'What a mess,' she repeats.

She waits for my breathing to calm. 'How's your hand?'

I have completely forgotten about my hand. 'Hand's fine.'

'Think you can play today?'

'Yeah.'

'Good, I think you should.'

'Sorry, Lise, I haven't even asked how you are?'

'I'm fine. We can talk about me another time. What are you going to play?'

'I don't know.'

'I bet you do,' she says quietly.

I don't know how long I sit there after we've said goodbye. Long enough to decide to turn off my phone. Long enough to realise I should get out of these wet clothes. When I finally stand, I head straight towards my violin. The rest of my living room is out of focus. I clutch the case to my chest and breathe in the familiar earthy smell.

—

Two teenagers board the tram and sit in front of me, staring at their phones. They look roughly the same age, even their clothing is similar, but I can't tell if they know each other. I watch the screen over the shoulder of one of the kids, expecting the usual Instagram litter – reels by therapists explaining codependency in 45 seconds, Marcus Aurelius quoted in the same breath as Taylor Swift – but this kid is watching a video on a loop. A standing man talks to another version of himself, who sits on a sofa (this could also be his twin, though I suspect he has edited the film so that he appears twice). The man on the sofa leaves, the standing man takes his place, and the clip starts again. And again.

The internet loves 'loops'. Occasionally, the dregs of TikTok leak into my own Instagram feed, and I watch cyclical videos like this. Round and round. Perhaps the loops give us permission to stay in a moment. Like music. Everything else moves on too quickly.

I'm already at the opera house. I'm already in the empty lift to my favourite floor. The opera corridor is empty, too. No angry old men. No harassers in headbands. No star cellists or flaky conductors. My phone's still off. It's going to stay off for as long as I need to be in this room. I place a tiny card on my music stand with the words 'brilliant, truly' written inside. I lift my violin from her case and tune her facing the window. Vienna's vicious evening wind lashes a tree outside as rain scrubs the city. A group of Mozarts have taken cover by the pillars. The *Technik* men are still smoking.

'We know what we're going to play, don't we?' asks my violin.

'We do. I just need a minute.'

'Take your time,' she says, nuzzling into my neck.

I lean against the golden wall and close my eyes. *Alright,* I tell my body or my brain or whatever part of me remembers all the details, *let's go.* My hands are on the handle of my memory drawer and I pull. The room fills with:

My mum in her scrubs, looking past me.

Lisa's hand, covered in pen, checking the temperature of the bath water.

Josh's drunk, blurry body on a rooftop.

Elsa's earrings shimmering like tiny chandeliers in the rehearsal room.

Lucia's body decorated in patches of soft mandarin light.

The crunch of Davorin's jaw on my fist.

The cold, dark church where we mourned Professor Forrest.

Running through the park, blood between my toes.

'Brilliant, truly', and a box of Jaffa Cakes.

The first notes of Brahms' violin sonata – *No. 3* – are playing in my head. The music begins almost mid-thought – *sotto voce* – a whispered melody that answers a question we'll never hear. Ascending fourth. Tumbling quavers. This music is urgent, but mysterious. Heavy with sorrow, but hopeful, mourning, tender. This music is grand because it doesn't seek grandeur. Arresting, but introspective. Sustained notes collapse into their neighbours, spontaneous yet, somehow, impossibly, self-aware. Perfect. Fucking perfect. My fingertips are tingling. I ready my bow. I already know which memory I'll pick. The ink is still wet.

MEMORY: SINCE THE WORLD IS ENDING, WHY NOT GO TO VIENNA?

Acknowledgements

The title of this book is inspired by a line in the Ben Lerner poem, 'Mean Free Path', which is referenced in his novel *10:04*, as well as the song 'If the world was ending' by JP Same (ft. Julia Michaels).

Maya and Josh's refrain 'suffering is absolute, not relative' is borrowed from Zadie Smith's *Imitations*. I am really such a fan.

The discussion about Rachel Cusk's writings about fiction vs non-fiction reference her *A Life's Work*.

Joni Mitchell's *Blue* is epic and legendary.

The art described in this novel is:

- *Judith* (1901), Klimt
- *Water Serpents I* (1904), Klimt
- *A Raindrop Which Falls into the City* (1955), Hundertwasser

To Judith Murray, my dazzling agent, this book would only exist on the back of a napkin if not for you. Our friendship is such a joy. I am so grateful to you for your meticulous work and generous care.

Chris White, Editor Extraordinaire, you've been the perfect partner on this novel. Thank you for your patience, vision, and for sharing your magnificent brain. It's been a life high-light working on this book and *28 Questions* with you. I feel exceedingly lucky.

Thank you also to Greene & Heaton and the whole team at Scribner / Simon & Schuster – it's been such a dream to work with you over the last few years.

I wrote big chunks of this book in the homes of Kathy Peacock/Matthew Carter, Ellie Shearer, Camille White, and Charlotte Jeffries over a nomadic 2022 summer – thank you for having me, wonderful, WONDERFUL friends.

This novel was raised by a village and I have a lot of people to thank:

To Saint Cambo, for your beautiful friendship, SM, S & A.

To Sylvia Greenberg and David Aronson, the OG Soprano and Conductor, thank you for your guidance and support.

To Robyn Parton and Anne Champert, who helped me fall back in love with music when things felt very hard and very bleak.

To Yoonjee Kim and Freya Müller, for our long, meander-ing conversations about music and language.

To Ros Dobson, yes, you, please. You are the best thing that's ever happened. You spark joy and inspiration. Thank you for making me laugh and swoon every day.

I will be forever grateful to you, Ellie Shearer and Jenn Schaffer-Goddard. You are both extraordinary. I'm getting emotional thinking about how much our writing group means to me, as per. Reader, if you haven't already, please buy and read their books. And then buy them for all your loved ones and read them again.

To my family – Schneider, Phillips, Stein, Benjamin, and Bass – the best and strangest people, who I am so grateful for.

To my favourite people, Lell and Pap, for your red and blue hearts and your unconditional love.

To my dad, Greg (Gregory*), who types with two fingers, whose favourite Shakespeare play is Ethelo, and whom I adore. Thank you for agreeing to never read any sex scene I write.

To my mom, Gabbi. I can't imagine writing anything without consulting your weird, magical brain. The force-o has always been with YOU-o.

I've poured my whole heart and soul into this book. Thank you to all those who work in this industry and to readers all over who make sharing stories possible.